THE FAR GRASS

JOHN MICHELL

The Far Grass © John Michell 2020

ISBN: 978-1-922460-58-5 (paperback)

Published in Australia by John Michell and InHouse Publishing.
www.inhousepublishing.com.au

Printed in Australia by InHouse Print & Design.

PREFACE

In 2019 I made a research trip to the UK, Germany and Russia, intending to refresh my memory of countries I knew moderately well and write a novel based on my travels.

On leaving Australia, I certainly had no plans to revive a manuscript completed in 2018 – my first book writing attempt. This initial manuscript had been gathering dust while I finalized my first published novel, *Dublin Zoo*. But once in Berlin, when I found myself scouting locations for the manuscript's opening scene, I recognized I was about to have a change of heart.

On return to Australia, therefore, I set about transforming this first draft, variable in quality as it was, into something better. The result is *The Far Grass*, a new slant on the traditional Cold War spy fiction novel that infrequently, and only with embellishment, draws on my experiences as an Australian diplomat from 1979–2012.

I sincerely hope that readers will benefit from the re-casting exercise by finding enjoyment in *The Far Grass*.

John Michell
Instagram: john_michell88
www.johnmichell.strikingly.com

DISCLAIMER

This book is a work of fiction. Comments or actions attributed to public figures are either inventions or loosely based on historical events. In the latter case, summaries and accounts provided are not intended to be of academic quality, accuracy or balance.

Otherwise, any character's resemblance in the book to any individual living or dead is purely coincidental.

By the author of

DUBLIN ZOO

'Don't depend too much on anyone in this world because even your own shadow leaves you when you're in darkness.'

— Ibn Taymiyyah 1263–1328

CHAPTER 1

KONRAD

It's Berlin. Wednesday 19 December 1973. East Berlin, actually. At dusk. I was standing on the corner of Warschauer Strasse and Stralauer Alle, just across from the forbidding darkness of the River Spree and the lights of West Berlin on the other side. The wind was whipping off the river. It was freezing, bloody freezing. I was hanging around trying to link up with a person I'd never met before and knew of only as Konrad. That was not his real name; it was his work name. It was all part of Operation Skyman, an undertaking by the British Secret Intelligence Service, MI6, to exfiltrate Konrad to the West. My small role in this was to provide Konrad with papers, a forged exit visa valid for forty-eight hours permitting him to make a single visit to the Western sector for work purposes.

The plan was for Konrad to walk past me towards the Café Tagtraum on Warschauer Strasse. The café was a shitty bolt-hole in the wall serving cheap East German beer. It was not well frequented on Wednesday nights and had been chosen for this reason. I had been briefed that Konrad is in his mid-forties and will wear a distinctive full-length brown overcoat with large side pockets. He was to carry with him in his left hand a cheap satchel of the type favoured by low-level East German bureaucrats. If Konrad carried the satchel in his right hand the mission was to be aborted.

Inside the café Konrad was to hang his coat on a peg in the vestibule separating the café's entrance from its main area. He was then to order a beer and repair to a bench to drink it. I was undercover as a Moscow-based British Foreign Office courier, freshly arrived in East Berlin earlier in the day. I was at a loose end and checking out the sights. That night I had decided to experience the gritty end of East Berlin life. I was to enter the café a few minutes after Konrad and hang my jacket in the vestibule. While there, I was to slip the slim sealed package of forged papers into one of the voluminous pockets of his overcoat. I was then to have a couple of drinks in order to confirm that Konrad, having finished his beer, had reclaimed his overcoat and made off into the gloom.

I was nervous. After months of waiting, and only recently activated, this was my first foray as an MI6 intelligence officer. Fortunately, a man I judged to be in his forties soon emerged from the haze and turned into Warschauer Strasse. There were not a lot of people about and none bar the man were wearing a heavy brown overcoat and carrying a briefcase satchel in their left hand. I studiously ignored Konrad as he passed. After forcing myself to count slowly to a hundred, I made my way up to the café.

I entered the Café Tagtraum vestibule. For a moment I was unable to see much in the dim light. As my eyes adjusted, I anxiously scanned the hung garments for Konrad's coat. The document was in my front trouser pocket, but first I had to wrestle off my thick jacket and stow my hat and gloves. Then, holding the jacket in my right hand, I fished out the package with my left. As I leant forward to hang my jacket, I was simultaneously to deposit the drop in Konrad's coat from behind the protective screen of my body.

At that instant the café entrance door opened with an enormous crash and in poured four very drunk and loud Russian soldiers. I stared at them like a rabbit in a spotlight. The noise alerted the café owner. A formidable German woman entered the vestibule from inside the café. She quickly established she had little time for inebriated Russians and, right then, transfixed imbeciles with idiotic smiles on their faces. 'Raus hier, raus hier,' she screamed as she waved the five of us into the street. I stumbled outside, hands shaking and heart pounding. The Russians were vodka-charged. They disappeared into the night laughing loudly without so much as a backward glance at me. The woman's scowling face glaring out of the café window forbade me from re-attempting the drop.

My composure slowly returned. I thought about fallback arrangements. If the drop could not be made, Konrad was to finish his drink and thirty minutes later position himself at the first tram stop north of the Bersarinplatz roundabout linking the southern and northern stretches of Petersburger Strasse. The walk to Bersarinplatz took about thirty minutes and was deliberately designed to keep Konrad moving lest a nosy policeman ask him why he is loitering.

Once at the tram stop, Konrad was to place his satchel on the ground and stand astride it to signal he was comfortable to be approached for a brush-by pass. He was to wait there no more than ten minutes. Reckoning that Konrad would take an additional ten minutes to finish his beer, I calculated I had fifty minutes to complete the job. I headed north up Warschauer Strasse.

It wasn't my night. Upon reaching the junction where Warschauer Strasse becomes the southern stretch of Petersburger Strasse, I found the road cordoned off for overnight resealing of its bitumen surface. *Fucking hell*, I thought, *what else can go wrong?* With growing agitation, I headed off looking for a parallel street from which I could backtrack to Bersarinplatz. All of a sudden there seemed to be people everywhere. I was reluctant to cut through the line of apartment buildings; if someone spoke to me I would be revealed as a foreigner and with a pocket full of forged documents that was the last thing I wanted. On and on I went, until finally I managed to make my way back to Bersarinplatz.

My detour had caused me to take over an hour to arrive at the tram stop. But I judged that Konrad would have run into the same problems with the road works. There were about six people in the shelter. A tram arrived and they all boarded. I hung about feeling increasingly awkward. Other people arrived and stared at me, sensing my discomfort. A second tram came and went. After twenty minutes, I concluded that Konrad had been and gone or wasn't coming. He would have to wait for another day.

Soaked in sweat, I slowly headed back to my hotel in Alexanderplatz. Along the way I rationalized my situation. *Konrad can't be that important otherwise why would they leave it to a novice like me to deliver his papers? There will be other opportunities to get him out.* Once in my room I felt sufficiently assuaged to take a shower. Then I rang the number I'd been given for Gloria Milford. Gloria was attached to the MI6 station at the British Embassy in East Berlin, operating under political section cover.

The phone line was scratchy when Gloria answered. It was assumed the East German secret police, the Stasi, were listening. 'Hello, Gloria,' I said, trying to sound relaxed and breezy, 'it's Joe Lambert the diplomatic courier from Moscow who got into town earlier today. I was wondering if you would like to come out for a drink?' The bit about having a drink was an arranged code advising I'd not connected with Konrad. Had I made the drop my invitation would have been for a meal. I will never be sure what, if anything, those listening made of Gloria's sharp intake of breath. But it sent a chill up my spine. I knew then my masters would not treat lightly my missing Konrad.

'Sorry, Joe,' Gloria said, giving the pre-planned response regardless of which message I used. 'I've just washed my hair and will have to take a rain check.' We bantered some more and hung up. I spent the night staring at the ceiling. My anxiety was well founded.

I had barely set foot in the embassy the next morning when I was told to get down to the secure area, *toot sweet*. The MI6 station head was a pompous individual called Stephen Maunder-Roberts. He had not paid me much attention the day before except to ask as I prepared to leave for my rendezvous with Konrad, 'Are you set?' At best, he gave the impression he preferred not to spend too much time with me. Now any semblance of nicety had disappeared. 'You fucking rank amateur,' he bellowed, his physical bulk belied by his curiously feminine habit of crossing and uncrossing his legs. 'I simply don't need useless cunts like you coming in here and making our difficult job impossible. I hope you're happy with yourself. If I have my way … MATE … you'll be drummed out of the Service. Now get the fuck out of my sight.'

I couldn't really argue and even if I could he wouldn't have listened. I had a 3 pm flight back to Moscow. With as much dignity as I could muster, I sealed my diplomatic bags and prepared the necessary paperwork. No one else from the station spoke to me. I was not very communicative with the garrulous embassy security officer who accompanied me to the airport to watch over the diplomatic bags in the aircraft's hold as I boarded, just in case prying eyes chose to ignore diplomatic conventions. He soon worked out something was on my mind and thankfully shut up.

———◆◆———

On reaching the embassy in Moscow, I sought out the station chief. He was already briefed. James Sim was a kindly enough man, a former academic in Russian and Far Eastern studies. All the same, he was transparently relieved I had messed up on someone else's patch and not his own.

'James,' I said, starting to try and explain what had happened. But he quickly shut me down.

'Joe,' he said, 'I can't sugar-coat it. All hell's broken loose in London. The target you missed was a big deal. The KGB pulled him in at some ungodly hour this morning. Maunder-Roberts has advised headquarters the agent planned to go over directly after last night's drop, had he received his papers.' Sim paused. 'You're being recalled,' he said. 'Permanently. The story for Russian and unindoctrinated UK staff is that you have an urgent family illness. Go home and pack. They want you back in London by the weekend.'

CHAPTER 2

RECRUITMENT

My recruitment into MI6 – or the Service as I came to call it – owed much to the machinations of UK politics. At the 1970 general election, Edward Heath's Conservatives surprisingly defeated the incumbent Labour government led by Harold Wilson. Wilson had called the election on the basis of opinion polls placing Labour well ahead. This decision, and the subsequent loss, placed his leadership in jeopardy, driving him into the arms of the Labour Party left wing. The Left regarded MI6 as a bastion of conservatism and thought it closeted, underperforming and insecure. In return for supporting Wilson continuing as leader, it extracted his promise to reform the Service when next Labour occupied the Treasury benches.

Wilson had agreed because he viewed the 1970 result as an aberration and, knowing that Heath was unpopular in Conservative ranks, fancied his chances of beating him next time around. But Wilson also knew the Service's formal reform was politically fraught. In 1971 he let it quietly be known in British secret circles that MI6 would do well to broaden its social breadth, hoping this would pacify the Labour Left when Labour did reclaim government.

I later saw a memorandum penned by an MI6 officer called Southwark. Citing Labour Party sources, Southwark detailed both Wilson's warning to the Service about needing to broaden its social breadth and his associated belief that Labour would return to office at the next election. Sir John Rennie, then the MI6 head, had annotated the document. This I know because his handwritten comments were signed as *C*, the Service chief's traditional sign off. Rennie's instruction was blunt and candid: *This warning is something we should heed*, he wrote. *Don't go overboard, but let's pull in a few people from further afield.*

———◆——◆———

I was born on 14 March 1948 in London. My mother liked to boast I shared a birthdate with Albert Einstein. There, I suspect, the similarities end. I lived only a matter of months in London. In November 1948 the family – comprising my parents, sister Elsie two years my senior and me – relocated to Bootle near Liverpool. My father worked as a wharf labourer, but his union activism eventually led to him being blacklisted by employers. The Bootle docks offered the work now unattainable in London. Unfortunately, the move did not end happily. But at least the port authorities took pity on us when a wayward crane boom killed my father in May 1949; we remained the tenants of our Knowsley Road, Bootle docks-owned house until my mother's death in 1967.

Our Bootle home was across from North Park, where I happily spent many summer days playing cricket. School was another thing. I just wasn't interested and never got into stride at any stage. Eventually, aged sixteen, I took up a labouring position on the docks.

My co-workers were not sainted warriors of the working class. Like any other group there was the good, the average, and the mad and bad. Being young and green, I attracted the attention of the mad and bad, a situation compounded by their apparent distaste for my fresh, pale complexion – the by-product of my father's Cornish origins – and wavy fair hair and clear blue eyes. I quickly grew street-smart, enabling me to talk the talk while avoiding physical altercations.

This was fortunate. I might have been just short of six feet tall and, as I matured, of reasonably solid build. But I genuinely feared violence. And unlike many others, I also had little inclination to dish it out. Half a lifetime later this aversion would suddenly revisit me, in the most extraordinary of circumstances.

———◆◆———

My mother's death from lung cancer, courtesy of her lifelong smoking habit, apart from being a harrowing time coincided with the worst of my adolescent immaturity. At nineteen and wanting to show everyone how tough I was, I didn't stay with my mother to her end. Instead I left a couple of hours before she died, and went drinking with my mates. I continued the pretence in public. But in the wee hours of the morning after my mother's funeral I woke to the sound of a howling animal, only to discover I was that animal. It was then the shame of my behaviour sheeted home. The guilt I felt over this failing in my duty became an everlasting burden.

We were given a month to vacate our house. I moved into rooms off Marsh Lane. Everything I owned fitted into two suitcases. My sister Elsie and I had never been close and we soon lost contact when she shifted to Manchester. I continued to work at the docks but became withdrawn. My mother's dying plea imploring me to make something of myself haunted me. Even though I had pledged to respect her wish, at the time of its making my promise was not made sincerely. I said what I thought I needed to say. Now with my conscience rendered increasingly fragile by the recall of my dereliction of duty, I knew I had to do something. In 1968 I began night classes at the Bootle Polytechnic.

I had no real idea what I wanted to do but decided to learn about business, whatever that meant. I took a course in basic business administration. It was hardly rocket science, yet I was pleased to do quite well. On the advice of the college, I applied for an assisted place at the Liverpool Metropolitan University. Eventually, a letter arrived advising I had qualified for university entrance, commencing in the 1969 academic year. After much indecision, I settled on a Bachelor of Commerce degree.

Being three or so years older than the bulk of my student intake meant I didn't form many friendships with classmates. Most were typical eighteen-year-olds and daunted by the age difference. Added to which, coincident with commencing university, I had experienced a noticeable blooming of the loner instincts that first emerged in the aftermath of my mother's death. Although I could still carry a social conversation and interact with people, I found I had little will to do so. The instinct to be alone was overpowering. Try as I might, I couldn't resist it, despite the sense of isolation it engendered. Many female students, especially the more mature, grew disdainful of me. In private, I felt their rejection keenly.

⎯⎯⎯◆⎯◆⎯⎯⎯

One of the tutors in my final year was a man called Bernie Odgers. Bernie was past his best. Alcoholic fumes radiated from his dark-puce, weathered face. But he and I got on well. He found young students too irritating and liked that I had some grip on the world. Bernie had been a prisoner of war. After two years in captivity, he was repatriated in an exchange of British and Italian POWs. Bernie said he became ill after he returned home. From what I could deduce he had suffered a nervous breakdown. But Bernie had paid his dues and was entitled to some dignity. The university acknowledged this by allowing him to tutor once a week.

Deep in the bowels of the MI6 personnel section Bernie's war service was also remembered. Nigel Wadsworth had been Bernie's company commander in North Africa. His Brigadier uncle had landed him an administrative position in MI6 headquarters after the war. But Wadsworth was not a strong performer. The Service old hands reasoned he would be the ideal person to scour the country in search of a few token provincial recruits. God knows you'd never give him anything important to do.

In early December 1971, while waiting for final exam results, I received a note from Bernie asking if I could meet him the next morning at Allerton Cemetery. The request did not surprise me; Bernie was eccentric and no stranger to unusual ideas. But this time when I arrived I was amazed to find him dressed to the nines, the erect collar of his dark blue trench coat around his ears. 'Important we're discreet, old boy,' he said, 'don't want to blow our cover.' Oblivious to the fact that he stood out like a beacon, Bernie told me in hushed tones, 'A Mr Sheppard in London would like to have a word with you.' Were I interested he would let Sheppard know.

I asked the obvious question. 'How would I know if I'm interested or not? I haven't got the faintest idea what this is about.'

Bernie seemed stumped, torn between telling me enough and telling me too much. Finally, he said, 'Joe, there's not many jobs around here; you will likely end up in London working in some civil service backwater. Dead boring. This is sort of civil service but mainly isn't. If nothing else you'll get a free run down to London.'

The idea of a day trip to London appealed. Mostly, I didn't want to disappoint Bernie who was obviously keen for me to go. *Why not?* I thought. 'OK, Bernie, tell this fellow I'll come to London and talk to him. But please tell him no guarantees. If I don't like what's on offer, I'm walking.'

So it was that lazy Nigel Wadsworth, aware of Bernie's tenuous link to the Liverpool Metropolitan University, had asked Bernie to talent spot for him. Paying scant regard to any objective criteria, least of all academic excellence, Bernie had nominated me.

━━━◆◆━━━

I met Wadsworth, whom I knew then as Sheppard, and someone calling himself Watts in a spartan office off Hampstead Road. Watts I later learned was a low-level pen pusher, real name of Coleman.

After preliminaries, Wadsworth took the lead. 'Have you ever travelled out of England?' he asked.

'No, I have not.'

'Would you like to live abroad doing work for government?'

Missing the cue, I replied as might any twenty-three-year-old asked whether he wanted an overseas holiday. 'How fabulous,' I said naively, 'I would love to see the Great Wall of China.'

Suddenly red of face, Coleman jumped from his chair with such force that I thought he was going to assault me. 'It's not all beer and skittles, you know,' he snarled, as if he had twenty-five years of field experience to draw on.

A few more questions on my preparedness to work abroad, which I now negotiated very cautiously, and the interview moved to general matters.

'What do you think is the biggest political challenge facing the UK?' Coleman asked, calm again.

Here's a chance to impress, I thought, recalling a lecturer once mentioning Lenin's theory of imperialism, something to do with the concentration of capital. 'The concentration of capital among the few creates inequality,' I said confidently.

'And?' Coleman said, cocking his right eyebrow.

My mind went blank. How I wished I'd paid more attention in class. My confidence evaporated and I panicked. 'Well, that results in no money being left over for others.' A pause as my nonsensical response was noted. I couldn't know it then but my botched attempt at sophistication was the answer Coleman was seeking – confirmation I had no ideological leanings.

Wadsworth took over. 'What do you think about the Soviet conduct in Czechoslovakia in '68?' I stared blankly, remembering once reading about the *Prague Spring*. But at least I had the wit to understand that Wadsworth's question ran deeper than this.

When I didn't answer, Wadsworth asked, 'Have you read any of Graham Greene's books?'

Graham who? I thought. Inside my head the wheels were spinning but there was no traction. All I could do was to sit mute.

Perfect non-answers as it turns out. More notes.

Finally, much to my relief, Wadsworth brought the interview to a close. 'Go home and wait to be contacted by mail,' he said. 'You are not to breathe a word of our discussions to anyone.'

On the return trip, I reflected on the interview. I'd clearly upset Coleman – who I thought was Watts – but the way they spoke as the interview concluded had the air of a *fait accompli*. I resolved to take the job were it offered. I had no family or friends in Bootle and accepting the position, I reasoned, would also honour my belatedly observed pledge to my dying mother to make something of myself. On arrival, there was a letter from the university waiting advising I had passed my final exams – just. *Joe Walter Lambert B.Comm, servant of Her Majesty's Government,* had a nice ring to it I decided.

CHAPTER 3

INITIATION

In the second week of January 1972 a letter in a Foreign Office crested envelope arrived. The message was terse: I had been selected for probationary employment in the Foreign Office research unit located at Century House on Westminster Bridge Road close to Lambeth North tube station. I was to report for duty in London on Monday 31 January. My worldly possessions now filled three suitcases, leaving me able to forego the removal assistance on offer. Accommodation for a maximum of three weeks would be provided at the Strand Castle Hotel. And 500 quid a year to boot!

On the night of 30 January I arrived at my hotel. My abiding memory of the next day at MI6 headquarters is of the security guards stationed at the building's ground-floor reception counter. Large, stern men all, I was later to know of them as wardens.

The first week passed in a blur of briefings and form signing. It slowly dawned on me I had joined the Secret Service. I could scarcely believe it. But I was young and robust and just rode the wave. From the outset the paramount importance of good security, principally the *Need to Know* principle, was rammed down the throats of my four fellow inductees and me.

The other newcomers, all males, were roughly my age. I didn't have much in common with them. Not only were they recruits from the Service's traditional universities, but they also wore a variety of expensively smart attire. Until I received my first pay and was able to buy a cheap suit on the never-never, I was forced to rely on the threadbare best of my student wardrobe. Two of the newcomers, whose names I can no longer recall, left the Service not long after completing basic training. The other two, Rupert Heneshaw and Frederick Ladler, were destined to become my sworn enemies. Both urbane young men, Rupert was slightly shorter, more thickset and of darker complexion than Frederick.

Heneshaw and Ladler first raised my hackles when we were told at one of our induction briefings that officers should always ensure the Service had their current home address and telephone number. I didn't have a strong Liverpudlian accent, primarily because at home my mother spoke in her native London tongue. But I did have the habit of occasionally ending sentences with *like*, which was a dead giveaway as to my background. 'I've still to find somewhere permanent to live,' I said. 'And when I do,' I added, memories of my rooms in Bootle still fresh in my mind, 'there's a possibility I may not have access to a telephone, *like*.'

Heneshaw and Ladler both sniggered at this unheard of revelation. 'No telephone?' Ladler said, feigning amazement.

Heneshaw responded in mock horror. 'Good Lord, I do believe we've a *lar* from the Merseyside in our midst.'

This resort to Liverpool slang highly amused Ladler. He and Heneshaw spent the next ten minutes exchanging looks and suppressing giggles. I briefly harboured delusions of conflict resolution Bootle docks-style, but instead sat there in simmering humiliation for the rest of the day. Rupert and Freddie made little subsequent effort to disguise their regard of me as a social inferior.

A silver lining, however, was the briefer introducing me to a Mrs Brooks who apparently administered Service property in and around London. She put me on to a retired Service couple living in Kentish Town. There I soon took up residence in a two-room granny flat in the garden of their Gatcombe Road home. It was a long haul back and forth to the office each day. I also had the feeling the couple was watching me. Old habits die hard, I guess. But at least my watchers understood the business. When informed I was going away for basic training, I was chuffed to be told with knowing smiles that no rent would be necessary for the duration.

In April 1972 our five-strong intake arrived at Fort Monckton, the MI6 training centre in Gosport, Hampshire. It was spring and the air was clear. It was an exciting time. But spring soon turned to summer and our workload increased. We were given all sorts of courses: in communications; dead drops; protecting against tails; and also unarmed combat. Life at the Fort was generally harmonious, although Heneshaw did take advantage of one of the unarmed combat sessions to sit me on my backside with excessive vigour, while all the while Ladler whooped in gleeful encouragement. I knew then that in Heneshaw and Ladler I had made enemies for life.

Back in London six months later, I was assigned to the Soviet operations area. A man called Martin Mumford was in charge. He had worked in Russia as a businessman, where no doubt he came to the Service's attention. A tall and wiry man about a decade my senior and decent to his core, he was destined to have a stellar career. He was also to have a profound influence on my life.

The Soviet operations staff were mostly young and a mix of men and women, a couple of whom were civil towards me in a guarded sort of way. The entire place reeked of ambition. I settled into a work routine blissfully unaware of the debate going on behind closed doors about what to do with me. In January 1973, as the first anniversary of my joining the Service neared, Mumford called me to his office. 'Joe,' he said, 'Service management is considering posting you to Moscow under a deep cover arrangement.'

Naively, I thought this represented acceptance at last. I was also so heartily sick of living at Kentish Town that had a posting to Mars been suggested I would have jumped at it. 'I would like that very much, Martin,' I replied, not stopping to think how I might become operational in Moscow without speaking Russian.

Mumford nodded. He was noticeably downbeat. 'We'll go and see head of Placements this afternoon,' he said flatly. Head of Placements was the Service's second-ranked administrator and known in MI6 argot as *Placements*. The position answered only to two others: the head administrator on the top floor of Century House and the head of the Service proper – the Director General – known for time immemorial by Service officers as the DG.

<hr>

'The Sovs,' Placements said to me, 'have recently embarked on a program to identify the MI6 officers in our Eastern Bloc embassies. Each time one of our diplomats leaves the building they have teams of watchers on their back. No staffing thresholds to worry about for the bloody Russkies. They're starting to sort the wheat from the chaff if you get my drift. The added complication is that, because visas take an eternity, we can't drop people into Eastern Europe at whim. This is causing us problems in providing the various bibs and bobs that certain assets need from time to time, often at short notice. We've decided to create a position in Moscow, which will involve you working in the embassy adminis-tration under Foreign Office direction and every couple of weeks doing a courier run of diplomatic bags from the post. You'll be going to all the benighteds; places like Budapest, Warsaw, and of course East Berlin when the embassy opens in April. As you'll already be in Moscow, you'll be able to obtain multiple entry visas for all Eastern Bloc countries.'

Placements glanced at Mumford, as if seeking confirmation his sales pitch remained on course. But Martin was impassive. With the hint of a shrug, Placements pressed on. 'The Russians will check you out on arrival,' he warned me. 'Don't expect to be doing any operational work for some months.' Placements glared briefly at Mumford before continuing. 'Most Foreign Office couriers like to get pissed,' he said, only to stop again and look directly at Mumford. 'It's not compulsory, is it?' Placements asked, his now demand for a response cloaked in humour. Seemingly mollified by Mumford's weak smile, he turned back to me. 'So you should do the same and, wherever you are, get out among the fleshpots and on the swill. If you get the clap, the umbrella up the eye of your John Thomas is not a cost the Service will bear.' Mumford brushed imaginary lint from his trouser knee as I politely tittered at Placements's joke. 'Provided you're suitably decadent, the Sovs will conclude you're nobody to worry about. We can ease you into some work thereafter.'

I still cringe when recalling how I had ignored Mumford's obvious misgivings. The truth is I was set on a posting and only too ready to accept Placements's homespun offering over Mumford's warning that some sort of bureaucratic malfeasance was afoot.

CHAPTER 4

MOSCOW

Unlike more benign postings, where the host government is friendlier, I found on arrival in Moscow in February 1973 that all British staff had diplomatic status, regardless of agency or position. But there were unofficially *A*-list and *B*-list diplomats. I was squarely a *B*-lister; the result being demotion in the pecking order when it came to embassy car parks, inferior office and living accommodation and often the incurrence of *A*-list disdain.

My courier work provided a reason periodically to access the embassy's secure area. There was not much moral support forthcoming from my MI6 colleagues within. In fact, James Sim the station head pointedly told me to avoid unnecessary contact with any of his people. He needn't have bothered; the nine others in the station ignored me as one. Time rolled by. I slaved away organizing furniture lots from Denmark for use in the embassy's staff apartments. In between, on average every fortnight, I travelled to most East European capitals carting my diplomatic bags. Out on the road, I was diligent in building cover, exploring the nightlife and generally trying to be seen as the life of the party.

After six months *en poste*, I started a relationship with a secretary from the American Embassy, an engaging Bostonian called Patsy. In Moscow's repressive atmosphere romances among Westerners bloomed easily and, on stumbling over her through my work, my affection for

Patsy sprouted in the environment. But once into the involvement, the initially strong spark vanished. The instinct to be alone was overpowering. In six weeks we were done. Loneliness and depression engulfed me. For a time afterwards I drank heavily, until the all too familiar bout of despondency had receded. Fortunately, the embassy caste system was such that no one who mattered was about to drop in and witness my maudlin behaviour night after night in the darkened confines of my hateful Prospekt Mira apartment. That was a secret between me and the microphones buried deep in the apartment walls.

———◆—◆———

How long I might have been left *building cover* is anyone's guess. But British politics again intervened. In two by-elections held in late July 1973, the Conservatives lost both previously held parliamentary seats. All in Westminster knew Edward Heath's government was doomed. Maurice Oldfield was now heading MI6. Oldfield had a keen political nose and was intent on avoiding trouble when Harold Wilson inevitably reclaimed the prime ministership. To that end, in September 1973, during the dark period following the demise of my liaison with Patsy and as I was beginning to see that Placements's aim in posting me to Moscow was to coerce me into disillusioned resignation, Oldfield sought an update from his head administrator on progress in expanding the Service's social breadth.

To his apparent consternation, Oldfield discovered that of the five yokels recruited, to use the label applied liberally throughout the Service to the likes of me, three had resigned and another had taken a home-based position. Only I was in the field. I say *apparent consternation* because later that day a *Secret* message *Personal for Sim from Oldfield* was flashed to Moscow: *As soon as feasible Lambert is to be given an operational task. Ready him.*

———◆—◆———

The Russian winter came early in 1973–74. One night towards the end of September I was hurrying to my car anxious to beat the evening chill. A member of the MI6 station sidled up to me. 'Joe,' he said, 'how are you doing?'

I looked at him warily. This fellow was an *A*-lister and had never spoken to me before. I thought he was an arrogant shit. 'Yes?' I said as coldly as I could.

'Old Jimmy wants an audience first thing tomorrow morning. As soon as you get free, would you mind dropping in?' I recognized the technique. By speaking disrespectfully of the station chief he was establishing a little bond between us designed to build rapport. 'Nothing to worry about,' he added before I had a chance to respond. 'Cheers.' And then he was gone.

James Sim at least had the decency to look embarrassed. 'Ah, ah, Joe, come in,' he said nervously. To his assistant sitting outside his office he shouted, 'Let's have some coffee down the back.' Down the back referred to a windowless room deeper in the already windowless secure area, where sensitive conversations were held. I knew of it but until now had never set foot in it. 'I've been watching your progress, Joe,' Sim began, 'and I'm quite impressed.' With this lie he was no longer able to hold my gaze. 'I've decided you're ready to get into something a bit meatier,' he said looking to one side. 'How do you feel your cover build has come along?'

'Well,' I said, 'every hooker in the lounge bar at the Polski Hotel in Warsaw knows me by name.' Sim looked at me as if I had just said something distasteful but otherwise let the sarcasm pass.

'Good,' he said without conviction. 'I'll recommend back to London it advise all Eastern Bloc station heads you are now an asset to be utilized.' That awkward moment over, Sim smiled a fatherly smile. 'Big career moment for you, Joe, your activation. Sabrina's having a dinner party this Friday night to celebrate. But for we people, of course,' Sim said, theatrically tapping the side of his nose with his forefinger, 'cover is always key. It'll be a pretend birthday party for some lassie at the Dutch Embassy. None of those wearing clogs will be in the know.'

Sabrina was Sim's right-hand woman, the one who had made us coffee. Beyond a cursory nod, she had never before acknowledged my existence. She came cavorting up as I left the secure area and placed a manicured hand on my forearm. 'Hope you can make it Friday night, Joe,' she gushed.

'B-b-be pleased,' I stammered. And with a conspiratorial wink and flashing smile she sent me on my way.

What did I make of all this? Well I knew I hadn't imagined my time in spying Siberia. Evidently something had changed, but as to what I was clueless. Where some of the station's males were close, I had no such relationship. Unsurprisingly, therefore, efforts to coax a reason for my activation out of my Service colleagues were not fruitful. Not until many years later did I gain access to the files and see the DG Maurice Oldfield's 1973 note to his head administrator querying progress on the expansion of the Service's social breadth, attached to which was Oldfield's subsequent message to James Sim. But at the time I ultimately gave up wondering and gratefully embarked on my new career direction.

A *Secret* cable from East Berlin station arrived in early December 1973 asking if *Leonard*, the code name given to my floating resource role, could be released to do a live drop in East Berlin on 19 December. The trip to East Berlin would be my third since arriving in Moscow. By now, so the theory ran, the Stasi would be inured to my comings and goings and not give my travel a second thought.

———◆—◆———

The excitement of my launch into operational work was just a distant memory as I jetted back to London with my tail between my legs. I resisted the urge to drown my sorrows with a few whiskies. The inquest into what went wrong in East Berlin would be bad enough without someone trumping up a story I was out of control on the sauce. It was the Friday night when I landed. London's Christmas lights cheered me temporarily. But booking into the Strand Castle Hotel, my mood soured when recalling my high hopes on arriving at the hotel nearly two years earlier on the eve of joining the Service. *What a fucking mess*, I thought. Sleep proved elusive that night. I was resigned to dismissal and sought refuge in such fatalism.

Head of Placements, Martin Mumford and a senior officer called Edis Aksu were waiting when I arrived at headquarters on the Saturday morning, 22 December. Placements's smouldering silence made clear his general unhappiness at being dragged into the office on a weekend. Mumford spoke first, addressing me. 'You may know,' he said, 'that Mr Aksu oversees the conduct of East German affairs. The top floor executive has asked him to undertake an in-house inquiry into the Konrad matter and report in early January.' Preamble over, Mumford moved to specifics. 'Konrad,' he said, 'was a low-level clerk in the East German Ministry of Finance. His job was to maintain his agency's files, enabling him for a time to provide us with an extraordinary range of unimpeachable intelligence. Our failure to protect him and get him out is highly prejudicial to recruiting other similarly placed sources. It will impede our East German efforts for years to come.' With that, Mumford paused waiting for Aksu to speak.

Aksu was reputedly of Turkish background, having come to England with his family as a child. A dark, slightly built man, he stared unblinkingly at colleagues when conversing. This was a natural trait but it unnerved his *confrères* all the same. Aksu stared briefly at me. 'Perhaps we should hear Joe's version of events,' he said, signalling my interrogation was about to begin.

— ✦ ✦ —

Wanting to remain strong and alert, I stared down the temptation to buy myself a bottle of whisky for Christmas. Time passed slowly. I had declined the offer of leave, figuring I could do with the payout when I was sacked, and spent my work days in the so-called transit lounge, a staging area within head office equipped with desks and other office paraphernalia where, as necessary, returning officers sat before taking up head office appointments. I found a small flat off unfashionable Albany Road in South London and moved in during the first week of January 1974.

I never formally heard another word about East Berlin. Many years later my access to the files, and by dint of that Aksu's report, revealed he had declined to scapegoat me – no doubt to the chagrin of Stephen Maunder-Roberts, the East Berlin station head who maintained Konrad intended to go West the same night he was to receive his papers. Instead, Aksu determined that Konrad's cover of a work visit to West Berlin dictated a less-conspicuous morning crossing at a time well after his pre-dawn arrest. This led Aksu ultimately to conclude that Operation Skyman's failure was immaterial. He had also somehow divined that East Berlin station knew suspicions about Konrad were emerging. Yet neither London nor Konrad was warned of this. *As a result*, Aksu wrote, *Konrad was left in place too long, possibly to enhance the career prospects of some in East Berlin station.* Aksu's report attached all blame for Konrad's detection to this. Konrad was shot just six hours after his arrest. I never did find out why he spied for us.

Maunder-Roberts had left the Service after returning from East Berlin. On reading the report, I came to understand this was the result of him mishandling Konrad. For his part, Aksu died prematurely, at age forty-five, almost five years to the day from the date of his report. Prostate cancer. He was not in the business of doing favours for anyone. But I owe a lot to him and his unstintingly objective inquiry. I shudder to think what might have happened had any of the other Johnnies around the place conducted the review, imbued in class prejudice as most of them were.

CHAPTER 5

SARAH

Sitting in the transit lounge in the first week of January 1974 I had no inkling as to the conclusions Edis Aksu would draw. I'd long given up any pretence of working and spent my time drinking cups of coffee and reading Harold Robbins's *The Carpetbaggers*. Then on the Thursday of the following week, head of Placements suddenly manifested in front of me. 'Wotcha reading, battlecruiser?' he asked, addressing me using the cockney rhyming slang for *boozer* and gibbering like the East End barrow boy he certainly was not. 'You got a minute?' he said without waiting for my answer.

I thought, *Mate, I've got the rest of my life*, but simply said, 'Sure.' On the way to his office, Placements talked about football and his love for Tottenham Hotspur. I was mightily confused by this time. I'd expected a summons and a curt sign this, get out of here and don't come back. Instead, Placements was treating me like we were long lost buddies. On reaching his office, Placements settled in one of his comfortable visitor chairs and invited me to sit in another.

'Joe,' he said, 'you've been good enough to come home early from Moscow to assist us with some pressing matters. We need to recognize this. Unfortunately, your departure from the embassy was too definite for you to go back.' I opened my mouth to speak. Placements held up a hand like a policeman stopping traffic. 'There is no further need to discuss these past events,' he said emphatically. With that, I shut up. I had no idea that Placements, in hot water with the DG for his unauthorized attempt to push me from the Service, had now been charged with making good in light of Aksu's findings.

'Now as I was saying,' Placements continued, 'there was a promotion round you might ordinarily have contested that closed just before Christmas. The lazy sods on the committee are all on holidays and won't report until the end of January. If you wanted to make an application it will be considered. Freehand writing is fine. No need to submit it through channels. Return it to me and I will process it. A couple of paragraphs will suffice. Get it to me before we finish tomorrow afternoon, there's a good chap.'

Placements smiled at me. I noticed the teeth at the extremities of his mouth were yellow from cigarette smoking. I wondered if I was the Service's only non-smoker – my mother's death had delivered me a stark warning about the evils of tobacco. Placements's announcement that he wanted to *look to the immediate future* withdrew me from my reverie. 'Have you ever been to Asia, Joe?' he asked, knowing full well I hadn't. 'Lots going on out there these days, especially in Dutch Indonesia. Seems the Sovs are still trying to cosy up to this Soeharto fellow.' I must have looked vacant. 'The strong man army general who became president half a dozen years back,' Placements explained impatiently.

With that, he abruptly jumped up and moved to the telephone on his desk where he dialled three times, indicating a call to an internal number, and spoke quietly into the mouthpiece. In a matter of seconds a tall, bespectacled woman entered the office. She had lank hair and wore a mien of intensity. 'Joe,' Placements said, 'I'd like you to meet Beverley Wellingham. Bev looks after our affairs in South East Asia.' Wellingham shook my hand forcefully, her body twisting as a result of the energy she expended. 'We'd like you to take up a position working on Dutch Indonesia,' Placements said.

'Actually, Cam,' Wellingham interjected, abbreviating Placements's first name of Campbell, 'it's not been Dutch Indonesia since 1949. It's now the Republic of Indonesia.'

Placements seemed to regard this as a mere technicality. 'Whatever it's called, Joe, we'd like you to spend six months in Bev's area to familiarize yourself.' He looked at Wellingham but spoke to me. 'We'll then give you a further six months to learn a bit of the lingo. By that stage you should be ready in the New Year to take up a posting with Jakarta station. What say you?'

'Yes … yes, that should be fine,' was all I could get out.

'Excellent,' Placements said. 'That's settled.' He never spoke warmly to me again.

———————

A lanky, prematurely balding man answering directly to Beverley Wellingham headed the Indonesia section. His name was Hanson Scott and his stock joke was to call himself Handsome Scott. Hanson had been a journalist in Indonesia and spoke the language well. He was good to me and made sure I was allocated a decent desk. I was granted access to reams of secret reports detailing Indonesia's turbulent past, as well as the cables from Jakarta station that arrived overnight while we were sleeping.

Soeharto, it transpires, was virulently anti-communist and extremely ruthless with it. Ever since he literally wrenched the presidency from his predecessor in 1967, the Soviets had experienced difficulty in gaining traction with him. But South East Asia was important to the Soviets – warm water ports high on their list of priorities. And with Soeharto decisively influential within the region, the Soviets were relentless in their efforts to cultivate him. Service interests in Indonesia, therefore, focused on Soviet efforts to get into Soeharto's good books – on how the Bear intended ingratiation with the regional colossus.

I stayed in the Indonesia area for six months as Placements had promised. Towards the end of that time, while lunching in the staff cafeteria with other section members, a Canadian exchange colleague joined us. Sarah Sutherland was about my age. She had long brown hair and beautiful hazel eyes. As would happen with me, some days I was more socially outgoing than others. For no good reason on this particular day, I was cleverly light on my feet. Our lunch turned into a laugh-fest, with me the lead funny man. I suggested to Sarah as we left the cafeteria we take in a film at the weekend. 'That'd be great,' she said in her soft Vancouver drawl.

Sarah lived in Cottesmore Gardens in upmarket Kensington. We went to see *Doctor Zhivago* at a cinema not far from there. I had spent only ten months in Moscow and, apart from two or three weekend trips, had never been elsewhere in Russia. Sarah let me impress her by telling her how nostalgic the film made me, although she was too smart not to recognize the licence I was taking. Afterwards we ate supper at a trattoria, while sharing a bottle of chianti and many laughs. Sarah and I kissed tenderly that night as we parted. For the next few days, I was flush with optimism. I was daring to think I had finally found someone whom I could love.

Sarah and I had agreed to have lunch on the Wednesday following our outing, to finalize plans tentatively made for the coming weekend. We had only an hour, so I booked a table at St Irvin's Hotel close to the office. Bad, bad mistake. Half the Service was there. Sarah was unsettled by the sly looks directed at us. My anxiety mounted. Lunch was a disaster, not helped by slow service, during which we sat in increasingly strained silence. Mid-afternoon back at the office my telephone rang. It was Sarah. 'I won't be able to make it this weekend,' she said. 'Something's come up.'

I was hardly a world expert on women but I knew the kiss of death when I heard it. 'OK, sorry to hear that,' I said. A pause, and the telephone went dead. I sat there stunned. In a blur, I stumbled to the men's toilets and locked myself in a cubicle. The tears flowed. I just couldn't reconcile the rejection. In all other things I was capable, robust and resilient; why was I so useless when it came to relationships? That night I self-medicated. Sucking mints to cover my whisky breath, I dragged myself into the office the next morning. Miserable and hungover I somehow got through the day, which ended with me in bed by 8 pm with a belly full of fish and chips.

Awaking early the next morning, I resolved to forget about relationships and throw myself into my work. Comparable priority would be afforded to no other thing. In the process, I reasoned, I would honour to the fullest my pledge to my mother to make something of myself. I knew that my orchestrated promotion – more meritoriously my not-so-good friends Rupert Heneshaw and Freddie Ladler were on the same list – was designed to shut me up. I also knew my posting to Indonesia, far from the Service's centre of gravity, was to keep me out of sight and hence out of mind. Unaware of the high-level political imperatives driving events, I was oblivious as to why all this had happened. But I had survived the Konrad farce in East Berlin, somehow. I was now going to make the most of my second chance, to the exclusion of all else.

A week later I commenced language training in the Service's language unit housed within the headquarters building. At the end of the allotted six months, I passed both my final spoken and written language tests with flying colours. Administrative arrangements finalized; the lease on my Albany Road flat terminated; and a lacklustre farewell in the office with my fellow Indonesia section colleagues, and I was done. In early March 1975 I boarded British Airways flight 388 for Jakarta via Hong Kong.

CHAPTER 6

NOUGHT

Using an embassy airport pass, Dan Milburn from the Jakarta station met me on the airside of the immigration and customs barriers. I was replacing Dan and would inherit things like his service-provided car and accommodation. We were to have a three-day handover. Dan's cover was as a political second secretary; as his replacement I was to adopt the same. We entered the diplomatic passport holder immigration lane. I bowled up to the counter. 'Selamat malam. Bagaimana anda?' I said in my best Indonesian.

'Aku baik terima kasih,' the immigration officer responded. 'Selamat datang di Indonesia.' I was ecstatic. In confirming his good health and welcoming me to Indonesia, the official had clearly understood my question and I, moreover, his answer.

Waiting for my bags to arrive, Dan was moved by my over eagerness to prick my balloon. 'Indonesian's a dead easy language,' he said in the manner the jaded reserve for the new and enthusiastic. 'It's all phonetic.' Dan's evident irritation also caused him not to bother much with a handover. But I was happy to make my own way. The apartment I acquired from Dan after he left was thankfully close to the embassy – travelling any distance in Jakarta's maddening traffic was not for the faint-hearted.

The station chief was a smooth Londoner named Noel Parfitt. He was declared to the Indonesians for liaison purposes, which meant the Indonesian Government had been advised of his true status. As with declared Service officers the world over, Parfitt's liaison centred on information exchange and, as required, inter-Service cooperation. The remaining three station officers, me now included, were undeclared. We were the field men charged with the station's clandestine work. As far as the Indonesians and many UK embassy staff were concerned, we were Foreign Office diplomats.

Parfitt called me in once Dan had gone. 'Joe,' he said, 'I want you to get out into the community. Where there's an opening of an envelope, you should be there.' This was a reference to the never-ending stream of invitations the embassy received to cultural events and diplomatic receptions.

I nodded agreement. 'Handsome Scott told me I would also probably do liaison with junior CIA staff at the American Embassy.'

If Parfitt detected my appropriation of Hanson's joke he gave no indication. Indeed, he fairly bristled. 'I manage all CIA liaison,' he said tartly. 'Your job is to be out there watching and noting. In everything you do, you are to keep me informed. You are not to move a muscle in anybody's direction without approval. If you see someone of possible interest tell me, or one of the others. Got it?'

Parfitt made no mention of the agents the station had on its books. But I knew from reading cables in London that Mike Milligan, one of my two subordinate colleagues, had a stable of agents. In those communications agents were referred to only by work names. Reading between the lines, though, most appeared to be either Indonesian academics or mid-level government officials.

The other of my subordinate colleagues was an extraordinary character called McNaught Collins. 'Call me Nought,' he said, 'as in zero. Everyone else does.' Nought was about to embark on his fourth year at Jakarta station. He had come to Jakarta directly from a three-year posting to Phnom Penh, reflecting he was not in great demand back in London. Nought was only fifty-six, but to me looked as old as Methuselah. He was apparently a wine connoisseur – and plainly the wine had won. Purple of nose, he was like a glorified in-house research unit. He did no work out of the office that I ever saw, principally because he knew the Service would put him out to pasture when he finished in Jakarta. For all that, he was the sagest person I have ever met. Nought's value to the station was his knowledge of the Indonesian bureaucracy. This seemed to come only from a close reading of the Indonesian newspapers. But he was like a walking encyclopedia. Ask Nought about this Indonesian official or that and he seemed to know him like a brother.

Nought and I shared an interest in cricket. The Australian cricket team was touring England in the summer of 1975. Nought and I bonded while sitting up half the night listening to scratchy BBC short wave broadcasts of the Test matches. We chuckled together at the rich bucolic tones of broadcaster John Arlott. Nought particularly enjoyed Arlott's evocative descriptions of solitary outfielders dispatched to the playing field's distant reaches. Soon Nought had coined the term *The Far Grass,* his means for referring to the location of isolated outfielders. I endlessly mimicked the expression, calling it *the foie gras* in a wordplay on the duck liver pâté that was all the rage at the time – a nod and a wink to the fact I couldn't stand the stuff. But I was callow at the time and never even considered that Nought might attach a more serious meaning to *The Far Grass* appellation. I grew to revere Nought. He became the only close male friend I ever had.

Meanwhile I did exactly as Parfitt had directed, unrelentingly so. I attended diplomatic functions most weeknights and every cultural event possible. I also filled the vacant vice-presidency of a UK–Indonesia friendship group, participants in which were a couple of pedestrian officials from the Indonesian Ministry of Culture and a variable smattering of Indonesian and expatriate British people.

Monthly gatherings were held in a ground floor room in the Ministry. These were generally desultory affairs, so much so I would have quit the group were it not for my unwavering commitment to career. About nine months into my posting, an annual general meeting, or AGM, was held and office bearers elected. Unsurprisingly, I was returned unopposed as vice-president. The Ministry hosted an after-meeting reception to mark the AGM's occasion. The promise of free food and drink had attracted a larger turn out than usual, including several people I hadn't seen before.

I grabbed a glass of wine and started to mingle. At receptions and the like, I was always on the lookout for talent. And although open-minded about whom, by weight of numbers my focus was usually on Indonesians. My attention turned to a small, well dressed Indonesian man of about forty speaking with three Western persons. 'Hello, I'm Joe Lambert, British Embassy,' I said muscling in on the group. This was not rudeness. Receptions worked like this. Two of the Westerners moved on, leaving me with the Indonesian and a tall woman in her mid-twenties. The man's business card declared him to be an employee of the Provincial Bank of Java, the PBJ. His name was Hartono Sumardi. The tall woman was Hilda Stadler, in-house counsel of the Jakarta office of Alberta Minerals Pty Ltd.

I launched into trawling mode, using Hilda as an initial conversation point but all the while focused on Hartono. 'Where is Alberta Minerals headquartered?' I asked Hilda.

'Calgary,' she said. 'We have interests in gold mining here. I'm from Edmonton. Opportunities in Canada for young lawyers are quite limited. An employment agency alerted me to this job.'

I smiled at Hilda before turning to Hartono, wanting to be sure he didn't feel left out of the conversation. 'So tell me about the Provincial Bank of Java,' I said, projecting interest.

'PBJ is a government-owned bank,' Hartono replied. 'It specializes in cheap, rupiah-denominated loans to foreign investors for meeting in-country expenses without converting hard currency. I've had past dealings with the friendship group and convinced Hilda to come along tonight.' Hilda smiled a tight smile suggesting she had mixed feelings about this. 'Hilda's company is a major PBJ client,' Hartono explained. 'We have a lot to do with each other.'

We talked generally about minerals exploration in Indonesia. As the conversation began to slow, I made my preliminary play. In training it had been emphasized that Service officers should have a social platform, such as a golf or tennis club membership. I couldn't hit a golf ball to save myself but was an adequate social tennis player. I had joined the tennis club at the Republic Hotel. 'Do either of you play tennis?' I asked.

'I'm reasonable,' Hilda said with frank confidence.

'I'm not so good,' Hartono volunteered coyly.

'Well, Pak Hartono,' I said, using the respectful Indonesian form of male address, 'that makes two of us. How about we three play this Friday night? I'm a member at the Republic. I'll book the court for 7 pm for an hour. It's lovely under the lights.' Hartono consulted a small diary before agreeing he could make it.

Ever since my arrival, whenever I suggested a possible target, usually an Indonesian, Parfitt and Milligan had pretended to consider the proposal before rejecting it. I had discussed this with Nought. 'The Indonesian political elite is ripping off the place blind,' he said. 'Spoils of victory; it's an era of excess. No wonder then that a lot of Indonesians further down the food chain – in government; the military; academia; you name it – are open to inducement. Who can blame them? Parfitt is content to have Milligan rely on these sources, even if in my opinion many of the agents recruited are of dubious quality, not to mention expensive to run. The base fact, Joe, is they don't want you muddying the cosy waters.'

'So what should I do?'

'What is needed,' Nought said, 'is a really big fish. Someone with direct access to Soviet thinking, thereby avoiding dependence on Indon sources. A source in the local KGB station is the ideal. That's why we're here, supposedly, looking for reliable insights into Soviet efforts to build standing with Soeharto.'

'OK,' I said. 'How do I get up close to an in the know Soviet?'

'It's difficult. The Sovs keep their people on a tight leash, usually only allowing them to leave the embassy in pairs or groups. My advice is to keep working on your tradecraft wherever you can. That way if the chance arises to nab a Soviet, you'll be ready for it.'

----◆◆----

With Nought's advice in mind, I made the decision to pursue Hartono without telling Parfitt or Milligan about him. *Apart from developing my tradecraft,* I thought, *he may appeal so much that they can't help but agree to a recruitment attempt.*

I had considered enlisting a fourth player for my tennis date with Hartono and Hilda in order that we might play doubles. But eventually I decided it would spread the conversation too thin. On the night, therefore, I suggested it would be too hot to be running around for the full hour and proposed we play round-robin singles.

Hilda's long legs took her speedily around the court. She mercilessly disposed of Hartono, so much so that when I stepped up I thought I should ensure I suffered the same fate. And when I played Hartono I deliberately let him win, just in case his ego was in anyway bruised.

Over a lime juice, Hartono and I joked about our lack of tennis prowess in the face of Hilda's onslaught. Hilda laughed along with us, appearing not to realize I'd been holding back. After allowing ten minutes more of chit-chat, I turned to cultivating Hartono. 'What's PBJ's book value?' I asked him conversationally.

'One hundred and fifty trillion rupiah,' he replied. By my calculation that was roughly fifteen billion US dollars. 'Please don't ask me how much of that is black money,' he added, laughing generously. 'We have a *don't ask* policy when it comes to deposits.'

Excitement coursed through me, overtaking caution and I didn't address the obvious – why Hartono was telling me his bank was corrupt. 'No, no, of course not,' I said. 'I wouldn't want to pry.' *Is he trying to impress Hilda?* I wondered. 'I bet though you've got some interesting names as clients?'

Hartono chuckled. 'We certainly do,' he said, looking earnestly at me, as if Hilda wasn't there.

My God, he's trying to impress me, I thought, initially astonished but then recalling Nought's advice about the current malleability of Indonesian officials. And the more Hartono stared at me, the surer I was of him fitting the mould. 'How about lunch next week?' I said. 'I have a commerce background and am keen to learn about the Jakarta business scene.'

'I will have to check my diary,' Hartono replied sharply.

At the time, Hartono's response struck me as odd, as if it were a reflex rather than a considered reply. But in my eagerness I was prepared to disregard the warning signal by treating his answer as the reaction of a man whose life revolved around his diary. After all, at the earlier friendship group meeting when I had proposed an evening's tennis, a check of his diary had similarly preceded Hartono's agreement to play. 'Fine,' I said, 'I'll call you next week.'

CHAPTER 7

LESSONS

In the week following our tennis outing, I set my sights on Hartono in earnest. As soon as I thought I could make contact without seeming too keen, I telephoned him at his office to ask if he would like to have lunch the coming Friday. 'Friday's not so good for me,' Hartono said. 'But why don't me meet at the Wayang Puppet museum on Thursday afternoon, about three?'

It's fair to say that Hartono's curious suggestion surprised me, coming as it did on top of his odd response when I had suggested lunch while having a drink after our tennis. But I wasn't about to turn him down. The museum was in Old Batavia, the Jakarta old town. In this discreet setting, I made my pitch. 'If you can provide me with a picture of the banking habits of any Indonesian minister,' I put to Hartono, 'I can arrange for a payment in return.'

Hartono barely blinked. 'I don't have much on political figures,' he said. 'But two or three Deplu officials might be of interest.' *Deplu* was the Indonesian Department of Foreign Affairs. 'I would prefer US dollars, cash,' he added, smiling genially.

I was fairly tingling with excitement. Not even Parfitt could ignore this opportunity. I told Hartono I'd get back to him shortly.

I raced back to the office – raced being a relative term in the Jakarta traffic. Both Parfitt and Milligan were out. I sauntered proudly around to Nought. 'Just hooked a nice little fish,' I said casually.

'Is that so?' Nought replied without enthusiasm. 'President Soeharto, I assume?'

'Not quite,' I said, a little peeved at Nought's sarcasm. 'A banker with info on payments made to corrupt Deplu officials.'

'Tell me the details,' Nought demanded curtly. I told him all about Hartono and how I'd come across him. 'Wait here,' he said, 'and don't say anything to anyone until I say so.' Nought returned carrying a folder. Opening it, he pointed to a poor quality photograph of someone alighting from a taxi. 'Is this your man?'

The image was grainy but Hartono's face was clear. The trouble was the file referred to a PBJ source called Hendra Sutrisno. 'What's going on?' I asked, my apprehension rising.

'Seems Hartono is chasing some extra cash on the side,' Nought said. 'It's not unheard of among agents. Milligan already has him on the books, but as Pak Hendra. Mike tries to photograph those of his recruits unlikely to appear in the newspapers and so forth. Hartono's clearly unaware of this because his key judgement is that you and Mike comparing notes will not undo him: silly foreigners confused by two Indonesians of similar names and descriptions who both work for the PBJ, that sort of thing. Hartono is probably his real name if, as you say, he uses that with Hilda who's a bank client. He's likely snared Mike by offering to sell him the political information he told you he doesn't have, adopting the Hendra name to protect his true identity. He would have known only too well the risks involved in snitching on the political class.'

I was still not convinced. 'But what if Milligan and I see him when together? I say Hartono and Mike says Hendra.'

Nought thought about this. 'I suspect Hartono's relying on a combination of our compartmentalization and Jakarta being a big city,' he said. 'Mike will be running him as a sensitive source, only meeting him alone and after dark, and somewhere obscure. Hartono would have demanded the same of you. And Hartono will engage with Westerners only when he knows it's safe to do so. Otherwise, out there in the kampong he's invisible to us. All this virtually eliminates the risk of you and Mike stumbling over him together.'

Nought was right. It was a strict Service edict that officers should never unnecessarily expose sensitive sources to other Service colleagues. Nought's assessment also caused me to recall that Milligan was away in Semarang the Friday night we played tennis at the Republic. Hartono must have had prior knowledge of this. That's why he checked his diary at the preceding friendship group event before agreeing to play. This exemplified Nought's point about Hartono engaging with Westerners only when he thought it safe to do so, while otherwise remaining hidden in his local community. 'OK,' I said, 'but why did Hartono attend the friendship group AGM? How could he be sure Milligan wouldn't have been there and seen he was calling himself Hartono? Once Hartono decided he needed to bring Hilda along as a foil he had no option to be anyone else.'

'Hartono has previously rubbed shoulders with the friendship group,' Nought said. 'He knows that no self-respecting British diplomat would ever bother with a motley lot like it. Your name and where you worked would have been on the paperwork circulated for the AGM elections. This told him you were Service and also there was no chance of Milligan attending. We were hardly likely to send two people to work so lowbrow an event. Hartono evidently calculated this was his chance to try and make some extra cash.'

'Even so,' I said, not wanting to believe what was becoming increasingly apparent, 'Hartono's scam seems pretty brazen.'

'He does sound desperate, I'd agree,' Nought said, laughing. 'Perhaps he has a gambling debt or maybe has purloined money from the bank and needs to pay it back in a hurry, who knows?'

I shook my head. 'The sneaky bastard wanted to sell me the Deplu stuff because he could ask top dollar for it. If he sold it to Mike as Hendra, he knew he would get little more than what he's already getting for the political intelligence he's selling him. And if we were to have Mike ask *Hendra* for the Deplu material he would have had fifty good reasons ready why that was not possible.'

'That's almost certainly true,' Nought said. 'But listen, we're in a position to stay shtum on this. Neither Parfitt nor Milligan know how advanced you got, and Hartono's not about to tell them when he doesn't hear from you again. Also take comfort from the fact that your groundwork was first class. You've gained a lot of valuable experience and will be a wiser man next time around.'

<hr>

I took leave in Singapore after completing a year at the post. It gave me a chance to step back. I reflected on the Hartono fiasco but took encouragement from Nought saying I had acquitted myself well. I resolved to ignore Parfitt's negativity and be ready to take any opportunity that arose. I returned to Jakarta my ambition to succeed fully restored. Nought was preparing for departure. He had a sister in Bath and was planning to retire close by, in Bristol.

We had a boozy night to say farewell. I was well in my cups when Nought mentioned I should get married. 'The Service prefers its men married, Joe,' he said, 'and preferably to good English stock. Hetero-sexual domesticity equals good security they think. It's a hangover from the Cambridge disaster.' I understood Nought was referring to the infamous Cambridge University homosexual spy ring, whose number included the former MI6 officer Kim Philby who had fled to Moscow thirteen years earlier. Nought shook his head. 'It's bollocks, total bollocks, but believe me being married is critical if you're going to advance much beyond your current level. Old divorced sots like me are a dying breed.'

Nought paused, as if debating whether to continue. 'You're hiding in *The Far Grass*, Joey,' he said finally. 'It's a natural trait; you're a loner and that's how you're made. Being unmarried will hurt your career, no doubt, ...'

The warning about career catapulted me deep into drunken contemplation. *So it's not a joke about duck liver pâté,* I thought. *He's warning that the Service could brand me as a loner and, based on the Cambridge experience, treat me as a potential security risk.*

My preoccupation was such that it blotted out Nought's second warning, seamlessly following his mention of career implications, '... but hiding in *The Far Grass* can also have ruinous personal con-sequences.' I heard the words and understood they had been said gravely. But they just didn't permeate. I was way too gone on the booze by this stage and reduced to doing one thing at a time.

My incomprehension convinced Nought to move on. 'They're going to send a woman called Penelope Hutton, Doctor Penelope Hutton, actually, as station chief when Parfitt finishes in six months from now,' he said. 'Penelope's an Islamic studies academic who has spent many years here teaching. Wonderful linguist. The Service will finally get a decent return on the station's liaison with the Indons now it has twigged to them filling Parfitt's head with nonsense. It's really a masterstroke. She's first rate. She'll want you to take the initiative and be active in looking for recruits.'

Nought topped up our glasses; Beaujolais I think it was. 'I'll see Penelope in the UK and put in a good word for you. She used to rate me back when we worked together and I was on. Why don't you ask headquarters if you can stay here until the end of '77? It'll agree. That'll give you around fifteen months of working with Penelope to use as a career launching pad. But remember, you need to find some tart and settle down. It's important.' The next morning Nought claimed he couldn't remember a thing past the opening of our third bottle. I didn't believe him for a moment. In a reputed quest for budget savings, he wasn't replaced when he left.

CHAPTER 8

BORIS

Penelope Hutton arrived in early October 1976. She was as Nought said she would be. In a matter of days the office atmosphere changed from cautious and restrained to relaxed and confident. Free of Parfitt's influence, Milligan became warmer towards me. By Christmas he had started to call me *Joey* and was happily responding to *Spike*. I returned from leave at the end of January 1977 imbued with enthusiasm to tackle the year ahead.

By now I'd grown to like the rank and file Indonesians whom I found polite, honest and kind in their dealings with foreigners. But liking the people was one thing and watching endless hours of traditional dancing, puppet shows and suchlike was quite another. The truth is, I guess, I wasn't sophisticated enough to appreciate its charms. But the cultural grind was at my cover's core. I stuck at it.

In early April I was offered the opportunity to travel to Surabaya, Indonesia's second largest city, with one of the embassy's senior Foreign Office diplomats. Primarily I was on hand to be the notetaker at his calls on local officials. But wearing my cultural hat, I had also arranged to attend a performance of traditional East Java dance. Although I had little interest in the dance rendition *per se*, I was keen to take up the embassy's invitation given my determination to explore every available opportunity. If nothing else, the event was a chance to keep an eye out for possible contacts.

The cultural performance, as it turns out, concluded with a reception on a riverboat anchored at a nearby canal. On boarding, I noticed a good-looking, fair-haired man, in his late thirties I estimated, speaking fluently in Indonesian to the event organizers. Speeches were made and refreshments served. Some speakers recognized dignitaries present in opening remarks. The blond man charismatically waved a hand when Mr Vasily Rykov, the Soviet Embassy's Cultural Attaché, was acknowledged. He looked briefly at me when well down the list plain old Joe Lambert from the British Embassy rated a mention. Vasily had two sullen colleagues with him. They stood silent and blank-faced, seemingly out of their depth while everyone, Vasily included, ignored them. The contrast with Vasily's easy charm as he set about working the Indonesians piqued my interest. I was sure Vasily would be of appeal to us, cultural man or whatever he was.

After a time, Vasily and I were invited to join the dancers for photographs. The troupe's leader, a man called Wahyu, was an especially enthusiastic photographer. He had a Nikon camera, small for the times. Seeking to conscript more photographic subjects, he placed the camera on a shelf behind the jerry-rigged speaker's podium and ran off to the room's far reaches. People were milling around and talking animatedly. Penelope had encouraged us to back our instincts, as Nought had foreshadowed. I made the split-second decision to walk to the back of the podium, where a huge public address speaker blocked clear vision of me. In the one action, I whipped the camera off the shelf and stuck it down the front of my trousers. My loose-fitting batik shirt covered the abnormal bulge in my groin. Sweating from the humidity but otherwise steeled, I locked myself in the boat's disgusting toilet. There I wound the film forward to protect it from exposure and removed it from the camera.

A moment of internal conflict suddenly overtook me. On one hand, I badly wanted to return the camera to Pak Wahyu. Like most

Indonesians he was a courteous man and had certainly done me no disservice. On the other, I knew if I left the camera to be found *sans* film Vasily would understand something was up. I looked in the fly-spotted mirror. To my surprise a hard-eyed, uncompromising face stared back at me. I knew then that profession trumped principle. Exiting the toilet, I walked to the starboard side of the boat where, on making sure the coast was clear, I dropped the camera into the murky water. I returned to the reception room to find Pak Wahyu searching for his property. Before too long he understood the camera had been stolen. His philosophical response masked his upset and satisfied his instinctive need to save face.

Spike and I developed the film when I was back in the Jakarta office. There were several good shots of Vasily. Penelope praised my initiative. There was no pushing me out of the way and taking the credit. We cabled London with Vasily's details and how he had come to our notice, photographs to follow by diplomatic bag. Before too long a reply arrived. Vasily was KGB to his bootstraps, real name of Nikolai Ivanovich Klimentov, born 1938 in Murmansk. He had previously served in Turkey and Iran. Headquarters gave us the go-ahead to check him out, allocating him the unimaginative code name of Boris. I was thrilled to be commended for my work.

❦

We began trawling for Boris at diplomatic receptions, looking for points of access to him. Penelope soon discovered that Boris had taken charge of a white Peugeot with gaudy red trim in which he drove colleagues to and from events. The Peugeot's diplomatic licence plate was *CD 37 167*, the numerals *37* informing those in the know the car belonged to a Soviet diplomat. Penelope told me to focus on Boris's vehicle and see where it led me.

The Soviet Embassy was located in South Jakarta. It occupied a huge compound fronting onto HR Rasuna Said, one of the many vast, congested and bewildering thoroughfares flowing through Jakarta's chaotic heart. As a form of internal control, all Soviet staff were accommodated on the embassy compound. My initial reconnoitring revealed that vehicles driven by Soviet diplomats usually left the compound via a rear exit on Jalan Denpasar, an unusually wide secondary road offering several vantage points to monitor comings and goings safe from roving Soviet eyes. Penelope and Spike both agreed that for a month or so, I should alternate my monitoring of the Sovs with the receptions and other events I usually attended. Just as I was beginning to think I was wasting my time, one Thursday night when on Soviet stake-out a Peugeot with a back licence plate of *CD 37 167* drove past me. It was dark inside the passing vehicle but my night vision binoculars made it possible to confirm the only occupant was the driver, Boris.

The numerals *15* on the diplomatic plates of the tiny vehicle I drove identified me as a UK diplomat. We had fished out a set of custom-made local licence tags held by the office, which I placed over the car's diplomatic plates when on stake-out. The subterfuge would not survive close inspection but in Jakarta's rough and tumble traffic, especially after dark, detection was unlikely. I gunned the engine and set off in pursuit.

Soon after passing me, Boris swung right and drove down a side street allowing him to turn left onto Rasuna Said. I followed, both hands tightly gripping the steering wheel as if willing my vehicle to overcome its lack of power. Boris drove like a madman, weaving through the traffic with all the skill of a local. I had done driving courses during training and vividly recalled one instructor telling me that the UK's star Formula One driver James Hunt had nothing to worry about from me. I was now beginning to understand what he meant. Before long, I was struggling to keep up to Boris. But equally I didn't want to get too close in case he spotted me. The combination of my car and me spared me this worry – I could not catch him even had I tried. If this solved one problem, it raised another in the distinct possibility that I might lose him. Fortunately, after each scare I again spotted Boris up ahead. For once I was grateful for the inestimable number of cars, motorcyclists and others locked in their perennial struggle for a slice of road space.

Boris continued along Rasuna Said, through an area called Setiabudi One. Shortly after, he took a left exit onto a road tracing a rough semi-circle. He followed it until he reached the entrance to the Wisma hospital precinct, into which he turned. There he skilfully squeezed into a parking space usually reserved for motorcycles. Boris sat in his car briefly, looking in the rearview mirror. He then locked the car and walked into the main hospital building. I would have liked to follow but decided to stay with his car having calculated I was bound to lose him if, after first trying to find a scarce car park, I sought to follow on foot. I pulled off to one side, ignoring the parade of cars and motorcycles blowing their horns as they eased around me. Mayhem was a fact of driving life in Jakarta and my obstinacy attracted no particular attention.

Boris reappeared after fifteen minutes. Without ado, he exited the hospital precinct but departed in the opposite direction from which he had arrived. I saw him leave but could not follow immediately; at least three other cars had pushed in and blocked my exit. Finally, as my anxiety levels were threatening to rise to code red, I reached the floodlit roundabout near Kuningan Village in time to witness Boris complete a slow rotation.

Only then did I recognize that Boris was engaging in tradecraft. The stop at the hospital was designed to detect any tailing person silly enough to be lured into the hospital building. I thanked my lucky stars. Had I followed him, as was my unrealized preference, Boris would have been sitting there waiting as I entered and the game would have been over before it began.

Conversely, the manoeuvre at the roundabout was to allow Boris to happen upon any suspicious-looking trailing vehicle, especially one driven by a Westerner. A second and larger sigh of relief escaped my lips. I had been lucky on two scores: had I not been impeded on leaving the hospital in all likelihood he would have spotted me at the roundabout; and if I had been delayed one minute longer, I would have lost him altogether. Fortune had shone on me.

Satisfied his back was clear, Boris turned right and wound his way along this route until he pulled up at a two-level, whitewashed villa nestled inconspicuously between apartment buildings. The villa's perimeter was protected by a fence made of rods of iron crooked at the top and clad with sheets of black steel preventing visibility into the dwelling's grounds. Two fixed sections of fence were inter-connected by concrete pillars painted white. Boris quickly opened a large sliding gate similarly constructed to the fence sections and drove inside, closing the gate behind him.

I parked my car about fifty yards past the villa and with the aid of passable street lighting monitored its entrance in my passenger-side wing mirror. A taxi soon pulled up. Its single passenger was a person whom I could make out was female. She activated an intercom near the gate, which opened just enough for her to enter.

The driver's side of my car was hard against a wall, obliging pedestrians to pass on the passenger side. Even so, people could see I was a foreigner, which unsettled the locals. After a time, some young males started deliberately bumping into the car. I could have offered an explanation for being there but that would have invited a barrage of questions. I tried to ignore the mounting interest in me, knowing I would inevitably be forced to move.

After nearly three hours, as the community's tolerance was about to exhaust, the same taxi returned. The woman emerged and quickly hopped in the back seat. I could not see her as the taxi passed slowly by, although I could make out the driver. He was an old Indonesian man wearing a Muslim skullcap. I began to follow, grateful to be moving. The taxi driver was oblivious to his tail. He drove along Rasuna Said before finally pulling into the Bek Murad Hotel. I followed into the hotel compound and parked my car.

The woman got out and the taxi drove off. I could see she was an attractive Eurasian. She did not enter the hotel. Instead, she walked back down to the footpath running parallel with Rasuna Said and crossed the freeway using the first pedestrian overpass she encountered. I followed on foot, keeping my distance. It was dark and there were people everywhere. But I knew I couldn't follow her indefinitely. I was a foreigner in a sea of locals and eventually she would become aware of me. I worried unnecessarily. Once over the overpass, the woman walked to the entrance of the Malaysian Embassy, was granted access and disappeared from sight.

———————◆◆◆———————

The next morning we agreed it was odd that a Soviet intelligence officer should be meeting one-to-one with an apparent Malaysian diplomat. With Soviet support, Soeharto's predecessor had opposed Malaysia's creation in 1963. Old wounds were still raw so far as the Soviets and Malaysia were concerned. We recognized, of course, the other party could be an agent Boris was running. But a three-hour meeting was a mighty long debrief. We were also bemused that Boris should drive to the safe house in a vehicle carrying diplomatic tags. This served only to invite the revelation the house he used was a Soviet safe house. We cabled London. It tasked us to see if Boris and the Eurasian met regularly.

We decided we needed to monitor the safe house. But clearly no Westerner could park in the street night after night. Penelope, though, had the solution. Part of her secret work while teaching in Indonesia had been to build a pool of ready-to-go Indonesian assets. The network had long been disbanded. But Penelope knew the whereabouts of some of its former Jakarta-based members.

Soon we had at our disposal a four-strong team of university students. All were critical of Soeharto, young and idealistic, and keen to infer that combating corruption by the Indonesian oligarchy was behind the task we set them. Each knew the hazards of challenging the state. Discretion was their byword.

The team got around on 125cc motorcycles, like the great majority of Jakarta's other residents. But we knew they could monitor the safe house only for about a week. Eventually, the locals would tag them as not from the area and assume they were criminals or other undesirables not to be welcomed in the neighbourhood.

The following Friday the team advised that the night before Boris had arrived alone at the safe house driving his Peugeot. A Eurasian woman visited him shortly after, staying around three hours. At this point, we knew we had to get ears inside the safe house. But the station had no resources for that. It was time to bring in our American counterparts.

CHAPTER 9
BETTY

London accepted our recommendation to involve the Americans. The MI6 station in Washington DC would approach the CIA. None other than Freddie Ladler, on posting in Washington, authored the station's reporting cable advising the CIA was interested. Its Jakarta office would be in touch with Penelope.

Chuck Lindergarten was a muscular, crew cut, pugnacious ball of aggression. He was also head of CIA station Jakarta. Only Chuck would know, at 4 am when supine in his bed, if Mr Self-doubt, he of the feet of clay, ever visited. But once on his feet, Charles H. Lindergarten Jr. made clear to all and sundry he regarded himself as indestructible. 'P,' he said, comfortably seated in Penelope's office, 'this'll be a piece of piss. We'll get a listening team in there in the blink of an eye and see what this mother-fucking Russkie's up to. We'll either bribe the pembantu, and tell her we'll cut her throat if she blabs, or we'll pick the fucking locks and be in there quicker than shit passing through a goose.'

'Sounds good, Chuck,' Penelope said with equanimity. Whether she took seriously Lindergarten's stated preparedness to threaten the maid with murder was not clear. 'We'll leave the detail up to you.' Seamlessly she added, 'Would you mind if Joe sat in on the op?' She smiled sweetly at Lindergarten. Chewing vigorously, he didn't seem to realize she was playing him. 'Joe's one of our bright young things. It'll do him the world of good to experience how a listening post works.' In truth, the request had nothing to do with my career development. Penelope was covering off on the possibility that our erstwhile allies may decide to withhold something from us.

'Not a problem,' Chuck replied expansively.

———◆—◆———

Two Thursday nights later I found myself in the enclosed back of a darkened van. The van's exterior declared itself in Indonesian to belong to *Comfy Removals*. Inside it was like a spaceship, with equipment mounted on racks welded to the vehicle's internal side panels. Bright dials provided the only light source. There were two American operators. They gave me a set of headphones and a stool to sit on. We were parked on a vacant block of land less than 150 yards from the safe house. The signals from the microphones the CIA had installed could be picked up from there.

We heard Boris arrive. He hummed gently to himself and put on softly playing music. The listening equipment gave signal strength indications for each microphone, enabling us to know which room Boris was in. All sound was taped. After a time, the intercom bell chimed. 'Come in Ibu,' Boris said in Indonesian, using the traditional formulation to courteously greet his female guest. In my mind's eye I saw Boris's charming smile. The woman, however, did not respond. The only sound we heard was footsteps as they walked upstairs. The microphone in the bedroom boomed at full signal strength. We then heard sounds of water running from a tap close enough to be coming from the en suite bathroom.

The Americans looked at one another with concern. Running water was the enemy of the microphone because it obscured the sound of voice, making what was said in proximity to the water source difficult to hear. More to the point, running a tap was often a sign that the target was aware of the microphone and taking steps to frustrate it. After some anxious minutes the water stopped. 'I think that's enough bubbles,' we heard Boris say. With relief, we realized that Boris and the woman had just run themselves a bubble bath.

The two must have been in the bath for a good hour. Goodness knows what they were doing. There was occasionally unintelligible murmuring and frequently the sound of water lapping. After what seemed an eternity the bedroom microphone picked up the rush of water gurgling as it ran down the drainpipe. The voices of Boris and the woman became clearer and we heard a bed complaining under their weight. Sounds of passion ensued, captured in all its exacting detail by the CIA microphones.

On and on they went. The woman occasionally cried out, in Chinese according to one of my American colleagues. Finally, with one last bellow from Boris, there was silence. After a long time a shower running could be heard, followed by inconsequential small talk as the couple re-clothed. They made their way downstairs. It had been a nearly two-hour stay in the bedroom. Over the next hour they appeared to drink a cup of coffee together. *All very civilized*, I thought. The evening culminated with the flicking sound of money being counted and the woman confirming, 'It's all there.' We heard her pick up the telephone. 'Pak Tasrip,' she said, 'I'm ready now. Can you come and get me please?'

◆━◆

Penelope Hutton's integrity shone through. She argued persuasively with London that I should be allowed to make the pitch to Boris. The Americans were Johnnies-come-lately; their claims to first dibs on him should be resisted. This worried me. 'Penelope,' I said, seated in her office, 'I hope you're not going out on a limb here. Frankly, I'm petrified I'll let you down.'

'Joe,' she said, 'Nought told me how with opportunity you would grow into a very good intelligence officer. I agree with him. It's now your time.'

It went all the way to the DG. He finally sided with Penelope but with a rider in his instructing cable: *Contingency hand holding plans approved at senior executive level to be in place by 8 May.*

Turkey celebrated Ataturk commemoration day on 19 May. Having served in Turkey, Boris was a good chance to be at the Turkish Embassy reception marking the occasion. And so it was. I sidled up to him. 'Nikolai Ivanovich, do you remember me?'

My use of his real name startled Boris, but only briefly. 'What do you want?' he asked in Indonesian.

'Friends of mine tell me you've been a naughty boy,' I said with more calmness than I felt. 'Little Chinese girl and so on. Your KGB masters in Moscow would be very upset if they knew.'

'You are mistaken,' he said, and turned to walk off.

'Find an excuse to meet me in an hour at the Blitar Hotel, room 404,' I said. 'Otherwise you're in big trouble, I promise you.'

Chuck and Penelope were enjoying tea in room 404 when I arrived. Chuck had brought two pieces of muscle with him in case Boris got ideas. Both carried machine pistols with silencers attached.

'What do you think, Joe?' Penelope asked.

'Hard to say,' I replied. 'But he got the message all right.'

A short rap on the door came forty-five minutes later. Muscle one ushered Boris inside and muscle two frisked him. Boris might have regarded himself as a modern-day Lothario but he didn't show much bottle. I wondered idly about boys' talk I'd heard to the effect that men who are good with women often don't have much heart. There again, Boris might have been pragmatically accepting the jig was up; or perhaps I was just self-consoling.

In good English Boris admitted that the Malaysian woman, Betty, had been an agent run by his predecessor. He had inherited her. The safe house had been used to debrief her while in service. 'But the recent arrival of a new ambassador, a Malay nationalist,' Boris said, 'resulted in Betty losing her job as the ambassador's secretary.' After a pause he added, with apparently genuine indignation, 'For no reason other than she was one-third Chinese.'

'And then?' Chuck asked.

'She was sidelined into a position of social secretary, meaning her access to secret information was lost.'

'Yet you kept up the association?' Penelope said.

Boris was suddenly coy. 'She knew too much and should have been sanctioned.' We all knew he meant she should have been assassinated. 'But she was an attractive woman and understood the reality of the situation. I suggested we remain in touch, *informally*.'

'You old dog,' Chuck said without humour. 'How did you manage that cosy little arrangement?'

Boris smiled briefly. 'It wasn't hard to pay her the same retainer by falsifying an entry in the agent cash log. There is no embassy oversight of this expenditure and few audits by the KGB in Moscow. Betty and I reached an understanding. She was to come to the safe house each Thursday night. If the curtain in the upstairs living area was open it was clear to come in. Betty uses an old Indonesian taxi driver. He treats her like his daughter and is totally loyal. She would meet him Thursday nights at the Bek Murad Hotel and later he would drop her back there.'

'And what about the use of your diplomatic vehicle to travel to the safe house?' Penelope asked.

'The Peugeot is cover,' Boris said. 'It's deliberately distinctive to convey I am a cultural diplomat with nothing to hide. The KGB station has a pool of nondescript vehicles carrying Indonesian plates for secret work requiring clean transport. But a file number must be recorded on sign out. That means if something goes wrong the file will tell the station which job the officer was on. An abominable Georgian peasant administers the car pool. I don't like him and he doesn't like me. I know he regularly checks on me. He would have come to realize that each time I went out I was operating solo, without backup, which is very rare. This made me reluctant to make false entries. I thought it safer to use my diplomatic car.'

'OK,' Chuck said. 'But what does the embassy make of you disappearing by yourself Thursday nights if you don't have the intelligence task excuse? How do you explain that away?'

'Ordinarily,' Boris said, 'all in the embassy are forbidden to leave the compound alone. But members of the KGB station have the authority to ignore the rule when they judge that operational needs warrant it. Naturally, this power is abused. The embassy hierarchy is wary of upsetting KGB people. Its compromise is to tolerate the abuse so long as the station officers concerned are restrained and discreet. Provided I go out alone only for a couple of hours once a week no one pays me any attention.'

'Even so,' Penelope said, 'you must have understood the risks associated with using your diplomatic vehicle?'

Boris shrugged. 'The diplomatic plates are no doubt an issue. But substituting local ones for them would protect only so far. The Peugeot is still distinctive. Anyone with an interest in it would know it is my car. That's why I take elaborate precautions against tails. I assume that despite this one of your people still managed to follow me to the safe house?' When Boris received no answer he said, lips tightly pursed and head slowly shaking, 'Trust me when I say whoever it was got lucky.'

Boris knew what was expected. We ran over plans for his weekly debriefing and how he was to pass us documents. He hardly argued. He knew for sure the combination of tipping us the safe house's location and pilfering of funds was enough for the KGB to shoot him, even before it debated the merits of his liaison with Betty. I ran Boris until the end of 1977 when my posting concluded. The Americans were not at all happy having to rely on our product, but they were pragmatic and used *the most heavy lifting* argument to gain first in access to other sources jointly recruited.

A year or so after I left Jakarta, Boris was posted to Ecuador, for no apparent reason other than to give him a break from the Islamic world. With that we, the Brits, sold him to the Yanks. The Americans pushed Boris hard. It finally got too much for him, or maybe he simply got sick of it all. Boris was found sitting in his living room with fragments of his skull and brain splattered on the wall like someone had dropped a watermelon. A KGB service issue pistol lay by his side.

CHAPTER 10

KATHLEEN

Despite the Service's all-encompassing emphasis on the *Need to Know* principle, word soon got around that Joe Lambert was a bit of a star. It came as no surprise in late 1977, shortly before I left Jakarta, when my name appeared on a promotions circular. I was overjoyed to be now at a level where I could head my own section – I felt I had earned it. My only disappointment was again seeing the names of Rupert Heneshaw and Freddie Ladler on the list.

On return to work in London in January 1978, I was placed in charge of Indonesia section, back where I had started. With Hanson Scott the former section head having moved on, this seemed an ideal arrangement given Boris was in play. In hindsight, it wasn't a great management decision. I became proprietorial about Boris and was never happy at the way the station was running him. I chafed at this and, in truth, became overbearing and full of perceived importance.

After one particularly bad day in late February 1978, I sat in my rented flat in West Brompton mulling over things. My thoughts turned to Heneshaw and Ladler. Jakarta had been a defining posting for me and I was no longer regarded as a yokel. But I still couldn't shake the impression that Rupert and Freddie were well ahead of me in the Service's pecking order for plumb headquarters jobs and overseas postings likely to lead to promotion. Yet in my estimation there wasn't much daylight professionally between the three of us. With that, Nought's advice about needing to get married, on which I'd done precisely nothing, rang loudly in my ears.

The next day I began to make discreet enquiries about Heneshaw and Ladler. Fortunately, Service people routinely shared gossip about their colleagues, free as it was from the strictures of national security. Heneshaw, it transpires, had married a Chelsea belle while on mid-term leave from his then posting in Bonn. In Freddie Ladler's case, he'd married *a big-toothed Texan* he met during his Washington posting. The evidence might have been circumstantial but something told me Nought had been right all along. He always was.

━━◈━◈━━

There was an office social forum of which I was aware called the Diners Club. Joining involved placing a short note containing a list of interests on a notice board in the staff recreation room. Interested persons contacted other interested persons to arrange dinner parties and the like. But the entire office had visibility of the notice board and I feared ridicule. Finally, though, Nought's wise advice won out. Shortly after my birthday in March 1978, I took the plunge and put up a notice: *Joe Lambert; age 30; interests: cricket, reading and stage plays; extension 235.* I had included my age hoping this may encourage contact with people of a similar age group.

A fellow called Robert Charters rang. 'I'm calling about the Diners Club,' he said. He was obviously quite young. I wondered if my age strategy had gone awry. Robert was very nervous. 'My girlfriend, Phoebe, has a second cousin a few years older than her who has just moved to London. Her name is Kathleen Pennington. The cousin, that is. Sorry, I'm rambling here.'

'Take your time,' I said. My instincts were responding positively to the cues I was picking up. I liked Robert.

'Kathleen wants to have dinner. Rather than lopsided numbers, I wondered if you would be interested in joining us? I must be clear that neither Phoebe nor Kathleen is Service, if that's of concern.'

'No concern at all,' I said, 'and dinner would be great. I assume you'll make the booking? I live in West Brompton.'

'Pheebs and I live in Highgate,' Robert responded.

Five demerit points for the Pheebs bit, I thought. 'Goodness,' I said, 'when I first came here I lived at Kentish Town and thought that was a long way out.' He laughed and I restored his demerits.

'It's not too bad. And look, don't worry about the booking. Kathleen lives in Mayfair so we'll eat nearby. What date suits you?'

My weekend diary was hardly full to overflowing, but to save face I did the let me check routine all the same. 'How about Saturday 8 April?'

'That would work,' Robert said. He told me he would book for 7 pm and let me know where.

——— ❖ ❖ ———

I presented washed and sober on the appointed night at the Ancient Islands steakhouse a stone's throw from Marble Arch. Robert and Phoebe arrived smack on time. They were the epitome of a nice young couple – clean lines; stylishly dressed without hint of ostentation; and impeccably mannered. Robert worked on one of the administrative floors. His work didn't allow him access to my area or me to his. It was the first time I had met him.

At 7:10 pm Kathleen arrived. I assessed her surreptitiously. She wore expensive couture and her fair hair was long with a flicked fringe designed to give her a lady about town look. God knows what Kathleen thought about me but she was politely friendly throughout. We wound up about 9:30 pm. Robert and Phoebe had to rush for a train. I offered to walk Kathleen home and nearly fell over when she told me her flat in Adams Row was owned by a family trust. That was serious money. The half-hour stroll to Mayfair was otherwise unremarkable. Our evening culminated with a chaste handshake and vague mention of staying in touch.

Proceeding past Hyde Park Corner and onto Kensington Road, I reflected the evening was like a nil-all football draw. You couldn't complain about the result but nor was there anything to get excited about. Why then did I write to Kathleen a week later suggesting an outing, just the two of us? The truth is I was desperate to avoid the Service pigeonholing me as a bachelor loner and the threat to career this entailed. I never gave so much as a millisecond's thought to whether the pursuit of Kathleen may also help avoid the other pitfall of hiding in *The Far Grass* – the ruinous personal cost to which Nought had fleetingly referred.

——◆◆——

Kathleen accepted my invitation to a Saturday matinee session of *The Mousetrap*. We had tea afterwards. She told me about herself, including that she was an only child who until recently had lived at home in Maidstone in Kent where her parents owned and operated a toffee factory. At the earlier dinner with Robert and Phoebe, Kathleen had disclosed she was a kindergarten teacher who had shifted to London to gain experience. Now over tea, she confided that the round trip of sixty miles or so had deterred her from commuting from the family home.

Kathleen also volunteered she was turning thirty later in the year. I was struck by her dread when admitting this. In some quarters in the late 1970s, unmarried women of thirty or more were still thought of as doomed to spinsterhood. Kathleen's evident trepidation over her impending birthday made clear she shared this outmoded notion. I made appropriately soothing references to more enlightened attitudes. The outing ended with a polite embrace and me pecking Kathleen on the cheek as we said our goodbyes.

And that's how it started. It would be wildly over-generous to say we fell in love. Rather, the relationship was decorous, really little more than a friendship. True, we did engage in petting every now and again. But sex was not on the agenda. The one time I mentioned the subject, Kathleen had responded firmly. 'Joe, that will come in good time,' she said. 'The church has taught me I must be a virgin when I marry and that's what I intend to be.' And in that regard, Kathleen's parents were taking no chances; whenever we were in Maidstone, I was accommodated as far away from Kathleen as the physical design of their massive house allowed.

When courting Kathleen I found that my loner instincts never surfaced, without which the relationship could not have progressed as it did. The reason was apparent enough. Although I was not uncaring about Kathleen, I had not invested much in the way of emotional capital in her and felt no need for emotional security. This convinced me that only in cases of substantial emotional outlay was my natural tendency to hide in *The Far Grass* likely to trigger. My reaction to Sarah Sutherland's rejection, the Canadian intelligence officer on exchange with the Service for whom I'd once held high romantic hope, told me that much.

My relationship with Kathleen also caused me to revisit the tentative conclusion I had reached years earlier – that my mother's death was somehow linked to my loner instincts. Psychological theories began to take hold, of how the trauma of my mother's death had sparked a drive to be safely alone from women of meaning to me. In the romantic context, I concluded, this translated into a fear of female rejection, a condition aggravated to morbidity by the Sarah Sutherland disaster. The thesis I came to accept was that when anxious to cement a relationship my emotional outlay was prone to exceeding a certain threshold, beyond which I was vulnerable to female rejection. On detecting this my sub-conscious pre-emptively sparked the need to escape to protect me from the threat. The subsequent distress and depression arising from the involuntary triggering of this defence mechanism was the result of losing what I badly wanted in the first place. Such was my circular introspection.

Meanwhile, I continued on with Kathleen. When her father began to offer me a weak whisky before dinner, I knew then I had been accepted into the fold. Kathleen and I announced our engagement in October 1978. I proclaimed the happy news widely and loudly in the office. The word spread like wildfire.

CHAPTER 11

FAREWELL

Around this time Penelope Hutton re-entered my life, via a telephone call from her Oxford University office. She had recently completed her stint as Jakarta station head and resumed academic life. 'Joe,' Penelope said, 'you should know that Nought Collins is gravely ill. He would like to see you. He told me so.' Penelope gave me a Bristol address, saying Nought refused to have the telephone at his home. 'If I were you,' she cautioned, 'I would get over to the West Country soonish. He doesn't have long left.'

Nought, being Nought, had not bothered to stay in touch as he'd promised upon leaving Jakarta. But I remained endlessly fond of him and was shocked by Penelope's awful news. Penelope had called on a Tuesday. A letter posted that afternoon would reach Nought by Thursday morning. I quickly wrote him a short note, explaining I would call at his home the coming Friday morning ex the London train. I then ran out to post the letter and on return to the office completed an application for Friday leave.

I arrived at Nought's home in Bristol at about 11 am. It was a small, single-fronted, red-brick town home. The tiny front yard was mostly paved over; what greenery there was had clearly not received much attention in recent times. I rapped the doorknocker and heard the echo of its sound reverberate throughout the house. Silence. I began to panic and wondered if Nought had received my letter. Finally, the sound of stockinged feet moving very slowly could be heard.

I hardly recognized Nought. He still had the bulbous nose but was a wizened relic of what he once looked like. 'Joey Lambert,' he wheezed. 'What a sight for sore eyes. Come in, come in.' The house was not untidy in a major way. Nought explained he had two nieces in Bath who came in week about and cleaned for him. 'They want to be sure they're in the will,' he said, smiling to show me he wasn't serious. 'Love to offer you a decent drink, Joe, but my innards have rotted. My sister has banned grog from the house as a condition of her daughters helping out. She knows I'd drink anything that was here. What the fuck have I got to lose?'

I made tea and we talked of the old days. After a time, I asked Nought if he remembered, on the night of our knees-up when he was leaving Jakarta, telling me I should get married.

'I do,' he said. 'And still valid advice too. Times are changing but the Service is a conservative outfit; it'll be the last to conform.'

'Well I've just become engaged.'

Nought's reaction was not what I expected. Rather, he just looked at me, shrewdly assessing what I had said. Finally, he spoke. 'I loved my wife but I was young, ambitious and intelligent. Brilliant some said. Too many other temptations. Never home and ended fucking up the one thing that matters in life: real and lasting love. Lost my marriage, got on the lash and eventually found my way to the scrapheap.' Nought heaved for breath. 'Do you love this bit of crumpet you've got your hooks into?' he asked.

There was no point lying to Nought; he was too canny for that. 'If I was honest,' I said, 'there have been other occasions when I've felt a more powerful attraction. This is a different relationship. It's steadier, more a matter of companionship and mutual support rather than an emotional rollercoaster oscillating every which way.'

Nought made no direct response. Instead he said, 'Remember I also told you at the knees-up you were hiding in *The Far Grass*?' He smiled sadly at the memory.

'Yes. For sure I do.'

'Did you ever stop to think what I really meant?'

'I thought initially it was just a joke, badinage as the Americans might say. But after that night I believed you were warning of the danger to my career in the Service regarding me as a loner because it thinks that's why Philby and Co. spied for the Sovs.'

'That's true, certainly. And it's still relevant to you. Although some day the Service will understand its thinking about the Cambridge lot is cockeyed and stop automatically putting anyone with loner tendencies in the same boat.'

Nought's eyebrows then knitted in a frown. 'But I was also trying to warn you about something a lot more serious. You weren't listening by then so I didn't push it. I wanted you to know that spying comes to destroy us if we allow it. It's the dark side of our dark business. You need to be aware, Joey, that total obsession with the black arts for too long will always lead to isolation and moral incompetence. One day we wake up and we're social outcasts; devious bastards unable to separate right from wrong, condemned forever to creeping alone across life's outer fringes.'

From over his teacup, Nought checked I was still listening. '*The Far Grass*,' he said, 'is the perfect metaphor for the damaged spy. That's because the cricketers who inhabit it are also cast out and left alone to pad across a vast expanse. Only pariah spies are excised not from the epicentre of a cricket match but from normal life, and what we're left to pad across is not bloody savannah but the endless, frozen landscape of spying. Understand, Joe, all that stands between we who succumb to spying and life eternal in *The Far Grass* is real love, the *real deal*. Nothing else can stop the otherwise inevitable. I should know. I tried every alternative, the whole fucking lot.'

I didn't respond, a little disconcerted by Nought's rawness. Instead, I reflected on him speaking as if still part of the Service, recalling he'd once told me of its capacity to claim people for life.

Nought stared at me with rheumy eyes and took another sip of tea. He knew his appeal to my sense of self-preservation still hadn't overcome my fixation on career. He also knew just how badly I wanted him to encourage me to proceed with the marriage. Grimacing, much like a caring father reluctantly conceding to his son, he said, 'I guess for now you should try to make those who count think differently about you.' After a pause he added, 'But do so knowing this brewing marriage you've come here crowing about is going to end at some point. I can tell you that with certainty because there's no glue there. You might last ten days, you might last a decade. But it won't last forever. Ride it as far as you can I suggest. The longer you stay married, the more progress you'll make at convincing the top floor you're something you're not.' He laughed an anaemic laugh. 'That's Uncle Nought's last pearl of wisdom,' he said. 'I'm fucked, over and out.'

I left Nought heavy of heart. His final words rang in my ears. 'Don't fret for me, Joey. I'm now in the acceptance phase. I know what's coming and all I want is for the pain and feebleness to stop. One final thing: I don't want you coming to my funeral. I mean it. I really want you to remember me as I was. But I do want you to have this.' He produced from behind his back a small rectangular item. It looked like a pencil case and was no more than a foot long and an inch high and wide. 'Been passed down in the Collins family from father to son since the time of my great-grandfather. But as I fucked up, the line stops with me. If you have a son, Joe, be sure to give him this.' The box's outer leather skin was aged smooth with time and embossed with the seal of the Austro-Hungarian Empire. I opened it. It was an exquisite, nine-inch antique silver rapier. The lump in my throat threatened to choke me as I realized the significance, and finality, of the gift. Nought could see this. He winked. 'Go well, son.' Then he shut the door.

On the return journey I couldn't hold back the tears. Those in my train carriage inspected me warily before retreating behind their newspapers. Back in London, I stopped at the off-licence on the way home. Sitting in the quiet of my flat I bid Nought farewell. Nought died eight days later. His sister telephoned to tell me the news.

PHOBIAS

Kathleen and I were scheduled to marry on Saturday 9 June 1979. I mean that literally; we didn't select the date. Kathleen's parents wanted a big bash and figured the first chance of decent weather was in June. Kathleen never said anything to me suggesting she thought differently. Her parents paid the bills and directed all traffic. They were not to be questioned. I was never consulted.

The Service decreed that officers could reveal their occupations to partners only once formally married, and subject to spouses first signing the Official Secrets Act. By 1979 the regulation was hopelessly outdated in the face of growing numbers of unmarried couples living together. Yet change was slow in coming.

As my June wedding date loomed, I made the decision I should not wait until Kathleen and I married. I needed to tell her beforehand exactly what she was signing up for. One Saturday night in mid-May we were scheduled to go out for dinner. I arrived at Kathleen's flat about 6 pm. With three weeks to go until the big day Kathleen by this time was in a state of high anxiety. She was in constant contact, and conflict, with her mother over the wedding arrangements. I was grateful to have been marginalized. Of the nearly 200 guest invitations sent I had invited not one person. I would have invited Nought. But he was dead. Robert Charters, who had first brought Kathleen and me together, was to be my best man.

'How are you?' I greeted Kathleen. 'You seem a bit frazzled.'

'Well, wouldn't you be?' she replied, a wild look in her eyes. 'I've been on the phone to my mother all afternoon and now there's some sort of problem with the flowers at the church.'

I could see she was close to tears. 'Sit down and catch your breath. I need to tell you something.'

'Yes?' she said distractedly.

I was now wondering if this was the right time and regretted not earlier deciding to ignore the Service's edict. But it was too late. If I didn't tell Kathleen now when would I? 'You know how I've told you I work for the Foreign Office?' Kathleen didn't answer. 'I actually work for the Secret Intelligence Service, MI6. Our role, broadly, is to ferret out information that other governments don't want the British Government to know.'

I found Kathleen's look disconcerting. 'Why are you bothering me with all this mumbo jumbo about information?' she asked with heat. 'Surely I have enough things to worry about right now?'

'Well,' I said, 'when we're married you'll have to sign the Official Secrets Act, which is a legal undertaking not to discuss my work with anyone.'

Kathleen looked at me uncomprehendingly. Then she dissolved in tears and collapsed into my arms, her shoulders heaving violently as she wept. I was taken aback. I stood there holding Kathleen, dismayed that my efforts to inform her should have distressed her so. Suddenly, Kathleen broke free of my arms. She was now cried out and angry. 'Do you enjoy upsetting me?' she spat accusatively. I shook my head in vigorous denial. 'Thanks to you, I'm now too upset to go out to eat. At times like this, I wonder why we're bothering to get married at all.' Kathleen glared at me. 'I'm going for a walk,' she said abruptly, stopping briefly before she left to rummage through her handbag and extract her purse. 'I'll buy us a pizza while I'm out. We can eat it here.'

Alone in Kathleen's flat, I tried to make sense of everything. I had long known I wanted to marry Kathleen only because I feared the Service tagging me as a habitual bachelor. But we had an awful lot of incompatibility. I began to get cold feet and wondered if I could renege on the wedding at this late stage. Then I thought of the career costs involved. From the grave, Nought resolved my dilemma: *Ride the marriage as far as you can*, he had counselled. And that, I concluded, was what I must try to do.

We ate the pizza in strained silence. Shortly after, I readied to go. I was surprised when Kathleen kissed me lightly as I left – but should not have been. Walking home, it dawned on me that Kathleen's going for a walk was her means for finding clear air in which to think. Kathleen was haunted by her dread of spinsterhood and marrying me met her perceived needs. Consumed by her entrenched anxiety, as I was mine, the conclusion she reached while out was the relationship should carry through to marriage and beyond. Neither of us ever mentioned that night again.

⁂

The Friday night before my wedding I caught the late train to Maidstone after finishing work, carrying my hired formal wear with me. Kathleen and her father met me at the station. Kathleen was upbeat. 'Darling,' she said. 'Have you eaten?' Back at the house, over tea and grilled cheese on toast, I was informed the marriage plans had come together well.

Our matrimonial day dawned sunny but crisp. The groom's vehicle deposited my best man, Robert Charters, and me at a beautiful old church in the Maidstone town centre about ten minutes before the scheduled 2 pm ceremony. Accompanied by her father, Kathleen was traditionally late. My knees trembled as the service got underway. The church was small and packed to the gunnels. Invitations fell into two categories: those invited to the church and reception to follow, and those to the reception alone. I couldn't help but think of the *B*-list diplomats in Moscow when first becoming aware of this. My memory of the service remains hazy. But all went to plan. Words were said, rings placed on fingers and then we were done: man and wife.

The reception venue was the nearby Town Square Hotel. Kathleen was overcome by excitement and squeezed my arm as we were driven away from the church. 'Fantastic service, wasn't it?' I managed to say as I tried vainly to come to terms with what I'd just done. The hotel's function room was overflowing to capacity with people swarming everywhere. Kathleen and I were seated in the middle of the head table. Food was served. Having hardly eaten all day, I bolted it down. Kathleen whispered I should eat more slowly; people were watching. I would have killed a man for a strong whisky at this point but all that was on offer alcoholically were sparse quantities of champagne. I didn't much care for the beverage but nonetheless rapidly sank two glasses of it, earning me a sterner rebuke from my spouse.

The official part of the reception went on forever. Kathleen's parents both made speeches, interminably so, followed by this uncle or that, seemingly by the dozen. Just when I thought it would never end, the speeches were finally done. But then Kathleen and I had to dance our bridal waltz, by ourselves in view of everyone. The last time I had danced was well over five years ago and even then I was inside a bottle of gin. I worried I might fall over or worse trip up Kathleen. To applause befitting the winners of the all-England ballroom dancing championships, we tottered around. Thankfully, after only a few solo rotations, other couples began to enter the square of parquetry demarcating the dance floor.

It was close to 10 pm before Kathleen's parents released us. They were not stupid and could see I was flagging. But I counted for little in their eyes. Not until Kathleen showed signs of running out of steam did they consent to our departure. While Kathleen was still gallivanting around the room inviting inspection of her wedding dress and generally being the centre of attention the show had to go on. I shrugged inwardly. Their little girl, I guess.

———◆——◆———

We were driven back to the family home to change. Our chauffeur then drove us up the M20 motorway towards London and on to our hotel near Heathrow. Kathleen was tired by now and not much was said en route. But she perked up a little when we arrived, loudly announcing at reception for the benefit of anyone in earshot that we had a booking for 'Mr and Mrs Joseph Lambert.'

In the room and alone we sort of stared at one another. Kathleen declined my offer to make her a cup of herbal tea. She changed in the bathroom and emerged in pyjamas, jumping straight into bed and turning out her bedside lamp. I'd packed a pair of short pyjamas and changed there in the bedroom. The back of Kathleen's head was the only part of her visible as I hopped beneath the covers.

I was exhausted but couldn't sleep. I summarized my position. Now we were married and to live together in Kathleen's flat, we no longer had the luxury of separate accommodation providing space for emotions to blow over each time we had a disagreement. Our relationship would soon be under strain. Yet if I went churlish on Kathleen we'd be done in no time. I had entered into the marriage only for the sake of my career. Having widely talked up the event within the Service, I would be the veritable Emperor without clothes if the union turned out to be stillborn. The blowback professionally and personally would be devastating. I had no option but to adapt.

No doubt both of us had end points beyond which the marriage would no longer have a purpose to serve. But it was impossible to predict how long it would be before Kathleen judged she had proved she was not a spinster. And I had no idea when being wedded would have satisfied my career needs. My focus could only be on keeping the marriage afloat while I needed it afloat. To that end I resolved, starting from the moment I awoke the next morning, to avoid aggravating Kathleen no matter what. Then I slept. Many years later when the BBC television comedy *Keeping up Appearances* aired, I marvelled at the similarity of my strategy to the attitude taken by the fictional character Richard Bucket to the relentless pretentiousness of his equally fictitious wife, Hyacinth.

❖

Our honeymoon involved six nights in Madrid and a further four in Barcelona. Once on the British Airways flight, our respective spirits perked as the holiday feel took hold and we polished up our limited Spanish. On arrival we changed money and caught a taxi to our hotel in downtown Madrid. After lunch we hit the tourist trail, returning tired and sunburnt in the late afternoon. Back in our room after an early dinner, I could feel Kathleen's tenseness as we readied for bed. Unsure whether or not to play the amorous husband, I settled for a goodnight brush of my lips against hers.

The next day some of the thrill of being in exotic Spain was starting to ebb away as Kathleen, not entirely without reason, began to complain about the rudeness of some of our many fellow tourists. That night Kathleen had a couple of glasses of sangria over dinner. This seemed to relax her and later in the evening, when in bed, we did finally consummate our marriage. Even so, we were both relieved by the time our honeymoon was over. Being together all day, every day had broken new ground for us both.

CHAPTER 13

EMILIYA

The timing of my wedding had been fortuitous in that it coincided with the departure of the person heading the Service's counter-intelligence unit. The unit's role was to recruit selected Soviet personnel stationed in or visiting Britain. Being home-based yet operational in nature, it was a much sought-after placement among Service officers at my level. I think my superiors had finally come to recognize that Indonesia section wasn't suiting me. Whatever, when I returned from my honeymoon and applied for the sideways shift to the counter-intelligence position, I was granted the move. I had no doubt that the success of my application owed much to my newfound respectability, courtesy of my recent nuptials.

My new boss was a woman called Sheila Whiley. She was tallish and thin, about forty with short hair. Sheila had not been long with the Service, having been promoted in from the Foreign Office around two years earlier. Super bright and collegiate, she was also all business, which suited me nicely.

My staff consisted of two analysts and four so-called positive action assets. The analysts were both young. Herman Brandt was twenty-six, slightly built and sported a wispy beard that resolutely defied proper growth. He was a mathematician by training and, being of German extraction, spoke the language perfectly. Harry, as we called him, had experienced some discrimination at the hands of older Service officers with memories of the war. On learning that Placements was having difficulty in finding a spot for him, I decided to take a chance on Harry. He had proved to be bright and diligent, and I know Harry appreciated that I'd been willing to take him on.

His counterpart analyst was Aneta Spa. A year younger than Harry, her surname was an anglicized version of her family name of Spasova that her grandparents carried with them when immigrating to Britain from Bulgaria. Aneta had a first in Russian studies and spoke Russian fluently. And although still a little green around the edges she was, like Harry, a valuable section asset.

My four positive action people, all ex-military men, were our muscle who drove unmarked surveillance cars, performed watcher duties and, as required, broke down doors and did other physical things. They all had cowboy tendencies and, collectively, two pet peeves. The first, they said, was the unit's lack of aggression towards Soviet spies in London working under diplomatic cover. 'They should be kicked in the balls and told to desist,' they argued.

My response was to remind my colleagues of the so-called gentlemen's agreement of which I had first become aware when in Moscow. On activation there I had been told of instances of Western intelligence officers returning home to find the kettle just boiled, indicating someone had very recently been inside their apartment. This type of psychological warfare was tolerated. But on both sides of the equation retribution was swift and brutal if the mark was overstepped. I had been briefed how this gave rise to a gentlemen's agreement between the Americans and the Soviets, which Britain and the Soviet allies closely followed. Namely, that the meting out of physical harm to intelligence officers and their families – narrowly confined to the spouses and children who usually accompanied married officers posted abroad – was off limits. But the agreement did not apply to deep cover agents or, depending on the circumstances, even people associated with intelligence officers. Here each side had open slather.

The associated matter concerning my positive action people was the Service's refusal to engage in what the Americans called *wet affairs*. *Wet affairs* referred to the CIA's practice of eliminating certain enemies of the American state, those not protected by the gentlemen's agreement, as and when usually extreme circumstances demanded. 'The Americans play across a larger positive action field than we do,' I explained, 'simply because they can afford it, which we can't.' I didn't get into complex discussions about *Pax Americana,* of the concept of the US being the guarantor of Western hemisphere peace and stability and needing to do all that was necessary to maintain its preponderance of power. In all honesty, I didn't understand it sufficiently to give a cogent account.

Thereafter, with my positive action staff quelled if not entirely pacified, the unit began to gel nicely. Even so, I was far from satisfied. I badly wanted to hook a source of high and enduring quality. Days became weeks as time meandered by. Then one day, when I least expected it, Emiliya entered my life.

◆ ◆

It all started routinely, as these things invariably do. It was the late summer of 1979 and the Home Office had just provided us with details of visa applications by a Russian trade delegation planning to visit London. The delegation comprised six men and one woman, Emiliya Dmitrievna Kuznetsov, born Nizhny Novgorod on 22 September 1951. We ran each applicant through our processes and came up blank. *Nothing known,* we reported back to the top floor executive. The delegation was planning an eight-day visit, arriving on the evening of Sunday 19 August and departing mid-morning on Monday 27 August.

Harry, Aneta and I perused the program the Russians had provided and decided how we would run the rule over them. We agreed the visit's duration was a smidge longer than necessary for activities beginning Monday and ending Friday morning, but judged the schedule was probably framed to allow the visitors some sightseeing on the last weekend. The delegation was to lodge at the Soviet Embassy in Kensington Palace Gardens, which was the usual arrangement for Soviet officials visiting London.

The visit began. MI5, the UK's domestic intelligence agency – known to us in the Service either as *Five* or the *cousins* – had a permanent watching post in a flat on Bayswater Road from which it monitored the Soviet Embassy. The watching post's mobile team followed the delegation on departure each morning and confirmed its arrival at its first scheduled meeting. We then took over. Our positive action people trailed the Russians to their other appointments and otherwise kept a close watch on the group. The evenings were not much more demanding. By Russian standards the six delegation males were quite restrained – most were tucked up in bed by 11 pm. Come the middle of the week, Harry, Aneta and I were all in agreement that the delegation seemed legitimate.

Emiliya was a serious young woman with a prosaic taste in clothes who wore her hair tied back in a fierce bun. Other than delegation duties, she kept to herself. Harry, however, had been reviewing positive action watcher reports. By late on Friday 24 August he had discovered that at various times, alone or with others, all six of the Russian males had consulted Emiliya on minor visit issues, such as car seating. 'Joe, these are chauvinistic Russian men,' Harry pointed out. 'They usually wouldn't speak to a female colleague, let alone seek her opinion. Yet even on base trivialities, they're all treating Emiliya as if she's an authority to be respected.'

I scanned the passages Harry had underlined in the reports. 'I see what you mean, Harry,' I said. *Strike one for thorough analysis,* I thought. I was convinced enough to brief Sheila, who by now was answering to none other than Martin Mumford, recently promoted from heading Soviet operations where I had first encountered him on returning to London from basic training.

I was in the office bright and early that Saturday morning of 25 August 1979. The day passed without any sign of Emiliya leaving the embassy. I began to wonder if we'd outsmarted ourselves; if our analysis had made a mountain out of a molehill. Nonetheless, I was still in the office early on Sunday, even if my expectations were low. About twenty-five after nine my telephone rang. It was Aneta who was duty analyst for the day. 'The cousins advise that madam' – meaning Emiliya – 'left home on foot a short time ago. She's on her own. Cousins are in touch at a respectable distance.'

'OK,' I said, my senses enlivened by Aneta's news of Emiliya's Sunday morning escapade. 'I'll get others in here. You get here ASAP.' I hung up and rang Harry, and then walked around to my on duty positive action man.

An hour later the four of us sat in my office. I rang Five on speaker. The voice at the other end was obviously that of a former policeman. 'Bayswater post without mobile resources 8 am to 10 am this morning due to one-off implementation of new shift roster. Perchance, five-person mobile taskforce en route to Israeli Embassy staging through post when target left home at 9:03 am. Decision taken to deploy this unit. Target initially walked west towards Notting Hill Gate, stopping briefly at Lloyd's Bank to adjust her blue raincoat. Asset one behind withdrew assessing possible window reflection back check. Asset two in front maintained touch. Target walked north, then east before entering Paddington underground. Asset three established contact and rode to Baker Street in target's carriage. Target spent sixteen minutes at Baker Street doing back checks. Asset four now in place had visual all the way to Euston. Observed target exiting towards Euston Intercity terminus. Asset five at Euston too late to attach, but while searching Intercity terminus chance sighted target boarding Birmingham New Street service departing platform eight. Station staff advise that target presented return ticket to Bletchley. Report ends.'

Five, I thought, *God bless their cotton socks*. Addressing my colleagues, I asked, 'Why Bletchley?'

Harry jumped to his feet. 'Bletchley services Milton Keynes and I recall seeing Milton Keynes mentioned in this morning's newspapers. I'll go and get the wardens' copies.'

We found what we were looking for in the *Sunday Times* – a short paragraph in a side column on page eight informing readers that a symposium on the future of UK nuclear technology was to take place today at the Great Linford Hotel in Milton Keynes. We didn't need to read past that. 'Right,' I said, 'let's go.' Turning to Aneta I said, 'Aneta, you're duty analyst and will have to stay in the office in case Five needs to contact you. Harry and I will go. While we're gone could you update Mumford and Sheila please?' It actually suited to have Harry with me. The place would be full of scientific eggheads and Harry fitted the stereotyped description. Our positive action man rocketed us up the M1 at a great rate of knots.

———◆——◆———

Harry and I entered the Great Linford conference centre and took seats towards the back of the room. We scanned for Emiliya. Harry spotted her on the right flank near the front. Her hair was no longer in a bun but cascaded down across her shoulders, and she wore a tight-fitting woollen maroon top. Emiliya's chair was turned inwards at forty-five degrees affording her line of sight to the speaker's podium. Her chair's position also allowed her to monitor the hall entrance with a subtle rather than dramatic turn of her head.

'If I'm not mistaken,' I whispered to Harry, 'that's tradecraft Emiliya is practising.' I was sure Emiliya would have seen Harry and me walk in. But presumably aided by Harry's appearance, we must have passed muster. *If in doubt, cut and run* was the golden rule of fieldwork. Yet there Emiliya was, still sitting there.

CHAPTER 14

KATYA

The Milton Keynes symposium featured eight speakers. Protestors in the audience chanting slogans and being generally disruptive frequently delayed proceedings. Security guards removed them. Around 4 pm the convener drew the event to a close. Emiliya had done nothing all day, bar sit there. But at the end of the event she made a hasty beeline for a wire-headed boffin, in his late forties I estimated, whom I knew from the program as Dr Geoffrey Tyler, a nuclear physicist from the Atomic Weapons Research Establishment.

AWRE was a top-secret agency housed within the Ministry of Defence. It was charged with developing Britain's nuclear weapon capability. We could now see that Emiliya had abandoned the overly long and loose-fitting skirts she usually wore for a short, tight-fitting navy-blue number. I couldn't hear what she was saying to Tyler but she was smiling broadly while touching and curling her beautiful mane of black hair. 'Harry,' I said urgently, 'go and find a telephone and ask that Mumford, Sheila and Aneta meet us halfway between here and London, at the truck lay-by at Luton. And also find out what time the trains to London run. We're going to have to move like lightning on this.' Harry disappeared.

Five minutes later, as soon as Emiliya had finished talking to Tyler and began to leave the hall, I charged into the ruck of people taking refreshment. 'Dr Tyler,' I whispered in Tyler's ear, 'I have to speak to you right now.' He stood there, startled.

A woman about twice the size of him descended. 'What do you think you're doing?' she asked haughtily. 'I'm Geoffrey's wife. Don't you come in here and start manhandling him.'

'Sorry,' I said. 'I'm with the house security detail.'

'What do you want?' she demanded.

'I'll tell you shortly but first let me speak to Dr Tyler.' I was grateful she had not asked for identification.

Tyler and I pulled to one side. Working where he did, he would assuredly know all about the Service. 'I'm MI6,' I said. 'That woman in the maroon top – what did she say to you?'

'Nothing much,' Tyler replied. He fished in his pocket. 'Here,' he said, handing me a business card in the name of Marie Brunelin. 'She's French and works for France's Atomic Energy Commissariat. There's a conference in Vienna in a fortnight. I'll present a paper and Marie will be an observer. She had to return to Paris tonight but wanted to introduce herself before Vienna. Her work deals with some of what we at AWRE are doing on Polaris.'

'The British Navy ballistic missile system?'

'The one and the same,' Tyler confirmed patiently, as if a headmaster talking to a dull student.

'Dr Tyler,' I said, 'I have to leave you now. There's some urgent business that needs my attention. Tell your wife I had received information suggesting the protestors here today were planning to target you as you left. Say it became obvious I was over-reacting once it was clear all I wanted to do was give you a general warning. Please do not say a word about this to anyone. The matter is very important to national security, I assure you.'

Tyler shrugged. I could only hope he was taking me seriously. I wasn't sure that he was.

Mumford and the others were already waiting at the Luton lay-by when Harry and I arrived. 'Emiliya is clearly KGB,' I briefed. 'She was all tradecraft and tits today. The Russians are obviously intent on springing a honey trap on Tyler in Vienna. They somehow knew the Five monitoring post had no call on mobile assets for a two-hour window this one Sunday morning and found out it coincided with the symposium. The trade delegation visit was mounted to allow Emiliya to make the initial approach to Tyler on the last day, believing she wouldn't be followed on leaving the embassy and nobody would know about her Milton Keynes jaunt. But they were dead unlucky. Even so, the KGB has done its homework. Tyler's wife is a harridan. Terrifying. Once Tyler's sexually compromised, the Russians think he will do anything to avoid upsetting her.'

Mumford interrupted me, asserting his authority and taking charge. 'Sounds like a whole lot of planning and effort has gone into Tyler's targeting,' he said. 'Views anyone?' he asked of all present.

I didn't want to make myself unpopular with Mumford or Sheila by imposing myself too much on the decision-making. Time, however, was critical. 'Look,' I said to Martin, 'it's really up to you and Sheila. But we've tumbled Emiliya and we should act tonight, while she's out alone – before she gets back to the embassy and is out of reach. If she's ever going to come across, it'll be now while we have the leverage of her delegation still being in England. She's bound to be on the train arriving in London at 7 pm; we should pitch at Emiliya then, when she gets off the train.'

Mumford and Sheila considered this. 'OK,' Mumford said, 'who pitches?'

By now I was in too far. 'Aneta and me,' I said quickly.

'Why you two?' Sheila asked, but not with hostility.

'One,' I said, 'if Emiliya comes the *I don't understand* routine Aneta can speak Russian. And two, I saw Emiliya in action today. I can make clear we know exactly what the Russkies are up to.'

'Let's move,' Mumford said. 'Sheila, Joe and Aneta, you travel in the same car as me. We can discuss tactics on the way.' This time we rocketed down the M1, Euston station our destination.

———◆—◆———

Aneta and I got to platform eight just as the 7 pm train from Milton Keynes arrived. Emiliya was now wearing her blue raincoat and had retied her hair in a bun. We followed her until she reached the concourse. 'Emiliya,' I called with enough volume to ensure she heard me. She turned. I could tell she was shocked but her eyes were defiant. 'There's something important we need to discuss.'

Ignoring me, Emiliya continued walking, quickening her pace. Aneta ran ahead and impeded her path. 'You'd better listen to what he says, bitch,' she said. 'Your life and that of your family back in Russia are both in grave danger.' With that, Emiliya shrugged and retreated to the concourse's darkened perimeter, where she waited for us to join her.

Driving down from Luton, Mumford said the biggest thing going for us was that Lubyanka marked hard. Lubyanka was the infamous KGB headquarters in central Moscow. 'Serious failure is effectively a death sentence,' Martin told us. I thought of Jakarta and how the threat to reveal Boris's litany of errors to his masters led him to agree to work for us with barely an argument. Martin also indicated that, owing to her relative youth, we should assume Emiliya's parents were still alive. 'What we don't need,' he said, 'is someone telling us to get knotted because they personally are stoic enough to take what's coming. We need to leverage off the family.'

'You cocked up today, Emiliya,' I said, with what I hoped was icy menace. 'We now know you're KGB and going after Tyler with a honey trap at the Vienna conference.' Emiliya's face remained impassive. 'There's two ways to play this. One is to get the media involved while the trade delegation is still in town. Just imagine how your Moscow bosses would react to all those television cameras and the questions about using the delegation as cover for a spying operation.' I looked stone-faced at Emiliya. 'Think of your mother and father if we do go public. You and I both know they'll be sent to the gulag in punishment for the fuss you've caused.' The brief blink of Emiliya's eyes told me the mention of her parents had touched a nerve. I knew then we were on the right track.

En route to London, Mumford had also outlined how a double-headed outcome was possible should Emiliya wish to avoid the publicity option. 'Tyler,' he said, 'will feed the Russians chaff but only once they start making their real information requests. Until then, he will comply with their marginal requests designed to hook him and leave him no way out.' I admired the simple genius of it. The substantive information requests made by the Russians, once confident Tyler was on board, would identify key gaps in their nuclear program. These we would fill with disinformation. The result would be catastrophic. 'And separately,' Martin said, 'Emiliya would become a rare and much sought-after Service asset, one spying for us direct from the KGB's heartland.'

'And the other option?' Emiliya asked softly. Her raising the alternative was telling. Despite her steely demeanour, Emiliya's subdued enquiry told me she was not far from being turned.

'You go back to Moscow tomorrow as per normal, then go to Vienna and execute the honey trap. After that, you will remain on our books providing what we ask for. Obviously, we'll be looking closely at the quality of the information you deliver. If you go cold on us, we'll not hesitate to tell your people how you bungled the Tyler entrapment from the very outset.' I didn't need to go on.

Puzzled, Emiliya asked, 'Besides recruiting me, you want the operation against Tyler to go ahead as well?'

'I'll spare you the details, Emiliya,' I said, 'but the short answer is yes.'

Emiliya stared poisonously at me. She knew the KGB would brand her as criminally irresponsible for alerting us to its intricately planned honey trap and bringing the Russians' duplicitous use of its trade delegation to the attention of the world at large. She also knew the unpalatable consequences of the denunciation. Faced with the choice of either condemning her family to a pitiless fate at the hands of a Russian kangaroo court or clinging to the hope of a reprieve, Emiliya took the only option open to her. With grim reluctance she nodded her agreement.

I wanted to finish soon. The delayed train excuse only ran so deep. If we detained Emiliya much longer her embassy masters would be wondering where she was. 'The arrangements for channelling information to us will be worked out ahead of Vienna and conveyed to you there,' I said. 'Now best you get home as quickly as possible.' I touched her arm as she started to leave. 'One last thing, what's your real name, date and place of birth?'

With something akin to military precision she replied, with pride I thought, 'I am Katya Vasilievna Lyubimova, born in the Hero City of Leningrad, 30 June 1952.' Aneta scribbled in her notebook as Katya spoke.

CHAPTER 15

VIENNA

Back in the office that night we shared a glass of whisky in our small conference room on the fourth floor of Century House. We weren't terribly upbeat because we all knew that planning for Vienna involved doing a lot in a short time. Mumford succinctly summarized the position. 'The national interest dictates the honey trap must go ahead,' he said. 'Without it Katya will be known to have failed and likely be eliminated. With that, we would lose the rare opportunity to sabotage the Soviet nuclear program while at the same time be denied a prized source within the KGB.'

Martin looked around the table, inviting input. Sheila spoke first. 'If Geoffrey Tyler is going to work for us,' she said, 'it may be prudent to ignore whether he takes up Katya's offer of a night in bed or if the Russians have to drug him. The realization that he's been compromised will be difficult enough to deal with as it is without him also thinking we are being judgemental.'

'Yes, that's sensible,' Mumford agreed.

'There's also the fact that I effectively told Tyler this so-called Marie Brunelin is a French spy,' I said with an apologetic shrug. 'We'll need to neutralize this before we get to Vienna.'

Mumford read my body language. He knew I was worried he would think I had overplayed my hand. 'The approach you took was perfectly understandable in the circumstances, Joe,' he said, putting my fears to rest. 'Let's not waste any more time on it. The important thing is how do we rectify the situation?'

'Well,' I said, relief bolstering my confidence, 'Tyler did appear to take what I said with a grain of salt. It makes me think he would be amenable to an explanation it is now clear that Marie is not spying for the Frogs. Sorry for the stuff up, etcetera.'

Martin considered this, his chin cradled between his thumbs and interlinked forefingers. 'Sheila,' he said finally, 'you should approach Tyler as soon as possible to explain away Joe's intrusion at Milton Keynes. Not formally in his office but somewhere unobtrusive. As Joe says, it's important that Tyler goes to Vienna without any preconceived ideas.'

With that, we uncapped pens and started listing tasks. Of course we all recognized that even should the disinformation sting get off the ground, it would not run forever. Sooner or later the Russians would wise up to it or tumble to the fact of Katya's spying for us. As a result, both inextricably linked operations would fall over together.

❖ ❖

The following Wednesday, Sheila reported that, the night before, she had collared Tyler in the carpark of the Tesco supermarket near his home in Brentford. Sheila had cast herself as someone humbly apologetic. She explained that my buttonholing of him at Milton Keynes was all a terribly embarrassing cock up; hence her informal approach. The Service hoped Dr Tyler would accept its sincerest apologies. Marie Brunelin was not a French spy. In the days since the symposium she had been thoroughly checked out. We'd be most grateful if you didn't mention our mistake to her – you know, English–French relations and all that.

Tyler was apparently contemptuous. 'I thought so,' he said. 'I think that character who set upon me at Milton Keynes was a sandwich short of a picnic.'

In the two days preceding, we had made low-key enquiries through the Ministry of Defence to determine that Tyler would be staying at the five star Erdberger Wien Hotel, walking distance from the conference venue, the Burgtheater. Sheila's account of her discussions with Tyler triggered Harry Brandt's immediate dispatch to Vienna, whereupon he booked into the Erdberger Hotel. Using his fluent German, Harry was soon able to confirm with staff that the hotel was holding a booking for Mlle Marie Brunelin.

The tumblers were falling into place. On receipt of Harry's advice, Aneta and I attended a local travel agent to book a double room at the Rose Hotel on Rilkeplatz. The booking was in the name of Mr and Mrs Jeffries, consistent with our Service-issued forged passports. The Rose was five of Vienna's huge city blocks from the Erdberger Hotel where Katya would be accommodated; close enough for her prompt return to the Erdberger if needed, but far enough away to be reasonably sure of not running into people we'd rather not. The conference was to be held over three days. When it broke on the first night seemed the best time for Katya to come to our hotel. Eight o'clock was the selected time. Sheila was to forewarn Katya of this during the conference's first day.

We knew KGB people would be around the conference and all over the Erdberger Hotel. But we inferred from the Milton Keynes exercise, where she operated alone, that Katya enjoyed a high degree of operational authority. We were confident she had only to utter the words *operational requirements* for any would-be watchers to back off. On Katya's arrival at the Rose Hotel, Sheila would shepherd her to the room where Aneta and I waited. I was acutely aware that Sheila was doing a lot of the legwork and me more the guts of the operation. But Mumford was calling the shots and Sheila seemed to accept his direction without question.

The day before the conference, Aneta and I flew to Vienna, travelling separately from Sheila. Our room had a small couch on which I volunteered to sleep. After breakfast the next morning, Aneta sought the concierge's advice on tourist activities and we set off ostensibly to do these, all the while looking for tails or people overly interested in us. The risk of Katya running a double game was at the forefront of our minds. We continued the trade work throughout the day. By late afternoon we were sure we were clean.

<hr>

Katya was nothing if not punctual. Sheila ushered her into the room on the dot of 8 pm. Harry arrived ten minutes later after watching for following foot traffic. At first nothing was said while Aneta frisked Katya. When the preliminaries were done, I told Katya to take a seat. 'When will the move on Tyler take place?' I asked.

Katya smiled briefly. I couldn't help thinking how beautiful she was. 'He's a conservative man. But ultimately he's a man. I doubt it will be tonight but tomorrow night I suspect it will happen.'

'You mean you think he'll get involved by choice?' I said, earning myself a withering look from Sheila that said: *We don't care how it happens, remember?* Without waiting for Katya's answer, I quickly moved on. 'Please tell us how Tyler will pass material to his handlers and be provided with information requests.'

'In London, mostly through dead drops,' Katya said. 'But when Tyler travels elsewhere in the UK, such as to weapons manufacturing factories, he will likely meet face to face with a controller, in a pub for example.'

'And what happens when Tyler's work takes him abroad?'

Katya shrugged. 'I suppose he will be required to carry material for passing over at the other end and will receive further instructions at the same time.'

'When will he be asked to begin supplying information?'

Katya understood my question. I found her intelligence seductive. *I really enjoy talking to her,* I thought, surprised to think this and distracted by the need to contain my galloping emotions.

'I don't know for sure, but my strong guess is he will be initially tasked to supply what the Americans call chicken feed.'

'I'm familiar with the term,' I said, doing my best steely Joe.

Katya stared intently at me, mocking amusement in her eyes. 'Maybe for six months,' she said. 'When Lubyanka headquarters judges he is in too far to back out, our demands will escalate.'

I looked at Sheila. I could tell that, like me, she was thinking how Katya's insights into running Tyler were a pointer to the quality of the information she would supply from inside the KGB. I hoped that Sheila wasn't reading my other thoughts.

I found it unnerving to watch Katya's resilience evaporate when I asked her about her family, transforming from defiance to fear in an instant and unable to disguise it. We later agreed Katya was not telling the truth when she claimed her parents were dead and that she was unmarried and an only child. The look in her dark eyes when I warned of the consequences for her family if she sold us out said it all. I wanted to put my arms around her.

Sheila then took over. 'Assuming everything goes to plan, you'll be back in Moscow on Thursday. On the following Saturday, go to the Russian State Library at 2 pm. Provided you think you are clean, fifteen minutes after you arrive you are to remove a scarf you'll carry in your handbag and tie it loosely around your neck. Thereafter, untying the scarf is the signal you will rely on if you detect trouble. After an hour, leave the library and proceed by metro to the Pushkin Museum of Fine Arts. Position yourself in the Numismatic Collection exhibition by no later than 4 pm. Someone will contact you there. If anytime during the exercise you report suspicions, we'll abort and have another go the following Saturday, same times plus one hour.'

'I understand you,' Katya said sullenly, her distinctly Russian pout further arousing my distinctly conflicting protective instincts.

Interview done, we stuck a document under Katya's nose. She signed it in her native Cyrillic language. Aneta saw her out. Sheila rang a tame number in London, a Service flat where Mumford had situated himself. 'The insurance company has agreed to settle,' Sheila said. To a question I didn't hear, she responded, 'Yes, the entire claim.' Sheila rang off. 'Right,' she said, 'let's jot down key impressions for our lessons learned debrief.' Reaching for her handbag, she extracted a bottle of whisky before adding with a broad smile, 'After which we can have ourselves a well earned drink.'

❦

I wasn't part of the delegation that met with Tyler in an obscure office in Service headquarters. That chore fell to Mumford and Sheila. Mumford apparently told Tyler it had come to the Service's attention that the Russians had pulled a stunt on him in Vienna placing British national security at risk. Tyler did not deny it and did not ask how the Service knew. He was never asked to provide a blow-by-blow description of how the honey trap unfolded. Presumably he thought we knew, which I think we may have thanks to my out of order question to Katya.

'He was anxious to confess,' Sheila told me later. 'When I telephoned him that morning he readily agreed to talk to us.' Tyler brought with him the photographs the Russians had foisted on him in Vienna. I passed when the chance to have a look at them came up.

According to Mumford, Tyler was most relieved when told there would be no sanction for allowing the Russians to copy the documents he carried to Vienna. 'He was equally relieved when I advised it was unnecessary for Mrs T to know about the Vienna events,' Mumford recalled. 'He knew that whereas we might forgive him his transgression, the home front was much less certain.'

Tyler apparently stiffened up when told that the Service's forgiveness was conditional upon him passing initially genuine and then doctored material to the Russians. An intelligent man, he was immediately suspicious of the Service's involvement. Martin told

Tyler straight-faced the Service had no knowledge of the compromise and could also confirm that the French scientist Marie Brunelin was similarly unaware of it. Rather, he said, it was simply a matter of the KGB noting his emerging friendship with Marie and deciding to take advantage of it. 'Sometimes this sort of lie is necessary, Joe,' Mumford later explained. 'The chance to feed disinformation to the Russians stands to put back their nuclear program for years, long after they discover Tyler's material is a con.' I understand Tyler cheered up a little when Mumford hinted that a word in the ear of the Queen's Birthday honours secretariat might be appropriate.

CHAPTER 16

BELLONA

A promotion round was held in early 1980. The list came out in the last week of February. When it did, my name was on it. And so was Freddie Ladler's. But not Rupert Heneshaw's. I indulged in some schadenfreude on that score.

The afternoon the promotions were announced, I literally bumped into Heneshaw when he entered the men's toilets as I was leaving. It was as if he could sense my pleasure over his failure to be promoted. As soon as he saw me he abandoned any attempt at avoidance and drove his shoulder into my chest. We stumbled back into the toilet block coming to a stop only when I became pinned against a bank of hand basins. A stalemate ensued: we were both about the same size and weight. Gripping the lapels of the other's suit coat with no one party able to gain the ascendancy, we became locked in a dance of death. Finally, the toilet flushed in one of the cubicles. We looked at one another, each knowing that neither of us could afford to be caught engaging in fisticuffs in the office. We released our holds simultaneously and went our separate ways.

Sheila had been away. She returned the day after my run-in with Heneshaw and came to my office, a broad smile on her face. 'Well done, Joe. I was convinced your lead role in Katya's recruitment made you a shoo-in for promotion.' I thanked her. I really did owe Sheila. She had cheerfully allowed me to be front and centre in the operation when many others would have elbowed me out of the way to take the glory for themselves. 'I've also received some good news on the career front,' Sheila said.

'Really?'

'Yes. Word reached me last night that I have been successful in a Foreign Office promotion round. I'm to head Europe Division.'

'Fantastic, Sheila. Just great news. Sincerely sorry to see you go all the same; really sorry, actually.'

'I'm happy to be going back to the FO, Joe. It values level and consistent performance, whereas this outfit requires notable, if not spectacular achievements. I'm not sure I want to spend the rest of my working life trying to destroy the lives of other human beings just to get a promotion.' I stood and we embraced awkwardly.

Sheila left the Service shortly after, whereupon I took over her former position. I occasionally saw her when over at the Foreign Office. But when we did get to speak we never reminisced. Soon we just waved to each other without stopping. Our work was our only point of commonality; it was natural that we grew apart.

❖ ❖

Three months later, I was summoned to a meeting with a man called Rodney Charlesworth. Charlesworth was a Service heavy, the head administrator who, along with the rest of the Service's senior executive, resided on the top floor of Century House. Charlesworth was ultimately responsible for the Service's many administrative needs, including its overall resource requirements.

I called the lift a few minutes before the meeting's scheduled start and stepped in to find Freddie Ladler and a man in his mid-thirties whose name I did not know also heading for the top floor. Ladler had been best man at Heneshaw's wedding back in 1974. From the day we three had joined the Service together, he and Heneshaw had been joined at the hip. Ladler's body language radiated hostility, prompting me to recall my contretemps with Heneshaw in the men's toilets the previous February. He stared at me coldly. Neither of us spoke. Stepping out of the lift, the third party extended his hand to Ladler and me in turn. 'Brian McGowan,' he said. 'Seems we're all off to see Charlesworth, eh?'

Charlesworth got straight to the point. 'This blasted government,' he said, his inborn instinct to protect his career against political backlash preventing use of a stronger adjective, 'is making life difficult. Cuts here, cuts there. Unless we can do more with less, our capacity to service our current commitments, let alone expand them, will be severely tested. That's where you lot come in.' McGowan smiled a relaxed smile. Ladler and I did our best impersonations of Easter Island statues. 'You three,' Charlesworth said, 'have been chosen to do a root and branch review of the Service. No holds barred. You'll have access to all areas, top to bottom. Your terms of reference are simple: cut costs while generating greater operational efficiency.' He paused to let his instruction sink in. 'You'll have until the end of November, six months from now, to complete your report. Don't waste our time. We want good, practicable and well reasoned recommendations.'

Nodding at Ladler and me, Charlesworth told us, 'We've chosen two operations people because you'll need to look at every country in the world where we have a presence and examine how processes can be made more efficient.' Turning to McGowan he added, 'Your job is to conduct a comprehensive cost estimate for each individual recommendation. Whatever you arrive at, overall there has to be a demonstrable increase in operational efficiency married to a reduction in costs.'

Charlesworth went on to advise we'd be accommodated in offices down the corridor from his. We'd be starting the next Monday. A scribe would be provided to assist in drafting our report. 'Any questions?' he asked, with just enough aggression to make clear he didn't want any. 'Perhaps I shouldn't say this,' Charlesworth said as we began to leave, 'but you three have been handpicked by the DG to do this review. I don't need to spell out what a feather that is in your respective caps.' With that, he looked down at his papers, already on to the next item in his in-tray.

We rode the lift down together. Nobody spoke. At the fourth floor, McGowan bade me a cheery, 'See you on Monday.'

'Will do, Brian,' I responded. 'Cheers.' I could see McGowan's look of puzzlement as the lift door closed; the tension between Ladler and me was all too obvious.

Back in the privacy of my office, I punched the air. Being handpicked for anything by the DG was a big deal. My selection to do the review signalled he thought I was management material. All things being equal, another promotion was not too far away. My élan faded a little with the realization I would have six months of working cheek by jowl with Ladler. But like Scarlett O'Hara, I decided to worry about that tomorrow. Sitting at my desk, I started to try and read a document. Soon, though, I was only staring at it.

A knock at the door caused me to lift my head. It was Trent Davis-Dennison, T double D as we called him, who now headed the counter intelligence unit and answered to me. Trent, in truth, had been promoted too quickly. I guessed he would toughen up in time; he'd better, otherwise the Sovs would eat him for breakfast. But I liked him. 'Joe,' he said, 'I have some news that may be of interest.'

'Yes?'

He hesitated. 'Well, a mate of mine who works on Soviet ops mentioned that a certain Service source, work name of Bellona, is no longer with us. He said you had a bit of history with Bellona.'

I could see Trent was now wondering if he would get his friend into trouble for telling me this. 'Double, don't worry old son,' I said. 'I'm not about to run off and tell anyone you've passed on a spot of harmless gossip.'

He smiled, relieved. 'Yes, apparently some rough treatment in Lubyanka before being put up against the wall.'

Bellona was the code name given to Katya.

I thanked Trent, while trying to remain impassive. He left. I shut the door and immediately began to shake uncontrollably. Katya had survived about nine months. The last of that time did not bear thinking about. I knew only too well what rough treatment in Lubyanka entailed. I thought about her recruitment. Through her defiance and later submissiveness, Katya made clear she would have had the fortitude to reject our approach but for the family consequences of her operational failure. 'She spied for us in order to give her loved ones as much time in the sun as possible,' I whispered softly, shaking my head in sad wonderment. 'She would have known that one day the balloon would go up.' The deeper I lapsed into rumination, the tighter I drew the shroud of anguish surrounding me. I held my head in my hands, momentarily overwhelmed by guilt. Then, mirthlessly, I smiled. Katya and Nought would have understood each other.

That night I decided to walk home to clear my mind of upset. I reflected on the loneliness of my marriage of convenience and why I entered into it. Usually I was able to push such thoughts aside. But tonight I could not. Sexual and emotional attraction to Katya fuelled by memories of her beauty and strength of character intruded and refused to budge. I tried to tell myself this infatuation was making me sentimental; my silly protective instincts were distorting my thinking. I determined to snap out of it. But each time I tried I couldn't get Sheila's parting words out of my head. I had destroyed this remarkable young woman, and in horrible certainty her family as well, all in the name of my career.

Returning to London on the train with Kathleen the following Sunday evening, after a day trip to Maidstone, I decided there was a silver lining in Ladler being on the root and branch review team. Since the news about Katya I had been consumed by self-disgust and disgust for my profession. For the first time since the Konrad debacle in East Berlin, I was questioning whether I wanted to stay with the Service. But the last people on earth to whom I wanted to reveal any weakening of spirit was Ladler and, by association, his boxing kangaroo sidekick, Heneshaw.

———◆◆———

The review soon bogged down. As soon as I suggested something, Ladler dismissed it as rubbish. I returned fire. About a month in, we had made precisely zero progress. Our fellow reviewer Brian McGowan began to exhibit signs of frustration.

One day Brian asked Ladler and me to come into our small conference room. He shut the door with a crash that would have been heard in the DG's office at the other end of the corridor. 'Right,' he said, hands aggressively on his hips. 'I'm sick to death of you two liabilities. You're both like children. If we don't get our finger out, this exercise will turn into a disaster for us all. I'm fucked if I'm going to sit here waiting for you two to grow up.' I noticed then for the first time that although Brian was naturally affable, he also had substantial steel in his backbone. It came as no surprise to me when eight years later Brian rose to become the Service's administrative tsar.

But for now, neither Ladler nor I spoke. We both knew what Brian said was true but each refused to be the first to concede. Brian came to our rescue. 'We are going to divide the world into two,' he said. 'Each of you will work independently of the other on one of the halves. We'll consolidate the notes you make so as to ensure there's no sign of the review being separately conducted. Clear?' Ladler and

I both nodded. 'Good,' Brian said. 'Let's get to it. There's a lot of time needing to be made up.'

Thereafter, Ladler and I worked hard as instructed. We didn't speak but nor did either of us seek to antagonize the other. I took on Eastern Europe, having served there. Ladler took the other high profile field, relations with the United States intelligence establishment. During this time I came across the files recording the political circumstances of my recruitment into the Service and later activation as *Leonard* while in Moscow. It was also when I saw Edis Aksu's report absolving me from responsibility for the Konrad disaster in East Berlin, which in the political climate of the day explained why the Service fell over itself to send me to Jakarta.

On discovering these files, I began reading them only when all others had left for the day. I called Kathleen to advise I would be home very late. Dawn was rising when I arrived back at the flat. I had a long shower. Kathleen was up by the time I emerged from the bathroom. She asked what I had been doing all night, seeming to enquire whether I'd been with another woman. But she appeared to sense I was telling the truth when I simply answered, 'Working.' After breakfast I headed back to the office. Riding the bus, it occurred to me that my career drive had rekindled, marking my recovery from Katya's demise. But as I entered the office, from out of nowhere a powerful sense of emptiness briefly engulfed me. After years of paying it absolutely no regard, I recalled like yesterday Nought's warning of the ruinous personal cost of hiding in *The Far Grass* and how the only thing standing between destructive moral incompetence and me was real love.

The report turned out a triumph. Our scribe had written it brilliantly – as though a team of happy campers compiled it. The DG put on an afternoon tea when the report, after first surviving Charlesworth's critical perusal, was presented to him in the first week of December 1980. I knew then we were in good odour.

Brian proposed we have a pint that night. I managed to get him to one side. 'This is a bit difficult,' I said. 'There's a lot of bad blood between Ladler and me. God knows I owe you a drink, but socializing with Ladler is unfortunately a bridge too far.'

Brian laughed raucously. 'Ladler just told me much the same thing,' he said, his body shaking with amusement. 'You and I should have a drink tonight. Freddie's got a bash at the US Embassy. I'll catch him tomorrow night.' Brian was still chuckling when later we met at the Three Stags pub near the Service.

CHAPTER 17
CHOWDHURY

I was still basking in the success of the root and branch review two weeks later as Christmas 1980 approached. With some leave in prospect, I was planning to suggest to Kathleen we take a trip to Scotland, where the combination of old age single malt whisky and a spot of fly-fishing appealed to me. The ringing telephone interrupted my daydream. It was the new head of Placements calling to say he wanted to send me to New Delhi as station chief in the New Year. India was where East and West frequently intersected making head of station New Delhi a prestigious Service assignment. He gave me a week to think about it.

I also learned on the Service gossip treadmill that Ladler had been offered Zimbabwe, formerly the British colony of Southern Rhodesia or, more commonly, just Rhodesia. Zimbabwe had attained independence earlier in 1980, with the UK leading the way. The fledgling country's prime minister, Robert Mugabe, however, was erratic and given to inflammatory Marxist rhetoric. The whole world was watching and Britain, as the facilitator of Zimbabwe's independence, suddenly had its own international reputation on the line. Insights into Mugabe's intentions quickly became critical. It was a sure sign of being held in high esteem by the top floor executive for any Service officer asked to be Zimbabwe station head.

The following weekend I casually mentioned to Kathleen that the Service wanted to post me to New Delhi. She had already knocked me back on holidaying in Scotland and I expected her to refuse point-blank on Delhi. This gave me cause to wonder if the end of our marriage might now be in reach. To my surprise, however, Kathleen began to wax eloquently about the wonders of the sub-continent. And her enthusiasm refused to wilt. She told anyone who would listen that we were 'off to Ind-yaar,' as she liked to say. I knew she had read Paul Scott's *Staying On* and wondered if the book's sympathetic treatment of India and the exotic images it conjured had influenced her thinking.

Whatever, come March 1981 we arrived in New Delhi to take up our assignment. India was a British Commonwealth country. I would be working out of a High Commission and not an embassy, although the difference was in name only.

————————◆◆————————

I was wondering how well Kathleen would manage being away from her familiar surroundings. The first few weeks abroad could be quite dislocating after the excitement of getting there had rubbed off. Most UK High Commission staff resided on a purpose-built compound also housing the High Commission office block and the High Commissioner's *Official Residence*. Owing to the nature of my work, we were located off compound. There were pros and cons to this. The upside was welcome avoidance of the endlessly unhappy compound politics, the downside being the house's erratic water and electricity supply.

We had two house staff: a dhobi who did our laundry and a bearer who cleaned the house and would have cooked had we wished. We also had a night watchman, our chowkidar, who gave new meaning to the concept of a static sentry. Kathleen found all this a novelty and, as if in some sort of time warp, began avidly penning letters back home describing the challenges of managing the staff. But the lustre soon wore off.

Kathleen's first stomach bug came just six weeks into the posting. The High Commission doctor prescribed antidiarrhoeal medicine, plenty of filtered water, and rest. Kathleen was instantly cured of posting life and began to miss her family terribly. But making telephone calls to the UK was a nightmare. It took Kathleen forever to get through and when she did the line seemed to be shared with a multitude of others, most babbling incoherently to English ears. Goodness knows what Kathleen's family in faraway Maidstone made of it all. It certainly didn't impress Kathleen.

Four months into our posting, in July 1981, Kathleen declared she was taking a trip home to see her parents. She was gone for a month before returning to Delhi. Three weeks later, she announced plans for another visit to Maidstone. The end of our marriage was now obviously in sight. We might well have struggled on much longer had we remained in England. But the pressures of living in a culture alien to us had hastened our shaky union to the precipice. In September 1981, close to the six-month anniversary of our arrival in India, I watched Kathleen board the airport bus taking her to the waiting British Airways flight. There had been no histrionics, but on noting her resolve I gained a strong sense of finality.

And so it was. For a time afterwards Kathleen never contacted me. I wrote her a letter but it went unanswered. After about six months, she wrote to have me arrange for her furniture in store in London to be released to an address in Maidstone. Kathleen had clearly moved back home. I complied. We never spoke again and when some months later the divorce papers turned up, I signed away any claim I may have to Kathleen's assets on the understanding she would do the same for mine. As Nought had suggested, the marriage had been ridden as far as it would go.

❖❖

For all the artificiality of our relationship, Kathleen's departure left me feeling empty and alone for a time. I didn't miss Kathleen *per se* and knew her return permanently to the UK was best for her, and me. All the same, I felt my isolation acutely. I refocused on my work with greater intensity. The staff thought I drove them too hard but I didn't care. 'Get out there and look,' I instructed them, reliving my diligence when doing the groundwork in Indonesia. 'I want every conceivable opportunity run to ground.'

This saturation approach soon paid dividends. At an insignificant event one evening in October 1981, one the station wouldn't usually attend, a man called Golam Chowdhury, a Bangladeshi, bowled up to Jessica Cole, the youngest and least experienced of my staff. 'I do not earn enough to put Khaled, my first boy and most important child, into the British school in Dhaka,' Chowdhury told Jess. Dhaka was Bangladesh's capital. 'I have access to information of high interest to your government,' he also claimed, this hint suggesting that Chowdhury knew Jess was Service and was offering himself for sale. Jess probed him on his connections to the Indian bureaucracy, which on face value seemed vast, and then parked him with the promise to get back to him.

It didn't take much to find out that Chowdhury was a declared member of Bangladesh's overseas spy agency, the National Security Intelligence. NSI was poorly resourced and, in light of Bangladesh's dire financial situation, paid very low salaries. We cabled London proposing that, on condition of Chowdhury agreeing to work for us, we provide a place for his son at the British school in Dhaka. London queried us on funding and a million other things. But, finally, we were given approval to explore the opportunity.

———◆◆———

The day of the recruitment attempt arrived. These were always nerve-wracking affairs. Chowdhury's was no different. Jessica had made the running on him and earned the right to make the pitch. She had arranged to meet Chowdhury late in the afternoon in the coffee shop of the Taj Mahal Hotel in Old Delhi. Philip Brownlie, another of my staff, was to ride shotgun for her. Time ticked by. I was waiting in the office when a visibly upset Jessica walked in, accompanied by Philip. Clearly, all had not gone according to plan.

'I had to park some distance from the hotel,' Jess said once she'd calmed down. 'Its car park is only small and was full. As I was walking back to the hotel, some young fellow jumped off his scooter taxi and groped me.' The effort of making the explanation caused Jessica to tip over. She dissolved into tears.

'I was a good way back watching Jess's back,' Philip said. 'By the time I got to where the commotion was taking place, there must have been 500 people gathered watching.'

'And then?' I asked.

'The hotel security eventually came down and took me into the hotel,' Jess sniffled. 'I told them I didn't want the police called.'

'Are you hurt?' I said. 'I mean do you want to see the High Commission doctor?'

'No, thanks. I'm browned off, that's all.'

'You've just experienced the big challenge of working in this city, Jess,' I said. 'Everywhere a Westerner goes there are a thousand pairs of eyes watching. It's particularly difficult for you because the majority of Indian street lads think that young Western women are promiscuous. It's a stereotyped image courtesy of our film, television and advertising industries.'

Jess nodded. 'Don't I know it?' she said bitterly. Turning to Philip, she asked, 'Did you get to speak to Chowdhury?'

'No,' he said. 'I looked for him in the coffee shop and around the hotel lobby but didn't see him. Presumably he'd taken off.'

'Let's not worry about Chowdhury right now,' I said to Jess. 'You get some rest and we will re-set tomorrow.' Jess lived on the compound. 'Philip, would you walk Jess home, please, and then come back here?'

Waiting for Philip to return, I counselled myself to hold my nerve. Fortunately, I had at the time an incomplete appreciation of Chowdhury's value. *Don't be panicked into taking control of the op yourself*, I thought.

'Jess has just fallen off the spy's equivalent of a bike,' I told Philip when he was back. 'And we need to get her back up in the saddle as soon as possible.' Philip nodded his understanding. 'I want you to find Chowdhury and bring him to my house tomorrow night,' I instructed him. 'I don't care what time. Just find Chowdhury and bring him there and Jess can pitch at him. It's not ideal, but let's see if we can prevent the op falling apart and Jess with it.' I told Jess of my plans first thing the next morning. She was determinedly grateful for the second bite of the apple.

Philip arrived at my home that night at 10 pm with Chowdhury in tow. I hadn't bothered to stand down the chowkidar; the mere thought of coming to work seemed to put him into a deep sleep.

'He took some finding,' Philip told me after Jess and Chowdhury had gone into my study. 'Eventually, I tracked him down at the Empire Club enjoying a few whiskies with some of his Intelligence Bureau buddies.' Philip's face took on a worried look. 'The Bureau guys did look strangely at me when I took him away.'

I nodded grimly but didn't say anything. I could hardly blame Philip. He was working on the run. But for the Indian internal security agency to be aware of our interest in Chowdhury was unhelpful, to put it mildly.

Jessica and Chowdhury emerged from my study after an hour. A deal had been clinched for a one-year scholarship for Chowdhury's son at the British School in Dhaka commencing in January 1982 and, starting immediately, a stipend of 250 US dollars a month to be paid to Chowdhury from our US dollar float.

I shook Chowdhury's hand. 'Good to have you on the team,' I said, pleased for Jess more than anything. But soon my thoughts turned to damage control. 'I understand you were with some Intelligence Bureau contacts when we dragged you away?'

Chowdhury read me like a book. 'Mr Lambert,' he said, 'are you familiar with the saying that my enemy's enemy is my friend?'

'I am indeed.'

'Well, suffice to say that India actively supported the emergence of the People's Republic of Bangladesh from the former territory of East Pakistan. This shared history causes the Indian security services to regard their Bangladeshi counterparts as trusted allies in the struggle against the despised Pakistan. My Bureau friends will not question any of my activities, of that I am confident.' He smiled roguishly, his head wobbling with such vigour in the distinctive South Asian manner that it defeated my pessimism.

True to Chowdhury's word, the Indians paid him no attention whatsoever, not even a cursory look. He roamed around New Delhi at will and had an amazing array of contacts, a veritable menagerie of sources from whom he extracted a stream of high-quality information, including on our key interest of Indian arms purchases from the Russians. But for all that, Chowdhury was to last only four months in service – after nearly seven years in Delhi, he was unexpectedly called home in early 1982.

Chowdhury's replacement was from the Bangladeshi elite, a thunderously wealthy young man who was easy to dislike. We tried but got little traction with him; he could have bought and sold the entire High Commission twice over. Nonetheless, while Chowdhury was in place we made much hay while the sun did shine. I derived enormous satisfaction from London head office handing the station a 1981 performance assessment of *Performing Exceptionally*.

CHAPTER 18

AGNES

A new High Commissioner arrived shortly after my thirty-fourth birthday in March 1982. An old soldier, Sir Aubrey Stevens was on his last assignment. But he was also a vastly experienced diplomat who knew the value of entertaining. I was just important enough to make the cut. Accordingly, two months after their arrival, I found myself one May evening an invited guest of Sir Aubrey and Lady Hanna at a dinner party at *The Residence*.

Sir Aubrey and Lady Hanna's guest list was eccentric, mixing ambassadors with also-rans like me. But *The Residence* dining table in seating sixteen, a smallish number by diplomatic standards, was still large enough to sort the sheep from the goats. The sheep at the top end of the table, along with the High Commissioner and Lady Hanna, were the Ambassadors of Ireland, Belgium and Greece, all with accompanying spouses, and a staid-looking couple, the male of whom was apparently a wheel from the Exchequer in London.

A woman called Shirley who ran the High Commission's passport office also had a jersey. A preposterous character replete with a monocle and cravat partnered her. I vaguely wondered how the two had met. At one point, the man claimed he was an exiled Polish Count. He and his consort sat opposite each other in the table's middle reaches as if, like me, the person in charge of the seating plan wasn't sure if the Count was for real. I tuned out when now and again he addressed those assembled as if holding court, while all the while Shirley looked on in unrestrained admiration.

Sitting with me at the goats' end of the table, remote from the ambassadorial company, were Sir Aubrey's deputy and her husband, and an English woman in her late twenties with long auburn hair called Agnes. I was on my best behaviour and drank sparingly.

I found Agnes an engaging personality. When she smiled her green eyes sparkled and her high cheekbones enhanced the warmth she exuded. Her business card declared her to be Agnes Huntington, Indian Operations Manager for an organization called HOPE, the acronym standing for Humanity, Opportunity, Purpose and Evolution. HOPE was a London-based, non-government aid outfit that, according to Agnes, did good works in the developing world. From what she said, her particular operation ran on the smell of an oily rag. Its focus was mainly on refugees in India. Agnes said her largest client group was displaced Afghans, who were especially disadvantaged because the Indian Government refused them refugee status. This caused my ears to prick up.

The Soviet–Afghan war had commenced in 1979 about two years before my arrival in New Delhi. By 1982 a pressing need had been identified in both Washington and London to quantify the scale of Soviet human rights abuses over the preceding three years. Indeed, the thirst for such knowledge had become unquenchable – in truth, it must be said, mainly for its propaganda value. All MI6 stations within reasonable proximity of Afghanistan had recently been tasked to gather information. Most displaced Afghans in India were from rural areas. The high probability was that among them were valuable sources of intelligence on Soviet conduct in the provinces. We were now actively trying to get alongside the Indian officials managing this human debris, but so far with limited success.

I must admit here that my motive was not entirely honourable. Rather, with Chowdhury having been in the picture only for four months, I was on the search for a new star source, someone like Chowdhury who was sufficiently productive as to convince head office that New Delhi station was continuing to perform above and beyond expectations. Agnes, I decided, may well be the key to this. I asked her if I could inspect the refugee centre HOPE had established on New Delhi's outskirts.

She smiled warmly. 'You are most welcome,' she said.

I do confess my heart gave a little skip in response before I quickly refocused on work priorities. 'I'll be in touch to make arrangements,' I told her.

The next day I decided to write to Agnes and arranged for a High Commission driver who knew the HOPE centre's location to deliver my note. His instruction was to wait for a response. He returned later in the day and gave me back my letter now annotated with Agnes's blunt reply: *OK for a visit next Thursday 20 May 2 pm.* It was signed in confident cursive script: *Agnes C Huntington, HOPE UK.* I found Agnes's handwriting inexplicably attractive.

❦

The drive to the HOPE centre took a seeming eternity. Finally, when we were about twenty miles from Delhi, we reached a collection of ramshackle buildings surrounded by a rickety wire fence. 'Welcome to the HOPE centre,' Agnes said, bounding out of the hut that served as her office, a huge smile on her face. Her hair was tied in a bun and as might be expected she wore no make-up. She was clad in trousers and a shirt and shod in heavy boots. The swell of her breasts against her shirt did not escape my notice. But I'd come with determination to act the hardcore professional and that's what I intended to do.

Agnes gave me a conducted tour of the facility. Along the way, I rehearsed my fabricated reason for wanting to visit. 'The Indian police,' I told Agnes, 'have recently warned the High Commission of persons suspected of being Afghans targeting the homes of Westerners in New Delhi.' I adopted a concerned expression. 'The sizeable British private sector community is among those most at risk,' I said.

Agnes pouted doubtfully when told this. 'I really don't think any of these poor beggars would have the means to get to New Delhi let alone rob anyone there,' she said.

I made my premeditated play. 'What if I gave you some names and descriptions? Could you keep an eye out for these people?' Indian officials had grudgingly provided this information. The names and background meant nothing to us. I could only hope that such persons actually existed.

Agnes became indignant. 'First thing,' she said derisively, 'I'm here primarily to worry about the welfare of these people. And secondly, what sort of description are you going to give me? Aged before their time, traumatized half to death, wearing rags around their heads, not to mention loose-fitting trousers? That should narrow it down to the last five million possibilities.'

I found Agnes's sarcasm strangely endearing. 'Tell you what,' I said, smiling at her, 'if you come across someone who was a village head, a teacher or similar, could you let me know?'

'OK, deal,' she said, shaking her head in exaggerated bemusement. 'Sorry, this job can be so bloody thankless.' Then, after briefly taking my arm to direct me, Agnes led me back to her office. Over a cup of tea and digestive biscuit, we swapped stories of life in India. Finally, it was time to go. We shook hands. The cool firmness of Agnes's handshake was like an electric shock but with difficulty I remained po-faced. A feeling of elation washed over me as my driver started to wend his way back to New Delhi.

The following day I sent Agnes a note asking if she would like to see a film during the next week, at the US Embassy cinema. *The Sting* was showing. Agnes's response simply said: *Sounds good. See you there at 7 pm Tuesday.* It generated far more excitement in me than the words could ever have possibly warranted.

———————

People often tell me *The Sting* is a great movie. I'll have to take their word for it because even though I sat through it, I have no recollection of it. Rather, all I can remember was the pleasure it gave me to sit in the cool of the theatre with my shoulder intermittently touching Agnes's. Above all, I recall the scent she wore. Like everything about her, I decided, it was perfect. The movie finished and I walked Agnes back to her car. An old Indian man was waiting. Agnes introduced him as *Gulam, my driver.* Gulam reverently opened the back door for her.

Gulam's deference took me back to Jakarta and the loyal old Indonesian taxi driver who drove Betty, the Malaysian conquest of my first major intelligence success, the KGB officer, Boris. But the memory did not swell me with the warm feeling of professional achievement. Rather, it was the diametric opposite. I now realized that my obsessive search for a replacement for Chowdhury, and the hoped-for spying triumph that would represent, had been replaced by total preoccupation with Agnes. I asked Agnes if she would like to have dinner next week. It seemed like the natural thing to do.

'I'd really like that,' Agnes said, causing my heart rate to quicken. 'Before then, though, I'm having drinks at my house this Friday night. Why don't you come along?' Before I could answer Agnes said, 'Bring a bottle of booze if you like. Mathura Marg, second house on the left. Any time. Thanks for a lovely night, Joe.' I watched the car slowly drive off, resisting the urge to run after it.

———————

I arrived at Agnes's house on the Friday night to be greeted by her offering congratulations on my ability to find the place. 'Not easy in the dark,' I said, 'but I've got reasonable radar.' The radar fib was harmless enough but an egregious falsehood all the same – it'd taken me over an hour to find her street.

Agnes accepted my bottle of wine. 'Come in,' she said. There was a mix of European and Indian guests. I proceeded to mingle. After a while, I felt a tap on my shoulder. It was Agnes. She handed me a glass of wine. 'Let's go outside where it's cooler,' she said, smiling. 'You can tell me all your darkest secrets.'

We sat on a bench under a Banyan tree. Agnes told me she once owned her own development company. 'But I mixed the personal with business,' she said. 'Neil was my partner in both spheres. It wasn't a good arrangement. After a time unemployed, I got this contract with HOPE. It expires in September 1984.'

'Do you have any ill-feeling towards your ex-partner?' I asked.

'I was never angry with Neil,' she said. 'I have a relentlessly forward-looking philosophy. It's best to forgive and be rid of all that negative energy. Anger's such a counterproductive emotion.' *Forgiveness; no negative energy; anger's such a counterproductive emotion.* Not until many years later did I understand why these sentiments struck a chord with me.

Agnes smiled at me. 'What about you, Joe?'

I explained I had been a diplomat since 1972. 'I was married once,' I said. 'It ended not that long ago.'

◆━◆

Agnes and I went out three times subsequently, including on 10 June to celebrate her thirtieth birthday. Mid-meal at her birthday dinner, Agnes suddenly became serious. 'What do you think of the work I do, Joe?' she asked. 'Is it worthwhile or just a waste of time?'

I looked into Agnes's intelligent eyes, sensing this was a make or break moment. *Straight down the line*, I thought, *no fudging.* 'I admire what HOPE does,' I said truthfully. 'It is addressing a humanitarian problem the Indians choose to ignore and, moreover, it's doing so without the help of the UK taxpayer.'

Agnes considered this and I discerned her trust in me mount. I knew then I'd passed some sort of character test. She smiled and a cascading waterfall of happiness swept over me. 'Good,' I said. 'Now we've cleared up that, let's sort out Arthur Scargill.'

Scargill was a polarizing UK trade unionist. Agnes shook her head and laughed. 'That's so funny,' she whispered.

I left Agnes that night feeling like an excited schoolboy. Sleep was impossible. The next day I wrote to her to suggest Saturday dinner at the Agra Diamond restaurant. Rupee for rupee, the Agra was arguably Delhi's best dining experience. Agnes and I were close to fusing and I wanted the evening to be a resounding success.

On the Friday preceding dinner, however, I received a note from Agnes saying she was beset by a stomach bug and confined to bed. It was unlikely she could do Saturday evening. I wrote a return note encouraging her to rest and saying I would come over on Saturday at 6 pm in any event. I then rang my bearer, who now doubled as my cook, and asked him to roast a chicken and make naan bread and potato salad. 'Wrap it all in foil and put it in the refrigerator, please,' I said. 'I will be needing it tomorrow night.'

Agnes was sitting up in bed when I arrived on the Saturday night. She had just showered as her damply falling hair revealed. Spontaneously, I kissed her lightly on the forehead. 'Poor baby,' I whispered. Agnes showed no surprise. Like me, she knew our relationship now extended beyond a simple friendship. I unpacked the food I had with me. 'Let me get you a plate and bib and prop you up,' I said. 'Eat as much or as little as you want.'

Agnes brightened. 'That's wonderful of you, Joe. The food smells beautiful. I can already feel my appetite returning.'

There was only the one bedside light. As dark came its glow reflected softly on us. The surrounding gloom had the effect of isolating us in our own cocoon remote from the outside world. It was still and quiet. I removed the soiled utensils and sat next to Agnes stroking her hair. She took my hand and I kissed her fully on the lips. Agnes drew me to her. My hand found the inside of her nightdress and caressed her firm breast and jutting nipple. 'Joey,' Agnes whispered as I took away the bedclothes. The smell of her perfume was intoxicating. I woke the next morning with Agnes still in my arms. I felt like the happiest man in all of India.

CHAPTER 19

SHUKHOV

As head of station, I was declared for liaison purposes to the Indian overseas intelligence agency, the Research and Analysis Wing, or RAW as it was better known. This was my meat and drink, although in parallel I also supervised the station's covert work, activities such as Chowdhury's recruitment. Being declared to RAW made it inevitable that my status would become widely known among New Delhi's intelligence community – this being the transactional cost the Service was prepared to pay to conduct liaison with the Indians. Early into my posting, in May 1981 to be precise, the KGB station in New Delhi, alerted to me by its RAW contacts, had routinely reported my presence to its Lubyanka head office.

I happen to know this thanks to a senior KGB officer, a Russian who in 1990 became a Service source. What's more, the source's material went far beyond a tidbit about the KGB station reporting on who and what I was. Rather, the Russian was to explicitly detail the KGB's subsequently central role in my story, thereby explaining the many baffling events that, commencing in October 1983, came to dog me. For now, I'll call this KGB source *our source*.

The KGB's Directorate *K* was responsible for keeping tabs on rival intelligence services. And, as *our source* was to explain, since the exposure in May 1980 of Katya, the KGB agent whom I'd uncovered at Milton Keynes in the summer of 1979, the Directorate had no task before it more important than to identify her recruiter.

When reporting my presence to its head office in May 1981, the KGB station in New Delhi had also supplied Lubyanka with a colour photograph of me obtained from RAW contacts. But in a rare mistake, the image was misfiled in Moscow and only reached Directorate *K* in mid-1982. Katya did not know my name. Under interrogation, however, she had earlier provided the Directorate with a description of me as the architect of her recruitment, from which a Photo-FIT had been constructed. In particular, Katya had noted my clear blue eyes, pale complexion and the fact that I was left-handed.

Our source said Directorate *K* immediately noticed the resemblance between the Photo-FIT and the RAW photograph when finally it got to do a comparison. The KGB station in New Delhi was urgently tasked to ascertain if I was left-handed, just less than six feet tall and spoke with a slightly bastardized London accent. I understand the station was able to confirm these characteristics via a source in the UK High Commission, work name of Basil, most likely one of our local Indian staff reporting directly to the Soviets.

On receipt of the station's response, the Directorate examined my history. An educated guess was made that I was in London at the time of Katya's recruitment. More substantially, my cover as a junior officer in Jakarta until the end of 1977, when contrasted with taking up the senior role of station chief in New Delhi in March 1981, indicated I had made significant career advancement over this period. The Directorate identified that suborning Katya was the type of achievement necessary to power such progression. On weighing all before it, Directorate *K* concluded I was Katya's recruiter. This led it to categorize me as a *Person of High Interest*, the elevation automatically triggering a request to the KGB's New Delhi station for a detailed personal assessment of me.

By late 1982, *our source* told us, the Directorate had a report before it indicating I had separated from my wife subsequent to arriving in New Delhi and was now involved with an English woman heading a private UK aid organization. The report recorded for the benefit of the KGB psychologists that upon entering into this relationship, my general demeanour had become noticeably buoyant. An assessment of my potential for recruitment was rated at low to negligible. My assessors also concluded I was a moderate drinker, leaning towards teetotalism – how this dovetailed with monitoring conducted during my Moscow days I never found out.

———◆—◆———

As March 1983 approached, Agnes and I began to discuss my return to the UK. I had sought a year's extension from head office. But citing strict adherence to the two-year New Delhi posting rule, born of the health risks abounding in India, the Service denied my request. I was aware of the real reason: after an impressive 1981 my performance in 1982 had tapered off, principally because of my preoccupation with Agnes.

One morning shortly before leaving New Delhi, I told Agnes I wanted to spend the rest of my life with her. She responded by solemnly kissing me before saying she loved me too. I had reasonable savings by this time and was earning a salary whereby servicing a mortgage was feasible. 'I'm going to buy us a house, Aggie,' I said, using the sweet nothing I often cooed in Agnes's ear in our most private and intimate moments.

'Where?' she giggled.

'Somewhere in London,' I replied, gesturing vaguely. 'And more to the point it's going to be OUR house, not my house.'

Agnes was suddenly serious. 'Joe, are you sure? I want to be with you forever. But you know I have to see out my contract with HOPE. They were very good to me when I was nearly down for the count and I feel that I owe them.'

I knew Agnes was effectively asking me if I thought our relationship could survive eighteen months of commuting, to September 1984 when her contract with HOPE expired. I was unfazed by her caution. Agnes was unquestionably a strong and intelligent woman and usually my loner instincts would be on a hair-trigger. The litmus test was whether they would kick in and I would again be overwhelmed by my cursed need to escape. But nearly a year into our relationship, there was no sign of this. On the contrary, I lived for Agnes and hated being apart from her.

I surmised that whereas with Kathleen my natural inclination to hide in *The Far Grass* failed to trigger because my emotional outlay fell beneath a lower threshold, with Agnes there was no trigger because my emotional outlay had exceeded an upper threshold. But in Agnes's case, the suppression of my loner instincts, my sub-conscious protection mechanism, saved me from *The Far Grass* differently to that with Kathleen. It was the serenity, inerasable calm and sense of emotional security that set the Agnes experience apart. Nought had spoken of the *real deal*, of the power of real love. I now knew what he meant. It was an exhilarating and liberating feeling.

———◆◆———

Around the time I departed New Delhi for the UK, on the fourth floor of KGB headquarters on Lubyanka Square in central Moscow, General Sergei Shukhov, head of the KGB's First Main Directorate, called the Directorate's operational steering committee to order. *Our source* was in attendance. As described by *our source*, Shukhov was a giant man, stretching some six foot, four inches into the air. At fifty-three he was physically fit and mentally sharp, and ambitious and ruthless with it. For all that, Shukhov was a heavy smoker. He claimed it helped him think.

Topic four on the agenda referred to MI6 officer Lambert, Joseph. 'You will have read Directorate *K's* report,' Shukhov said on reaching the item, simultaneously enveloping his colleagues in the foul-smelling smoke of his Latvian-made cigarette. *Our source* dwelt on Shukhov's smoking habit. Rumour had it that the Latvians substituted linoleum for a portion of the tobacco going into the manufacture of the cigarettes they were obliged to export to Russia. This had two advantages from the Latvian perspective: it reduced production costs; and expanded the incidence of smoking-related illness among the Russian populace. If Shukhov had heard the rumour he appeared unconcerned by it – apparently he smoked forty of the filthy things each and every day.

Shukhov had given his colleagues half a minute to refresh their memories before continuing. 'Directorate *K's* assessment is that Lambert would be difficult to recruit at this time. But he has caused untold damage to our nuclear weapons research program and orchestrated the leakage of vital intelligence on KGB global operations. We cannot and will not let this go unremarked. This takes us to the psychiatric report at annex B.' *Our source* told of Shukhov waiting impatiently while the other committee members caught up. 'You will see our chief psychologist assesses that Lambert is unusually emotionally dependent on a woman he is now involved with following the breakdown of his marriage.' Rifling through his papers, Shukhov said, 'Yes, here it is. Agnes Claire Huntington, born Hungerford UK on 10 June 1952, an employee of an English non-government aid organization.'

Shukhov stubbed out his cigarette and folded his hands letting them rest on the table in front of him. He spoke earnestly, *our source* said. 'My proposal is to eradicate Huntington, creating an emotional vacuum in Lambert's life to be exploited. That is, into the vacuum we will insert a woman whom we assess will provide Lambert with the same emotional fulfilment as Huntington does currently. Our operative will ultimately be tasked to recruit him. The aim,' Shukhov had said, twinkling as *our source* put it, 'is to recruit Lambert while posted to an important head of station role, where he will enjoy access to high-grade American, NATO or other alliance material.' Shukhov invited questions. But nobody spoke.

'Good,' Shukhov said, turning to the Spetsnaz Directorate representative. 'You are to task your people to implement an operation to eliminate Huntington. This involves no breach of unwritten protocol. She falls outside of the gentlemen's agreement we have with the West applying to intelligence officers and their families.' *Our source* thought Shukhov had deliberately paused to underline the point. 'The elimination must take the form of an accident, one that arouses no suspicion,' Shukhov continued. 'If Lambert so much as thought the Soviet Union was responsible for her death, he would assuredly refuse to work for us.'

With that, Shukhov addressed the head of the so-called Active Measures Department. The Department was an elite KGB unit that handled the most difficult and complex problems. The man heading it was a KGB colonel. He was also later fated to become *our source.* 'The chief psychologist predicts that after Huntington's death, Lambert will sink back into his work,' Shukhov said. 'This was his response to his marriage breakdown and at his age it is unlikely his behavioural pattern will change. The operation I intend involves your Department assisting Lambert win promotion to the next level in MI6. Only then will he be eligible for the positions we want him in before recruiting him, the likes of head of station Washington, Brussels or Bonn.' Shukhov looked around the table, again inviting questions. But neither the colonel nor any other spoke.

———◆—◆———

In the first week of April 1983, I returned to work in London head office. Placements had assigned me to a job in charge of the Balkans region. As fate would have it, Rupert Heneshaw, by now promoted to my level, was my counterpart, heading a sister area responsible for a suite of Central European countries.

Heneshaw and I didn't see each other much and there was little overlap in our work. We did, though, have a weekly meeting every Monday morning with our jointly shared boss, an insipid character by the name of Reggie Sullivan. Reggie had come into the Service at a lower level some years earlier from the RAF. He was widely regarded as the worst performing of the Service's eight middle managers, so-called because organizationally they sat between the top floor executive and the rest of the Service's workforce. It remained something of a mystery as to how Reggie had been promoted to so senior a level.

Usually I would have chafed at working for Reggie; he was not the right person to be supervising you if it was promotion you were after. But I didn't care in the slightest. I was full of joy and nothing could worry me. I now knew where my priorities lay.

Agnes and I wrote to one another every day. The New Delhi High Commission's archivist who managed receipt and dispatch of the post's diplomatic mailbag, and with whom I was passing friendly, had agreed to act as our go-between, placing Agnes's letters to me in the diplomatic bag to London and passing on my letters to Agnes when the bag arrived in Delhi. The exchange of letters was a second-best option but better than nothing. Each letter from Agnes I devoured hungrily, sleeping with them while they were fresh so that I could keep the smell of her perfume in my nostrils as long as possible. Agnes was next entitled to leave in late October and would return to the UK for its duration. I began counting the days.

In the interim, I scanned *The Times* classifieds for houses to buy. I was dismayed by the price of anything decent. Nothing at my limit looked remotely suitable. One sales agent suggested I look further out than central London and its near environs. A week or so later he alerted me to a listing in Brent Cross that met my needs. The house in question had a small rear garden and was situated on the left flank of a six-house terrace row set back from the main thoroughfare of Clitterhouse Road. Directly opposite stood the large expanse of the Clitterhouse Playing Fields.

Boyhood memories of playing cricket in North Park in Bootle flooded back. I was sold. This is where Agnes and I would set up home. I saw my bank manager during the week and signed a contract to buy. I moved in on Saturday 17 September 1983, whereupon I took endless photographs and wrote Agnes a long, heartfelt and no doubt utopian letter. The following Friday, once the photographs had been developed, I lodged the letter with the diplomatic mail people and began waiting with keen anticipation for Agnes's reply. How sweet was life.

CHAPTER 20

AGGIE

I was in a deep sleep. Something had awakened me. It was the telephone on my bedside table. We had some business going on in Albania at the time and my first thought was that something had gone wrong there. The crackling line, on which other conversations in Hindi were clearly audible, soon made me realize the call was from India. I looked at my watch. In London it was 2:30 am on Monday 3 October 1983. That made it 7 am the same morning in Delhi. Agnes never called. It was too difficult and expensive. But I assumed she was making an exception, calling at this odd time in a rush of excitement having just received the house photographs. I was instantly wide awake. 'Hello, hello,' I yelled into the receiver.

'Joe, Joe, can you hear me?' came the reply from an English woman, but not one who was Agnes. 'Joe, it's Heather Willmington from the High Commission in New Delhi. I've been trying to call for ages; it's taken an eternity to get through.' Heather was the go-between for the letters Agnes and I wrote to each other.

A cold chill washed over me. I tried to remember Service techniques for remaining calm. 'What's going on?' I yelled.

Suddenly it dawned on me that Heather was crying. I could hear her sobbing and gulps of breath as she sought to regain control. 'Joe, there's been a terrible accident. Agnes has been killed. A runaway lorry hit the HOPE bus on the Delhi ring road last night.'

I tried to speak but couldn't. I honestly thought I was dreaming. How long I sat on the edge of the bed holding the telephone handset, hearing scratchy speech coming from it but not comprehending anything, I don't recall. My next conscious memory was violently vomiting the contents of my stomach over my knees. Then I cried, my wailing coming in heaving waves that strained my rib cage. I fell to the floor and lay there in my own vomit praying to the God I didn't believe in that this was all a horrific mistake.

I spent the remainder of Monday in an incoherent state, stumbling around the house in unceasing distress. The Service was always alert to unexplained absences from the office. It packaged this as a staff welfare concern but it would not be too cynical to say its real motivation was a morbid fear of an MI6 operative suddenly popping up in Moscow: twenty years on, the ghost of Kim Philby was alive and well. I have a vague recollection of the telephone ringing throughout Monday but just ignored it. I now accepted that the news of Agnes's death was no mix-up.

✦✦

It was dark by the time a team of wardens assisted by a Service locksmith entered my house to find me lying dishevelled on the kitchen floor. An ambulance was called and I was shuttled off to a remote ward in the Croydon Heights private hospital, a facility regularly used by the Service. After forty-eight hours of sedation, the Service's now administrator-in-chief, the top floor's Richard Sampson, came to see me on the Thursday morning. By this time I was coherent enough to tell him what had happened.

'You've had a severe shock, Joe,' Sampson said. 'We want you to stay here until you're fully recovered. We can then talk about getting you back to work.'

'I need to go to India, to New Delhi,' I said, 'to find out exactly what happened. I want to bring Aggie back home.' I instantly regretted using my privately affectionate name for Agnes and the fact that saying it nearly caused me to dissolve into tears.

Sampson looked at me without expression. 'Agnes's family was notified of the accident,' he said. 'They agreed that Agnes should be cremated in India. Her parents travelled there to attend the funeral ceremony and are bringing Agnes's ashes back to the UK with them.' I understood the need for cremation to take place as soon as possible – bodies went off very quickly in India.

'Even so,' I said doggedly, 'I need to go there and see what happened for myself.'

I detected the slightest hint of irritation in Sampson. 'You know the Service rules, Joe. We can't agree to you returning to New Delhi.' He paused. 'We have to be firm on this point given your … uh … emotional state. Sorry.' His jaw set in resolve.

I exploded. 'Well the Service can stick their rules where the sun don't shine. You and the rest of them can fuck off. I'm going to go to India and that's that. I will resign if I have to.'

Sampson was now the hard-nosed bureaucrat he needed to be to become the Service's administrative top dog. 'You have signed legal obligations binding you for life. This gives us the authority to confiscate your personal passport, or even to physically restrain you from travelling. If you know what's good for you, you won't force us down that path.' He stood to leave. 'New Delhi station has obtained a copy of the police report into the accident. Against my better judgement, I am prepared to let you read it, if you wish.'

The Service courier arrived with the police report the next afternoon. I propped myself up with pillows and began reading. The report's gist was that around 6 pm on Sunday 2 October 1983 a HOPE minivan travelling along Shantipath had collided with a truck while merging onto the Delhi ring road. Shantipath ran through the middle of the New Delhi diplomatic precinct. I had merged off it onto the ring road many times, recalling the act demanded a close watch for speeding, poorly maintained heavy vehicles inexpertly driven. Anil Kunderan, a HOPE employee, was driving the minivan. Its passengers were Agnes and two other local HOPE employees. The minivan was reported by one eyewitness, and confirmed by another, to have veered *seemingly unsighted* into the path of oncoming traffic. Dusk was falling but conditions were otherwise clear. The lorry was carrying a load of clay bricks and the driver's attempts at braking had little effect. The minivan was pushed 100 yards up the road killing all four in it on impact.

The report appeared comprehensive. I lay back in the hospital bed exhausted from reading it. Dinner was served but I pushed it away. Something other than the obvious was bothering me. I finally realized my concern was that Agnes would not allow a careless driver behind the wheel of a HOPE vehicle. She would drive it herself before permitting this. It followed that Kunderan, the minivan driver, drove competently. Yet the police report indicated he had merged into oncoming traffic without taking adequate care. There it was, the piece of the puzzle not making sense.

———◆◆———

Of course, I didn't know then the lorry driver received 1,500 US dollars for his part in the accident, the two eyewitnesses 500 dollars each and that the acting sub-inspector who compiled the police report accepted 1,000 dollars in return for not addressing why the minivan's drag marks as it was pushed up the freeway began in the merge lane. Nor could I have known that within six months the lorry driver would die while supposedly drinking toxic home-brewed alcohol and the two eyewitnesses would have vanished from sight.

———◆◆———

Lying there in the quiet of the hospital ward, I thought long and hard about what to do next. I decided to write to Agnes's personal driver,

Gulam. I knew that no UK official would have spoken to him. Apart from the fact he was not involved in the accident, this was how the world of international relations worked. The death of Agnes and her colleagues was a policing matter. Jurisdiction to interview anyone in relation to it resided with the Indian police. The Indian Government would complain bitterly if, uninvited, a British civil servant sought to usurp this authority. Richard Sampson's anxiety about me returning to New Delhi was driven by this concern.

Suddenly, I had energy and purpose. The night nurse found me some writing paper and envelopes. My letter to Gulam was written in the knowledge he would not understand English and the expectation that the person reading it to him would have only basic comprehension. Thus I phrased it in child-like sentences and hoped this would cause no offence. On both the envelope containing the letter and at the head of the letter itself I wrote: *Please arrange for an interpreter to read this letter to Gulam.* The essence of my correspondence was to seek Gulam's opinion on what had happened.

I then considered how best to get the letter to Gulam. I had no address for him, did not know his surname and in any event placing reliance on the chronically inefficient Indian mail service was out of the question. I would have to rely on HOPE passing the letter to him. My instincts told me that as a result of my outburst to Richard Sampson, there was a good chance the Service would vet any letter I sent to the High Commission. I elected, therefore, to write to HOPE's head office in London using the Ladygate Lane in Ruislip mailing address I found in the phone book in my bedside cabinet.

My letter to HOPE described how Agnes and I were intending to marry and told of my hospitalization on hearing of her death. I also explained Agnes's relationship to Gulam, including that he treated her like a daughter and how Agnes would want me to commiserate privately with him. This calculated tug of the heartstrings was aimed at ensuring HOPE's best efforts in delivering the sealed envelope

I had enclosed. I concluded by asking HOPE to forward any response from Gulam to my Brent Cross home address.

I was now on a roll and decided to write to Agnes's parents. There was not much I could say beyond offering condolences and noting my own intense sense of loss. Finally, as midnight came and went, I wrote to Heather Willmington the High Commission archivist to thank her, sincerely, for contacting me and to say, for the benefit of anyone reading my mail, that the comprehensive police report I had seen explained everything. I put aside the letters to Agnes's parents and Heather Willmington for the hospital chaplain to post. Word would reach the Service I was writing letters and no doubt it would like to know to whom. The letters to Gulam and HOPE I secreted away; no one needed to know about these.

My letter writing signalled I was on the mend. The medical people sent me home the following Monday, a week after I had been admitted. I was to have two weeks of home rest before returning to work. As soon as the Service-provided taxi was out of sight, I dashed to the corner post box and posted my letter to HOPE containing my letter to Gulam. My house felt like a mausoleum. Without Agnes, buying it suddenly seemed pointless. It crossed my mind that I should sell the house. But I knew I could not, for one vital reason – I wanted to see if there was any response from Gulam.

A deep melancholia gripped me in the ensuing days, which only deepened with the arrival of a letter from Agnes's mother, included in which was a vial of Agnes's ashes. Four days later my spirits marginally revived upon receiving a letter from the HOPE CEO, one Rebecca Normington. Rebecca's letter expressed sympathy for my loss. She also provided a welcome assurance that a HOPE staffer imminently to visit India would deliver my letter to Gulam and arrange for an interpreter to read it to him.

I had been back at work for over six weeks. Christmas 1983 was fast approaching. On return home one night I found a large envelope bearing HOPE's insignia among my mail. Inside it was a smaller, unstamped envelope addressed to: *Mr Jospet Lambart.* The handwriting was barely formed, seemingly written by someone very old or young – or unaccustomed to writing in English.

I tore open the envelope. The letter's opening sentence read: *I am Ranjane. I write for Gulam S V Gaekwad.* Gulam's letter was formulated in the bygone style of colonial India, as if a lower caste Indian man writing to an English overlord. He was of that generation. This convinced me that the contents of Gulam's letter accurately reflected his thoughts. Anything too confidently phrased would have suggested something else.

When I got to the letter's substance, I staggered backwards, nearly falling. Knees trembling, I re-read the text. *Rusavasi they kill her. Cousin lari man tell my friend. Rusavasi pay lari man and 2 his drink wallah. Also pay pulis.* Rusavasi was the Hindi word for Russians; lari the word for lorry; and the *drink wallah* reference explained that both witnesses were the lorry driver's drinking companions. *Pulis* meant police, but Gulam did not expand on his allegation of corruption. Nor did he offer any theories on why the Russians had killed Agnes. But from deep in my bowels I knew his information was correct, deriving as it did from the Indian street where nothing bar nothing escaped the myriad onlookers.

With chilling realization growing to horror, it instantly hit me that the murder of Agnes and her colleagues related to my work and how, of my two major intelligence coups, Katya was the critical issue. Whereas Boris from Jakarta had committed suicide without revealing me as his compromiser, Katya would have described me to her interrogators as her principal recruiter. The nuclear disinformation we fed the Russians through the scientist Geoffrey Tyler and Katya's treasure trove of intelligence from within the KGB had badly hurt the Soviets and seriously dented the KGB's pride. Retaliation against the Service was inevitable. But revenge against a Service officer with no attendant intelligence benefit was unheard of. To do so was to be uselessly vindictive and further no intelligence interest. Even were the individual cowed, the parent organization continued on institutionally unimpaired.

At another time this might have told me something. But buried by grief I gave no credence to the possibility that Agnes's death was anything but a straight-out tit for tat revenge killing. It was a belief to which I clung tenaciously for ages, years in fact. But now in the moment, abject desolation began to mount. Just as my career ambition had caused Katya's death, so too had it now caused Agnes's. 'God help me,' I whispered. 'My career. My pointless, bloody useless career. Forgive me Aggie, please forgive me.'

CHAPTER 21

RONNIE

I sat at my kitchen table all night, thinking. Despite the freezing cold I did not turn on the heat, not even a light. Still in my suit and wearing my overcoat, I moved only when the bedside alarm went off at 6:30 am, its sound resonating around the house on the chill morning air. The lack of sleep seemed to have no effect. I felt awake and alert. My nocturnal contemplation had told me I now owed a solemn duty to Agnes. The Russians might well have acted with unconscionable vindictiveness – to the extent that they thought it necessary to use the smokescreen of the accident to try and disguise this. Even so, my self-absorption with career had provoked their conduct. My indubitable obligation was to find out who in the Russian system gave the order to kill Agnes and then kill that person. After that, it was no longer important if I lived or died.

For several hours throughout the long night I had considered how best to find out who gave the kill order. Finally, I decided it was through a defector. For every Russian who defected to the British or other Western allies, ten others defected to the United States. I needed to ingratiate myself with the Americans. This involved two aspects. One was becoming known to and trusted by them. The other was to be able to request defector information from the CIA additional to the defector debriefs the Agency routinely shared with the Service. Washington station chief met both criteria. But this was a much-coveted assignment. Further complicating matters was that obtaining the appointment necessitated my promotion to middle manager, the level insulating the top floor executive from the rest of the Century House staff.

The Service's long-standing practice was to appoint the Washington station head from the pool of eight head office middle managers. But the next rotation shaped to be different. Of the eight middle managers currently in headquarters, two had already done the posting; one I knew was earmarked for Bonn; and Brussels would have to be filled soon. Rumour also had it that Martin Mumford was about to be promoted to the top floor executive. Two others, I calculated, would want to stay in London to maintain profile in pursuit of the same promotion. And then there was Reggie Sullivan who was going nowhere. I decided that someone at my level would be specifically promoted to take up the Washington appointment, due in February 1985. Working backwards, I calculated this promotion would have to be announced within eleven months from now, by November 1984, to allow the selected officer to prepare.

I was certain that if I put my best foot forward at every opportunity, I could see off most of my peers aspiring to advance to middle manager in the next while. But I also knew that to realistically seek elevation, I would first have to repair my standing with the Service. There was for one thing the psychiatric angle. I resolved to point out that my breakdown on hearing of Agnes's death was the result of personal trauma, not the consequence of work pressures, and how I had bounced back in a week. A related issue was trickier. From my hospital bed, I had railed against the administrative overlord Richard Sampson, to the point where I was sure he would have instituted measures to prevent me ducking off to India and creating problems. This insubordination would be a certain impediment to promotion. It had to be addressed, somehow.

As for the actual appointment, I eventually concluded Freddie Ladler was the major stumbling block. The more I thought about it, the more I was sure that up on the top floor the highly regarded Ladler was already earmarked as the Service's next US point man. He would have cultivated a host of CIA contacts during his earlier posting to Washington, many of whom would now be rising through the ranks. He also had close links to the CIA's London station, aided by the fact that he was married to an American. And I knew Ladler would soon threaten promotion. He was now back in London directing Service intelligence gathering on Zimbabwe, having finished his posting there in July 1983, preparing others to continue this vital work. But it was common knowledge that Freddie was slated to return to the US theatre. I needed Ladler out of the picture. Only then could I confidently compete with the other contenders.

I shaved, ironed a shirt and put on my best suit. After which I walked to the station with resolve and purpose, exhaling billows of steaming breath as I went. Coincident with angling for promotion and a posting to Washington, I would seek to discredit Freddie Ladler – just how I did any of these things I did not know yet.

⚫━━◆━◆━━⚫

I took no leave over Christmas and New Year. The office was virtually deserted for that week and into the first week of 1984. There was little work to do; it was as if all the spies in the Balkans had gone to ground. I used the time at my disposal to take stock of what little I knew about Ladler. I decided I should try to find out more about his personal details. But bowling up to personnel section and requesting a look at his file was clearly out of the question, and I wasn't about to start making inquiries around the Service into things like his politics and financial affairs.

I did recall, however, that many Service people had entries in the Foreign Office Staff Appointments Handbook, widely known by its nickname of the Breeder's Guide, or the Breeder's for short. The Breeder's was not classified but nor was it freely available, much less publicly accessible. Copies were usually distributed to senior Foreign Office managers, to give them ready access to staff background they could consult as required. The idea for Service officers was an entry in the Breeder's added an extra layer of cover for when they were posted abroad under the guise of Foreign Office diplomats. To be sure there were copies of the Breeder's located within the Service. But the personal assistants to the top floor executives held these. In keeping with Service mores, copies were kept under lock and key and had to be signed out. My operation against Ladler, however, had one non-negotiable rule: *no footprints*.

I rang Ronnie Waterson at the Foreign Office on spec. Ronnie had been in New Delhi for some of my time there. We were not close friends but he knew my status and we had got on quite well professionally. I was pleasantly surprised when he answered his telephone. Ronnie explained he and his wife were planning to ski in Italy in February and he wanted to preserve his leave. I could tell he wasn't sure whether or not to mention Agnes. I saved him from his dilemma. 'You will have heard about my recent loss,' I said.

He agreed he had.

'I hardly need tell you,' I said with a deliberately maudlin air that wasn't hard to contrive, 'it really gutted me; knocked the stuffing clean out of me.'

'Well you wouldn't be human if it didn't,' he commiserated.

'True enough,' I said. 'But I'm slowly on the mend, which brings me to the purpose of this call.'

'Go on,' Ronnie said. I could sense his apprehensiveness.

'It's a bit embarrassing actually, Ronnie, but man-to-man I have to tell you I'm feeling extraordinarily lonely right now and in need of female company. There's someone at the FO I am considering approaching with a view to forming a friendship. Let me hasten to add that I'm not chasing a quick roll in the hay here. That's the last thing on my mind. It's just that right now ...' I let my voice trail off. It all sounded a bit lame to my ears.

But Ronnie was sympathetic. 'How can I help?' he asked.

'Do you mind if I duck over to your office this afternoon and have a quick peek at the Breeder's? It's like getting into Fort Knox to get hold of a copy here.'

Ronnie laughed, relieved. 'Of course,' he said. 'I was conjuring all sorts of things for a moment.'

I laughed back, companionably I hoped. 'Thanks ever so much, Ronnie. I'll see you about 3 pm.'

———— ✦ ✦ ————

Ronnie ushered me into his office at the appointed time. We chatted idly for a few minutes. Fortunately, he appeared not to have realized that on the telephone I had deliberately built the impression I was going to ask him for something major only to make a relatively simple request, resulting in his eager agreement to my lower level proposition. But now Ronnie was in a bind. When I suggested I'd best have a look at the Breeder's and be on my way, he fidgeted uncomfortably. 'Look, Joe,' he said eventually, nervously wringing his hands, 'I'm not sure I can informally give out private Foreign Office employee information. The practice is to share this stuff on a strict official needs basis.'

I did my best to look crestfallen but said nothing.

'Tell you what,' Ronnie said, 'if you give me a name and indicate your interest, I may be able to read you some of the entry.'

I pretended to brighten. 'How about I tell you who it is but you let me read the entry myself? The truth is I'm not entirely sure what I'm looking for. I'm a bit muddled as you can imagine.'

Ronnie looked doubtful. I raised my eyebrows and smiled a sad smile. 'OK,' he said, shaking his head. 'Who's the lucky girl?'

'Sheila Whiley,' I replied.

Ronnie looked at me incredulously. After a considered pause, he said gently, 'Joe, you know she bats for the other side I take it?'

'It's the company I'm after,' I said. 'We did some good work together when she was over with us a while back.'

Without another word, Ronnie handed me the book. To my great relief, he then stood and said, 'I'm just going to the gents. I'll be back in a tick.' Trying in my mind to stay one step ahead of our conversation, I had been unable to decide how I would look under *L* when Ronnie, were he watching, would have been expecting me to go to *W* at the rear of the publication.

Ladler's entry was brief: Frederick Godfrey Ladler, born 28 September 1948 in Walton-on-Thames; educated at Cambridge University where he read for the Law Tripos; married Mary-Beth Quinlivan on 8 July 1977; one son, Barrington James born 1980, one daughter, Julianna Felicity born 1982. The rest was a chronological recitation of bogus Foreign Office placements, interspersed by entries indicating diplomatic postings in Washington and the Zimbabwean capital of Harare. I scribbled down the details and had just flicked to the *Ws* when Ronnie returned. I handed him back the book. 'Perhaps you're right,' I said. He smiled grimly.

Returning to the office, I summarized what I had. Ladler had been born in the Surrey stockbroker belt, suggesting a conservative family background; was better educated than me; and his American wife, with whom he had two children, was of Irish extraction. I reflected on the monumental effort expended to obtain not much. *Almost certainly not worth it*, I thought, *but who knows?*

CHAPTER 22

RHODESIA

That night at home I sat disinterestedly watching television. The 10 pm news came on. It carried a report on Zimbabwe and referred in passing to the arch conservatism of a white Zimbabwean politician, the Opposition Leader Ian Smith. I sat bolt upright. There, as the analysts liked to say, was the triangulation I was seeking. Smith the far right conservative; Ladler from a likely conservative background in Britain; and by dint of his current position calling the shots for Service intelligence gathering on Zimbabwe. *Tomorrow*, I thought as I headed to bed, *I'm going to start making progress.*

I was in the office by 6:30 am. The first thing I did was to consult my area's card index system. Explained simply, if an issue arose between a country for which I was accountable and one for which I was not, Brazil for example, a dated entry on the accountable country's index card would be made under *B*. These entries directed the enquirer to a file where details of the matter could be found.

For each of my countries of responsibility, I looked under *Z* for Zimbabwe. Nothing. I did the same for *R* for Rhodesia. The Yugoslavia index took me to Belgrade station cables from 1967 reporting on Yugoslavia supplying items to Rhodesia in breach of UK sanctions. The sanctions had been imposed by the Harold Wilson government in November 1965 in response to Ian Smith, then leading a whites-only regime managing Rhodesia's internal affairs, unilaterally declaring Rhodesia an independent country.

I sat back and admired my handiwork. Less than two decades had elapsed since Smith declared Rhodesia sovereign. And although the declaration was ignored internationally, there had to be a good chance that, predominantly among white Zimbabweans, support for Smith would have existed during Ladler's tenure as Zimbabwe station head. I was also aware that Smith was an RAF pilot in World War II. This caused me to think that just as there was likely a rump of Smith supporters alive and well in Zimbabwe, the combination of his war record and politics would mean the same applied in Britain.

The resilience of the support for Smith in the UK and Zimbabwe, I reasoned, would depend a lot on how Zimbabwe had fared since attaining internationally recognized independence in 1980. Not well was the conclusion I soon reached. The credibility of the country's leadership was in tatters, much to the disappointment of those anticipating the growth of representative democracy. Not only had prime minister Robert Mugabe signed an agreement with distinctly undemocratic North Korea to train and equip the Zimbabwe army to put down a spate of tribal unrest, but he had also advocated for a one-party state. Added to which, Zimbabwe's economy was in free fall. These were all factors bound to have Smith's supporters saying, 'We told you so.'

Zimbabwe's evidently parlous state of affairs prompted a final, speculative piece of research involving the *UK Who's Who*. Under *Ladler*, I found five entries. But much to my interest only one, Godfrey Randall Ladler, Principal Partner of Phoenix Investments PLC, was chair of the Elmbridge Borough Conservative Committee. Walton-on-Thames, where the Breeder's told me Freddie Ladler was born, was located within Elmbridge Borough. Also recorded were a marriage to Coral Howlston-Browne in 1944 and three unnamed children, two sons and a daughter. 'That's Ladler's old man, I bet,' I whispered excitedly, this seeming unearthing of his father's company and the apparent proof of Freddie's conservative background now convincing me to press on.

The 1984 working year began in earnest the next week. On the Monday morning, 9 January, after Heneshaw and I had our usual start-of-week meeting with our jointly shared boss Reggie Sullivan, I returned to my office. Phoenix Investments specialized in offshore investment. I rang its listed telephone number. 'Good morning,' I said in my best upcountry brogue. 'It's Clarrie from UK Parcels. I have a package here addressed to a Mr Frederick Ladler. But the address is care of his father Godfrey at your company … yeah here it is, Phoenix Investments, 44 Tachbrook Street, Pimlico. If we dropped the parcel around would it be going to the right person?'

The Phoenix Investments switchboard operator was a young woman of pleasant disposition and disarming guilelessness. She laughed lightly. 'Yes, I can confirm that Freddie is Mr Godfrey Ladler's son. Drop it off and we'll make sure it gets to Godfrey.'

'Thanks, darling,' I said, and I meant it.

The next day, 10 January, I told my staff I had a lunch meeting. Proceeding to Waterloo Station, I entered the men's toilets on the concourse level. In a booth I changed out of my suit into jeans, a dirty shirt, sports shoes and an old parka. I stuffed my office attire into the brief case I was carrying and put it in a locker. Moving as quickly as possible without running, I caught the tube to Green Park and then on to Pimlico, watching my back as I went. Halfway up Tachbrook Street, I found the Phoenix Investments office. I told reception I was interested in an offshore investment because of the potential tax breaks it offered.

After a short wait, a thickset man in his late forties with crinkly hair came out and ushered me into a side office. He introduced himself as Dennis Davison. 'What can I do for you?' he asked.

'Well, I anticipate coming into some money soon,' I said.

Davison raised his head sceptically. 'How so?' he enquired.

I adopted a smug expression. 'Daddy's about to head to the afterlife,' I said, smiling at Davison's blank face, 'and has a house in South London likely to fetch around 200,000 quid.'

'Where is it exactly?' Davison asked.

I was ready for that. '198 Rodney Road.'

Davison made notes and then asked for identification. In 1984 driver's licences with embedded photographs were still a couple of years off. The absence of photographs made the illicit use of the paper licences of the day a less onerous undertaking. I produced a licence in the name of Brian Spinks with a Putney address. Davison jotted down its details. 'The address is an old one,' I said. 'Haven't got around to changing it just yet.'

———◆—◆———

After confirming on Monday 9 January that Frederick Ladler was Godfrey's son, and now set on visiting Phoenix Investments, I had begun to think about carrying phoney identification. The Service held a range of bogus documents for its various operational needs. But these had to be signed in and out, which would infringe my *no footprints* rule. There was also the trifling matter that use of Service clandestine property for personal reasons was a criminal offence.

Owing to these complications, I may well have chanced it without identification had I not recalled Heneshaw mentioning in our earlier meeting with Reggie that he had authorized a junior to draw a bogus driver's licence for a training exercise in the week.

I cornered the junior in the corridor after lunch and told him in hushed tones I needed the licence that afternoon for a one-day *Need to Know* purpose. He was very green, but nodded resolutely when I said he was not to mention this to anyone. 'Good field training for you,' I said with a wink when later he slinked by to give me the document. But what I didn't count on after returning it to him the next day was the junior asking the domestic documents registry to note the issue card to reflect my possession of the licence from 9–10 January. I was only to learn of this many years later.

For now, however, on taking back the licence from Davison, I pretended to be suddenly indignant. 'Listen, what's this got to do with me? All I want to know is where I can safely put 200 grand.'

Davison wasn't fazed. 'We need to be sure you're serious.'

'I'm bloody serious, mate, trust me.'

Davison's body language told me he was far from convinced. But my producing identification had convinced him to push on for now. 'Fine,' he said. 'Where do you live currently?'

'Got a bird,' I said. 'We live out back of her olds' house.'

'Address?'

'12 The Grange, Kilburn,' I told him. It was a vacant block.

'Telephone number?'

'Mate, we're in the fucking granny flat. Who has a phone in there?'

Davison shook his head slightly. 'Did you have any particular investment preference or destination?'

'In mining,' I told Davison. 'A mate of mine suggested I try some African country. Can't think of it right now. Starts with Z.'

'He probably means Zambia,' Davison responded. 'There's copper mining there. But the political risk is through the roof.'

'No, no, wasn't Zambia,' I said, pretending to rack my brains. 'It's on the telly. I seen something on it myself just the other day.'

'You don't possibly mean Zimbabwe, do you?' Davison asked.

Uncurling my left index finger and pointing it towards Davison's chest, I exclaimed, 'That's it, mate, that's it.'

Davison closed his notebook. He had given up on me. 'Sorry, Mr Spinks,' he said, 'but we do not recommend investment in Zimbabwe. There hasn't been a decent business environment there since the 1960s.' He turned the palms of his hands upwards. 'And now the political risk is off the scale, much worse than Zambia. Phoenix Investments chose to sidestep Zimbabwe some time ago.'

I looked puzzled. 'Well, what the fuck is Wally on about?'

Davison stood. Our interview was over. 'That,' he said, 'you'd have to ask Wally.'

❖ ❖

Originally, I had hoped to start smoke and fire rumours that Freddie Ladler was passing Service information to Smith's allies in the UK and Zimbabwe in support of Smith's return as prime minister. The gutter press thrived on this sort of stuff, especially when spies were involved. There was no great difficulty in anonymously feeding the tabloids allegations and flimsy evidence. They were tooled up for it and for circulation's sake prepared to splash around headlined innuendo. And the mud, once thrown, always stuck. But I soon came to realize I had one big problem – that Mugabe was so obviously on the nose. A very real risk existed, I decided, of some in the Service thinking Zimbabwe would be better off with Smith in charge and tacitly admiring Ladler's perceived daring.

On discovering Phoenix Investments, therefore, a link between it and Zimbabwe became indispensable. That's how I would convey via the tabloids that altruism was the last thing on Ladler's mind. People loved to think the worst. They would still perceive of Ladler using his inside knowledge on Mugabe to aid Zimbabwe's reversion to an Ian Smith government. But the mere hint of an economic benefit would also persuade them this support for conservative white Rhodesia was squarely aimed at enriching his father's company. Human nature being what it is, it was unnecessary to spell out how or when this would be achieved. I had allowed myself to believe the critical link would exist. It was a body blow to find it didn't.

Reggie Sullivan swept into my office even before I had time to hang my suit jacket. He was fraying at the seams. 'The DG has just bumped up Martin Mumford to the top floor executive. Mumford wants a full brief on our current state of play by 3 pm tomorrow. I'll need a Balkans activity report by the morning, please, no later than noon. Rupert's nearly finished his Central European update.'

Reggie rushed off. 'I'll show you,' I fumed, offended by Reggie's implication that, unlike me, Heneshaw was not slacking off. 'Somehow I'll get over today's setback and get back on track.'

Resolve restored, it occurred to me that Mumford's promotion was an opportunity to begin repairing my standing with the Service, damaged by my insubordination to the administrative head Richard Sampson at the time of Agnes's death. Postponing Reggie's brief until first thing the next morning, I instead sat in my office drafting and redrafting a letter to Mumford. Only when satisfied with the content did I turn to its presentation. My handwriting needed to be ragged but not illegible and convey that I had dashed out the letter in about ten minutes, rather than taking all night as had been the case.

My letter did not overly flatter Mumford. He was too grounded to be seduced by sycophancy. I simply congratulated him, noting his promotion came as no surprise to me. With careful calibration, I mentioned Agnes's death but emphasized I was fully recovered. I said I was keen for another overseas assignment, one taking me away from London and the bad memories. The US was my prime interest. The ideal would be to get promoted and go there as station chief. That done, I returned to Martin's promotion, squeezing all the text onto a single page. The truth is I would have mowed his lawns for a year if it had helped my case. But Martin was his own man. I had to hope my light touch kiss of his backside did the trick.

CHAPTER 23

TRANSRHO

Unbeknown to me at the time, Dennis Davison of Phoenix Investments fame was also something of a secret agent. It all stemmed from a private arrangement he had with a lawyer called Harold Elgin. Not that Dennis thought of himself as a spy. What he did was simply a variation of the *commission received for product sold* model that underpinned his income stream.

Elgin was London-based, but had been born in the South African province of Transvaal. He had a long-standing retainer with the so-called Vereeniging group, named after the provincial city in southern Transvaal of that name. The group comprised sixteen members, all of whom were born in Vereeniging and had lived there most of their lives. By 1984 fourteen members were in their mid-to-late seventies and two were over eighty. Between them they owned sixty-eight per cent of the issued script in a company called TransRho. TransRho's name reflected the Transvaal origins of its major investors and that the company's main asset was a diamond mine in Rhodesia.

At first, TransRho had been a very successful operation. But things changed in November 1965 when Ian Smith declared Rhodesia an independent country. The sanctions subsequently imposed on Rhodesia by the UK left TransRho unable to export its diamonds. With that, the company was destroyed. By 1968, when the London

Stock Exchange halted trading in TransRho shares, the share price was one halfpenny, down from a 1964 high of twelve pounds, four and six. But creditors were paid from the Vereeniging group's private funds and the company was never wound up.

As TransRho first began to decline, the Vereeniging group had forcefully lobbied the British Government. And when these pleas fell on deaf ears, the group members all went down the financial gurgler together. Upon Zimbabwe's independence, however, and the lifting of sanctions, prime minister Mugabe had made repeated references to stimulating mineral exports. But he had also hinted at compensation-free acquisition of resource deposits. Blinded to this threat by their eagerness to recover their losses, Vereeniging group members had reactivated Elgin's retainer. He was to report on any interest in the UK for investing in the Zimbabwe minerals sector.

———◆ ◆———

It was from *our source*, the KGB colonel heading the elite Active Measures Department who became a Service asset in 1990, that I learned about Elgin, his relationship with Dennis Davison and the Vereeniging group. *Our source* would later explain how it was that a seemingly trivial item, the driver's licence I had used during my visit to Phoenix Investments, came to spark a series of events destined to become the very essence of my story.

———◆ ◆———

The agreement Harold Elgin had with Dennis Davison was that for every expression of interest in the Zimbabwe mining sector of which Dennis became aware, Elgin would pay him ten pounds for the basic details. Dennis had contacted Elgin after the *Brian Spinks* visit to Phoenix Investments. He provided Elgin with the address of the house supposedly worth 200,000 pounds and the nominated Spinks home address, neither of which, as Elgin found, existed in the form

I had represented. Dennis also gave Elgin the number of the licence that as *Spinks* I had used for identification. Elgin had a low-level source in the Driver and Vehicle Licensing Agency. His contact was later to inform him the licence holder details could be obtained only by written application to the DVLA director.

In early February 1984 Elgin telexed all this in a report to the Vereeniging group. The report drew the erroneous conclusion, based on the evident subterfuge, that the Spinks charade was an attempt at commercial intelligence gathering on behalf of unidentified persons seeking to assess the potential for future investment opportunities in Zimbabwe. It also contained the details of the bogus driver's licence, with Elgin simply noting it had not been possible to verify Brian Spinks as the registered licence holder.

By prior arrangement, Elgin's telex went to the de Bruyn real estate office in the Johannesburg suburb of Saxonwold, owned by the son of one of the Vereeniging group. Its transmission took place at a time when the Soviet Union was without diplomatic representation in South Africa, having severed relations in Cold War strategic opposition to South Africa's policy of apartheid. It was also an era when the Soviets, in search of widespread political support on the African continent, were financing black South African movements, principally the African National Congress.

A black South African man called Jacob worked as a driver for de Bruyn real estate. Jacob had been told to drive the Elgin report to Vereeniging. He did so, but not before detouring to Soweto where his ANC controller had photocopied it. The Soviets were particularly interested in Western country efforts to access Southern African minerals. When told by the ANC of the Vereeniging group's wish to reactivate exports to the West, the Soviets had urged that a source be found to inform on progress. Jacob had been recruited because the ANC knew the de Bruyn real estate office was the Vereeniging group's window to the world.

ANC operatives subsequently smuggled the copy of Elgin's report to the KGB station in the Soviet Embassy in Maputo, Mozambique. The station sent it to Moscow. A Lubyanka analyst, intrigued by Elgin's inability to confirm the licence holder details, astutely decided further investigation was warranted. After consulting *our source*, she tasked the KGB's London station to get to the bottom of the matter.

<hr>

KGB London station had on its books a Sergeant Bruce Branton of the London metropolitan police. A competent policeman with a wife and two young sons, Branton nonetheless had a weakness for horse racing. The station had become aware of this in 1982 through a starting price bookmaker who extended Branton credit. It had snared Branton using a Czech intelligence officer called Tusar. Once entrapped Branton had nowhere to go. This was long before enlightened times when gambling addiction came to be treated for the illness it was. Branton knew he would lose his job and be publicly humiliated if his employer became aware of his problems.

Our source was initially unaware of Branton. This is because Branton had always complied with the KGB station's demands, as made through the Czech, Tusar. Branton was sick, not stupid. He understood that Tusar could not have interests sufficiently broad to warrant all the requests he made. But the KGB station calculated it was easy money – in the pre-computer age accessing police records left no electronic trail. The judgement was sound. Branton did not quibble when Tusar told him he was working the Czech émigré community selling his services as a procurer of useful information.

Our source became aware of Branton when Tusar reported Branton's claim to have no access to the licence information sought. This deepened the mystery first raised by Elgin prompting *our source* to order that heavy pressure be put on Branton. The following day

Tusar revisited Branton bringing with him a man from the KGB London station, a splayfooted thug from Siberia whose job specifically was to intimidate. Forty-eight hours later Branton told Tusar the driver's licence was a bogus issue held by MI6 and on 10 January an MI6 officer named Joe Lambert had possession of it.

Branton also told Tusar that, shaken by the Siberian's threat, he had that morning resigned from the metropolitan police. *Our source discussed this with General Shukhov, the man who had ordered Agnes's execution. The normal response would be to shop Branton to the UK authorities, as a warning to any other waverer among London station's stable of compromised civil servants. Eventually, however, Shukhov directed Branton be let go. His swaying judgement was that with the emergence of my name, it was best to avoid arousing the interest of the security services. Branton's was a case of a happy ending. In the world of spying it was a rare event.

Branton's version of the matter came to light many years after his exchange with Tusar, when a senior Service officer interviewed him, the same officer who also debriefed *our source*. Branton said the Siberian thug had threatened his family if he didn't supply the information required. Branton also said he recognized the threat was real; as a policeman, he knew a hard man when he saw one.

Branton said he had initially discovered the licence file was protected, meaning that either MI5 or the Service was the licence custodian. That is why he told Tusar he had no access. Now under duress, Branton rang a Thelma Morton in the Service's domestic documents registry. Branton and Thelma were professionally friendly. Thelma confirmed the licence belonged to the Service when Branton said it had come up in a traffic context on 10 January. She was allowed to say that. But then Branton had said, 'On the QT Thel, who had it signed out; best I know in case there's a next time?'

Thelma should have clammed up. But on studying the licence issue card, she saw an annotation that she herself had made earlier. 'There's a note here,' Thelma had said, struggling to read her own writing. 'Ah, yes, that's right,' she whispered to herself, still holding the telephone handpiece to her mouth, 'Joe Lambert had the licence on 10 January.' Much later, a contrite Thelma would own up to the Service. 'I told Bruce I'd spoken inadvertently and had him promise not to mention Joe Lambert's name to anyone,' she was to explain.

Within six weeks of resigning from the metropolitan police, Branton and his family had relocated to Edinburgh, home to his wife's maternal grandparents. Branton overcame his addiction and went on to be a successful executive with a local security company. It was in Edinburgh that the senior Service officer interviewed Branton, after a Service other had earlier tracked him down.

CHAPTER 24

LADLER

In late April 1984 General Shukhov received a follow-up report from the KGB station in London. It expanded on the station's earlier advice that Joe Lambert, an MI6 officer, had made enquiries to a private company about investment in Zimbabwe using an alias supported by a bogus Service driver's licence. Shukhov shared the update report with *our source*. It conveyed that the principal partner of the company in question was one Godfrey Ladler, father of Frederick Ladler an MI6 officer who had come to the KGB's notice when head of station in Zimbabwe. The KGB station, however, remained unclear on my motive for approaching the company. But given one possible explanation, it did provide details on a certain Jeremy Waller and the minutes of a meeting held in London in June 1979. Shukhov also told *our source* that his search request to the KGB registry, instigated on receipt of London station's update, had now produced a newspaper article on a man called Duncan Dales.

'By all indications,' Shukhov told *our source*, 'Lambert appears to have engaged in rogue conduct. We need to know why he went to Phoenix Investments. Let's get an asset to approach Lambert face to face. If our London people are correct about what he is up to, and provided we can live with his end objective, this shapes as a golden opportunity to assist him gain promotion.'

Our source described how Shukhov's intensity had visibly mounted; soon his eyes were burning. 'This is the key moment,' Shukhov had said, 'the chance to set Operation Oblast in motion. I can feel it in my moody Russian soul. Use only your best assets,' he instructed *our source*, 'and don't fuck up, no matter what.' Operation Oblast was the code name of Shukhov's plan to exploit my emotional vulnerability and eventually recruit me. *Our source* threw Shukhov a crisp salute. But the gnarled Russian Bear had just waved him away while lighting another of his vile cigarettes.

——◆—◆——

It was a Sunday afternoon in early May 1984; the first hints of summer were in the air. My front door bell rang. I opened it to find a small woman of around sixty on my doorstep. She carried a large handbag about half the size of her diminutive torso. 'Yes?' I said with aggression, thinking she was some variety of religious nutter.

'I am Valerie O'Hare,' the woman answered in a thick Irish accent. 'I wish to speak to you. You may call me Mrs O'Hare.'

Taken aback, I stood to one side allowing Mrs O'Hare to skip nimbly by me. We stood in my sitting room. 'It has come to my attention,' she began immediately, 'that, posing as some buffoon, in January this year you called on a London investment company of which Mr Godfrey Ladler, father of your MI6 colleague Frederick Ladler, is a partner. Please tell me why you did that.'

I don't know what stunned me more – the knowledge she had or her audacity. 'Who the fuck are you?' I asked angrily.

'Don't get any ideas of throwing me into the street, sonny boy,' Mrs O'Hare cautioned. 'My driver's a young tough who would dearly love to be invited in here to belt the living tripe out of you.'

I moved to the window but could see no car. 'I represent people who have suffered untold harm at the hands of the British authorities,' Mrs O'Hare said to my back. I turned to face her. 'One of our number heard of your Phoenix Investments antics. But they had no details other than your alias. We were able to find out it was you who made the approach and subsequently discovered the Frederick Ladler link, including that he is a colleague of yours.'

Mrs O'Hare was now comfortable enough to sit down. 'It's as plain as day Mr Lambert that you are up to some sort of shenanigans. A decision was made to assist you achieve your objective provided the outcome involves a black eye for the British Government.'

'No doubt this act of kindness was decided on by the Provos in a safe house up the Falls Road?' I said sarcastically.

'Something like that,' she responded, seemingly confirming she was working for the Irish nationalists.

My head was spinning. Why would the IRA want to help me? I decided to tell Mrs O'Hare I thought Freddie Ladler was mixed up in a pro-white Rhodesian insurrectionist group and wanted to make enquiries before going to the Service chiefs. But Mrs O'Hare was no pushover. 'Joe, Joe,' she said, as if my great aunt, 'what was going to Phoenix Investments supposed to tell you about that? Stop playing games and let us help you. Otherwise, this whole damnable thing will blow up in your face.'

Many things flashed through my mind. But mostly I thought of Boris in Jakarta and his tame capitulation. Now I understood. Faced with this resolute woman who could not be deflected, like KGB Boris I was boxed-in. 'I was trying to discredit Frederick Ladler,' I said softly, 'because I want him out of contention for a position I am after. Ladler has carriage for intelligence gathering on Zimbabwe. My first instinct was to paint him as aiding those working to overthrow the Mugabe Government. But Mugabe's making such a hash of things, I worried that some in the Service might actually give Ladler credit for going out on a limb to assist his opponents. I decided I could discredit Ladler only if there was a hint of personal gain involved. That's where his father's company came in.'

'I see,' Mrs O'Hare said. 'And the position involved is?'

'Head of MI6 station Washington,' I heard myself reply.

'And the reason?' Mrs O'Hare asked. 'Why are you so keen to do Ladler in the neck, Joseph?'

Only my mother ever addressed me by the longer form of my name and Mrs O'Hare's use of it irked me. Resentment stoked my failing resolve. Anything to do with Agnes, I decided, would remain in my confidence. 'Ladler,' I said, 'is a privileged prat who thinks people of my background shouldn't be in the Service. Like me, he wants to be Washington station head.' Mrs O'Hare's eyes narrowed as she listened intently. 'I intended to show that Ladler was prepared to assist white Rhodesians regain power in Zimbabwe because of the economic benefit to his family. My plan was to feed a sniff of this to the tabloid press and let it do the rest. That would have put the bastard back in his box and opened up the Washington job to me at his expense. But on visiting Phoenix Investments I found it had no ties to Zimbabwe on which to base the suggestion.'

Mrs O'Hare did not press the point. Instead, she removed an envelope from her oversized handbag and held it in the air. 'We do have some clever people. The essence of your plan to publicly link Frederick Ladler to conservative white Rhodesia was a popular theory among our thinkers, even if the reason why was not clear. That's why I brought this with me.' Opening the envelope, she produced a *Rhodesia Herald* newspaper clipping dated 17 June 1981. The caption below the photograph dominating the article read: *Pictured at a recent private party marking his fiftieth birthday are the host, Mr Duncan Dales, and Mr Frederick Ladler of the British High Commission.* I studied the picture of a smiling Freddie Ladler warmly shaking hands with a stocky individual, a half-smoked cigarette insolently hanging out of the man's mouth.

'Dales was a white Rhodesian,' Mrs O'Hare said. 'He owned a tobacco processing plant near the capital and treated his black employees appallingly. He fled to Portugal in late 1981 after several of his workers died in a company dormitory fire. Dales was later sentenced in absentia to ten years imprisonment for negligent man-slaughter.' In spite of my stress and confusion, I laughed to myself. Here was Freddie Ladler freshly arrived in Harare in mid-1981 and out and about trying to work out who was who in the zoo. Somehow this Dales character got his hooks into Freddie before Freddie realized he shouldn't be seen associating with him.

I started to speak but Mrs O'Hare held up her hand. 'Your want to discredit Frederick through his family was sound enough. But you were looking in the wrong place. Frederick's mother, Coral, has a half-brother called Jeremy Waller who is rabidly pro-Ian Smith. There is much publicly available evidence of this.'

'Well a bit bloody late to be telling me now,' I complained.

'Despite Jeremy's extremism,' Mrs O'Hare continued, ignoring me, 'he hasn't been disowned by the Ladler family. Coral apparently thinks blood is thicker than water and forbids it. Jeremy, therefore, still gets invited to family soirees and the like. But that will change when all and sundry come to know of Jeremy's familial ties to the Ladler clan, including that he is Frederick's dearly beloved uncle.' She chortled briefly at the thought.

'It matters not that you found no basis for your economic benefit story,' Mrs O'Hare said. 'The photograph with Dales is perfect grist to the mill where Waller and Frederick's family link is concerned. People will note Frederick's conservative background and choose not to believe in coincidence. The separate Dales and Waller associations will each reinforce the other's perception that he is indelibly linked to people who couldn't give a tinker's cuss about the welfare of black Zimbabweans. Now that you've confirmed our suspicions, we'll make sure the whole world knows about Frederick, his rabid uncle and the black-hater Dales. I can assure you that once the tabloids are finished no one will be thinking Frederick is a sainted soul wanting to do right by Zimbabwe.'

Mrs O'Hare paused and looked earnestly at me. 'I now want you to listen closely to what I have to say next.'

'OK,' I said, perversely intrigued by what was to come.

'The story about Ladler will break in the press next Wednesday. The following Friday, 11 May, at 3:30 pm, you will receive a telephone call at work routed through from the Foreign Office. It will be a man named Cuthberson. He will offer you a document. You will arrange to meet him that evening to accept it. Take careful note of what Cuthberson says so that you might tell your superiors.'

'Is this really necessary?' I said irritably. 'Why can't you just get the bloody thing from him and give it to me? Anyway, what's so important about it?'

'If you allow me, I will explain,' Mrs O'Hare said reprovingly. 'A second press leak would be too blunt, too orchestrated. Thinking minds would focus on this and not the document's content. Your giving it to your Service gives it gravitas and will ensure your people take it seriously. For that reason, how you come to take possession of the document will be the subject of intense scrutiny. Receiving it from Cuthberson will survive that examination.'

'If you say so,' I replied superciliously.

'I do say so,' Mrs O'Hare echoed firmly. 'Cuthberson will give you the minutes from a meeting of a now defunct group known as WRR – White Rule for Rhodesia – held in London in June 1979 just days after international pressure forced Ian Smith to stand down as Rhodesian prime minister. WRR's resolution calling for Smith's reinstatement is not important. But the list of attendees is. One you will find is Jeremy Waller. And it may aid your quest to be posted to Washington to alert your superiors to the fact that one other was a Mr Reggie Sullivan, another of your colleagues, I believe.'

Mrs O'Hare checked her watch and declared it was time she left. I sat there bewildered after she had gone. So many questions flowed through my mind. I had a stiff drink. I didn't know much about the IRA but doubted it had the intelligence network to gather the information this Irish woman had thrown at me. Surely it was a Service operation designed to elicit my confession, something I'd done meekly notwithstanding my reticence about avenging Agnes?

I waited for the knock on the door and Special Branch's command to lie on the floor and not move. But nothing happened. I drank some more. Midnight. Nothing moved. *Maybe they're coming for me at 4 am,* I thought, *that's when a person's resistance is reputedly at its lowest ebb.* Eventually, I fell asleep on the couch. At 6 am I stirred and made a cup of coffee. Convinced I would be arrested on arrival at the office, I shaved, showered and headed out.

The wardens gave me a cheery welcome and people I passed in the corridor wished me good morning. I looked and felt like shit. Reggie Sullivan appeared at my office door and the sight of him startled me. 'Food poisoning,' I told him. 'Takeaway curry.' It was a long day. I went home smack on the 5 pm official finishing time.

Mrs O'Hare had stopped at a phone box shortly after leaving my house that Sunday afternoon from where she rang her KGB controller. Raven's report, to use Mrs O'Hare's work name, was flashed to *our source* in Moscow. It advised that my stated objective in visiting Phoenix Investments was to discredit Frederick Ladler because he thought me socially unworthy of being an MI6 officer. To that end, Raven reported, I wanted to deny Ladler the head of MI6 station Washington position by taking it myself. The report concluded with Raven's assessment I would be OK by Friday, when the second phase was to occur.

Our source said Raven was a contractor, a mercenary who had never held a brief for either side of Ireland's sectarian troubles. He explained the logic behind using her was to give the approach to me a readily identifiable anti-British organizational context. This gave it credibility. 'Without the IRA pretext,' *our source* said, 'Lambert's mind may have wandered. Shukhov and I had agreed this could risk Operation Oblast's compromise, either by him not taking the bait or worse suspecting that Raven was working for the KGB.'

CHAPTER 25

SCANDAL

I spent most of Monday evening lying on the couch pondering my situation. One half of my brain was telling me to confess to the Service before my circumstances became even more precarious; the other was arguing that I owed Agnes and urging me to carry on. Overarching all of this was the pending IRA intervention. If Mrs O'Hare were on the level the hares would truly run on Wednesday when the tabloids went for Ladler. If she were not, I wasn't sure.

Was it an IRA blackmail play? *Unlikely*, I thought. I was of no use as an MI6 mole. The Service's Irish Affairs unit was a discrete outfit, comprising mostly paramilitary types. I was as remote from it as the conductor who clipped my ticket at Lambeth North tube station. Earlier thoughts resurfaced of Mrs O'Hare being a player in a Service operation against me. Was the Wednesday deadline set to give me a chance to come in of my own volition?

I slept Monday night with one eye open waiting for the knock on my door, which never came. Badly sleep deprived, but at least without a throbbing hangover, I staggered into the office on Tuesday morning. Everything and everyone seemed normal. But there again the Service was full of good poker players. I had two cups of strong black coffee and actually made inroads into my backlogged in-tray.

By lunchtime, however, I could no longer occupy my mind and was in a state of heightened anxiety. Time was running out. If I was going to own up to the Service, I needed to do so before the end of the working day. I studied the photograph of Agnes I carried in my wallet. Past memories overpowered me. Agnes was the only woman I had ever loved, the only woman for whom my affection continued to outweigh my debilitating loner instincts. She was the *real deal*, exactly as Nought had identified. I couldn't let her murder slide by, not when it had been my fault. At 6 pm I went home. From tomorrow there could be no turning back.

———◆◆———

Again no sleep. Again no knock on my door. I rose at 4:30 am and turned on the radio to listen to the 5 am BBC news. No reports of any scandals. I accepted then that Mrs O'Hare was the Service's stalking horse. Resigned to what was to come, I paid scant attention to the 6 am bulletin. Thus when the words *scandal* and *government* emanating from the radio permeated my fug, I wasn't sure what I was hearing. I rushed out of the house. The newsagent's shop was still in darkness. I waited impatiently for the 6:30 am opening time advertised on the door in gold lettering. The newsagent arrived seven minutes late, yawning and unenthused. I watched him through the shop window as he began slowly unwrapping bundles of newspapers he brought in from the shop's rear entrance. He looked up and smiled a weary smile when I opened the main entrance door, ringing the customer alert bell. 'Won't be a moment, sir,' he said.

I fixed on the unopened bundles of papers in the manner that a hungry lion sizes up an intended kill. Only with the greatest of willpower did I restrain myself from attacking them. I pretended to peruse the magazines, while internally screaming at the newsagent to hurry up. Finally, the papers were on the shelves. I scanned them at speed. The *UK News* and *The Examiner* went the hardest, both carrying the story in screaming, red-bannered front-page headlines.

I bought both papers and rushed back up the road into a doorway where I could read them without being too obvious. *Our Spies secretly working for Smith* was one front-page headline; *Racist link to UK intelligence* led the other. None too subtly both papers portrayed Ladler as a white supremacist holding to WRR objectives, emphasizing his family ties to Jeremy Waller and reproducing part of a rancorous letter that, in a WRR capacity, Waller had written to *The Times* in early 1979. Seamlessly, much mischief was made of Ladler's photograph with Duncan Dales and Dales's in absentia conviction for the manslaughter of his black employees. Readers were then apprised that Ladler was *understood* to be an MI6 officer with oversight for gathering intelligence on Zimbabwe, nakedly inviting the deduction he was using his position in aid of racist white Rhodesians. It was skilfully done, even if the tabloids had a lot of experience when it came to character assassination. Paying lip service to balance, both publications noted the Foreign Secretary had been unavailable for comment. I returned home and readied for the office. 'Remember,' I sternly instructed myself, 'act surprised by the news. Like everyone else will be, not least Freddie Ladler.'

The lights were burning up on the top floor when I arrived. Virtually everyone I encountered seemed to be carrying a tabloid newspaper. I saw Martin Mumford about to hop in the lift, heading for the top floor. He looked grim and tired, no doubt having been awakened in the early hours of the morning. But he was calm and measured at the same time; made of the right stuff our Martin. He held open the lift door as I walked by. 'Been meaning to thank you for your letter at the start of the year, Joe,' Martin said. 'Much appreciated. It's times like this you wonder whether getting promoted is worth it.' But he smiled and winked while saying it. I knew then for sure I was in the clear, for now. *God knows where this rollercoaster will end,* I thought, shuddering at the possibilities.

The Foreign Secretary refused to comment. His press secretary told enquiring media to do so would only dignify the fatuous nonsense that had been printed. In the end, as the press continued to bay, the government press office issued a low-key statement, its untroubled tone belying the welter of activity behind the scenes during the course of the day. The statement formally dismissed the allegations as baseless untruths and indicated the Foreign Secretary's full confidence in Ladler. Nor did the statement concede that Freddie worked for MI6, referring to him only as a senior and valued member of Her Majesty's diplomatic corps. The DG had then quietly moved Ladler to the Service's training branch. 'Just temporarily, for a couple of weeks,' I believe he told Ladler. With that, everyone settled back and waited for the matter to blow over.

My relief on realizing the Service was not behind Mrs O'Hare's visit was short-lived. I now had the IRA, or whomever it was, to manage around. I resolved to cope with whatever demands were made of me long enough to take retribution for Agnes's murder. Provided that was achieved, nothing else mattered.

In the absence of any other explanation for its hatchet job on Ladler and what was about to follow, I tentatively concluded the IRA had opted for a fox in the henhouse type of strategy. The government and Service had dismissed the newspaper allegations against Ladler for the patent nonsense they were. Without more, the matter would quickly fade from memory. But evidence forty-eight hours later of another senior Service officer, Reggie Sullivan, with ties to a ratty white supremacist group linked to Rhodesia would have the top floor beginning to second guess itself. The focus would be on a possible pro-white Rhodesia cell within the Service. I guessed the IRA's objective was to send the Service on a wild goose chase, hoping it would waste time and money trying to run the matter to ground and fall into tension with Whitehall in the process. Beyond burdening the Service with this relatively minor inconvenience, any outcome from the strategy likely to seriously damage the British Government escaped me. I metaphorically shrugged; presumably the IRA knew what it was doing.

I also took as incidental to the perceived IRA strategy the benefits befalling me: the praise coming my way from the Service for uncovering the minutes and Reggie Sullivan's connection to the WRR zealots; and the reviving in Service minds of the question marks that, courtesy of the press allegations, had briefly hovered over Ladler. After all, the IRA had no substantive interest in my wish to deny Ladler the Washington posting by taking it myself. Yet on the facts as I understood them, I benefitted more than the IRA. I was puzzled but reasoned I did not have the full story.

In any event, I was not about to look a gift horse in the mouth. Should everything be allowed to quieten, Ladler would return from his temporary exile and reassume pole position in the race for appointment as head of Washington station. The second intervention potentially offered a slight loosening of his grip on the job. And unearthing the minutes might also hopefully mean that my task of gaining promotion just got that little bit easier. My attention turned to the telephone call I was to receive on Friday.

CHAPTER 26

CUTHBERSON

At 3:35 pm on Friday 11 May the telephone on my desk rang. It was the Foreign Office switchboard. 'Mr Lambert,' the operator said, 'I have a Mr Cuthberson on the line for you.'

A click was followed by silence and then a weedy voice spoke. 'My name is Garrick Cuthberson,' he said. 'I was given your name by Anthony Delminico.' The name *Delminico* was familiar but I couldn't place it. Cuthberson jogged my memory. 'I understand you and Anthony worked together in an embassy in the Far East.' Then I recalled – Flight Sergeant Delminico had been attached to the office of the Air Attaché during the last year of my posting to Jakarta. Occasionally he was present when the station consulted the attaché on matters of mutual interest. Delminico was much older than me but we were both junior-ranked and a bond of sorts developed between us. He knew my real status.

'Yes, yes, that's true,' I said. 'How can I help you?'

Cuthberson was either a very good actor or genuinely nervous. 'I have a document I need to give to you. Anthony is now retired and lives in Brighton. I went to him initially and he told me to hand it over to the Foreign Office. He gave me your name.'

On the off chance the switchboard operator was listening, I strung Cuthberson along. 'I haven't spoken to Anthony in years. Can you tell me what this is about, please?'

'I'd rather not talk on the blower,' he replied.

I pretended to consider this. 'OK,' I said with a sigh of reluctance. 'I'll meet you at 6 pm in front of the WH Smith bookstore on the Strand. Please be punctual.'

'Yes, sir,' Cuthberson crisply replied.

— ◆ ◆ —

Cuthberson was waiting when I arrived. He wasn't hard to spot, and not only because he was the only person standing awkwardly in front of WH Smith with an expectant look on his face; he was also a rarity in that in person he looked exactly like he sounded on the telephone – tall and gangly with a prominent Adam's apple. He gave me a manila folder from his backpack. I opened it to find the minutes of the WRR meeting as Mrs O'Hare had promised.

'Two questions,' I said. 'How did you get hold of this? And why are you giving it to me?'

Cuthberson cleared his throat. He had clearly practised for the queries. 'In 1979 I was in the RAF and posted to RAF Northolt. I clerked for the adjutant to Wing Commander James Battersy, the Squad Commander. Battersy's dead now by the way.'

'Go on,' I said.

'Well, one day Battersy comes in with a ream of handwritten notes and asks me to type them up – nice like.' I nodded to Cuthberson to continue. 'That's them,' he said, pointing to the manila folder. 'I ain't real bright but knew I were typing up some sort of political stuff. I typed them on one of them new memory typewriters. After Battersy had gone, I printed a copy. I've left the RAF now but have kept the papers for some reason.'

'OK,' I said, 'that's how, what about why?'

Cuthberson took some time to collect his thoughts. 'A week ago, last Friday night, I got a phone call from Jenny Delminico, Anthony's sister. Totally unexpected. Never met her; never knew he had a sister, actually. Spoke like a Geordie. Said she was ringing on Anthony's behalf to ask if I still had a copy of the minutes I typed up in June '79. I said, "Yeah, I have as a matter of fact." I asked her why she wanted to know. She said she couldn't answer that; she was just enquiring for Anthony.' I opened my mouth to speak but Cuthberson beat me to it. 'I told Anthony about the minutes not long after I typed them. Showed him the copy I done. He didn't say much but I do recall him rolling his eyes and saying, "That fucking Battersy. The lazy sod." I wouldn't say Anthony was angry with me. He just warned me not to let on to Battersy about making a copy. "He'll kick your arse until your nose bleeds if you're not careful," he said. Anthony never raised it with me again.'

Warming to his narrative, Cuthberson pressed on. 'Anyways like I say, I kept the copy. Dunno why; just being bolshie towards Battersy probably. Put it away in my service trunk. For years now I haven't given them papers a second thought. It was only when Jenny rang that I remembered I had 'em. She says ring Anthony on this number on Wednesday afternoon and he'll explain why he now has an interest in the minutes. Then lunchtime Wednesday I was up the High Road and seen the *Examiner*. I shit myself. I thought fucking hell, the stuff in the newspaper is on the same gunk as in the minutes and here I have Jenny ringing about them. I ring Anthony, quickish-like. He was my senior NCO – you know, non-commissioned officer – when we was both working for Battersy.'

'I'm listening,' I said.

'Anthony's ill – heart or something like that. He told me he couldn't get involved but insisted I give the minutes to someone before I got into trouble. Ordered me, really. He didn't say why I'd get into trouble but I knew never to question Anthony. He gave me your name and the Foreign Office telephone number.'

'Tell me,' I said, 'why did you ring this afternoon and not Wednesday afternoon, yesterday, or this morning for that matter?'

Cuthberson looked at me, puzzled. 'Well it were you who asked to be called at half three today, weren't it?'

'But we've never spoken before today.'

'Yeah, that's true. But Jenny rang again, ten minutes after I'd spoken to Anthony, this time to tell me when you wanted me to call.' With that, Cuthberson started walking away. His intuition was sending him warning signals. He was scared and wanted out.

'How do I contact you?' I called. He made a shrugging motion as he walked but didn't turn or answer. I watched him disappear into the night.

Sitting in the saloon bar of my old stamping ground at the Strand Castle Hotel, I nursed a whisky, ice and soda as I tried to distil Cuthberson's explanation. The facts were this: the IRA, for want of a better name, had somehow learned that Cuthberson might have a copy of the incriminating minutes; someone pretending to be Anthony Delminico's sister confirmed he did; that same woman also arranged for Cuthberson to call Delminico so as to be given my name; and shortly after, she instructed Cuthberson when to call me to ensure that, as the IRA intended, the Service became aware of the minutes forty-eight hours after the initial Ladler allegations. Delminico's pretend sister with the supposed Geordie accent was part of the O'Hare group of this I was sure, almost certainly Mrs O'Hare herself.

But there were at least four other questions requiring answers. One easily guessed at was how did the IRA know of the existence of the minutes? Like every other amateur hour, ragtag group, WRR would have been a security shambles. There could be no doubt that many persons, IRA agents included, would have had access to its documents. Indeed, it would not have surprised me if secreted away in the police Special Branch files gathering dust was the very document I was about to spring on my Service superiors.

What, though, was the attraction to the IRA of a set of WRR minutes containing the names of Jeremy Waller and Reggie Sullivan? All I could think of was that, on discovering Ladler's family link to Waller and work association with Reggie, the IRA judged the minutes provided the fuel to convert this smoke into fire. The result, I mistakenly assumed, was its fox in the henhouse strategy to distract the Service. The decision on timing, to have the minutes surface forty-eight hours after the publication of the original dross on Ladler, was probably the final plank in the IRA planning.

But why rely on me giving the minutes to the Service? What happened if I dug in my toes and refused to cooperate? I recalled Mrs O'Hare saying that prior to her visit to my home her *thinkers* had made an educated guess my strategy was publicly to link Freddie Ladler to racist white Rhodesia. I decided the IRA's analysts had calculated that subject to confirming this intention, I would go along with delivering the minutes to the Service. It seemed high-risk to me. But the IRA apparently believed my handing over the minutes was necessary to generate the gravitas supposedly required for the Service to take them seriously.

On the link between the IRA and Anthony Delminico, however, I had no answers. How did the IRA find him and was it he who alerted them to Cuthberson? And crucially, in directing Cuthberson to me, did Delminico act voluntarily or was he prevailed upon? The simple solution would be to ask him. I now wished I had asked Cuthberson for Delminico's telephone number.

CHAPTER 27

DELMINICO

Back in the office, I rummaged around until I found the Brighton telephone book. There were two *A Delminicos* listed. I rang the first number. A man answered. 'Siapa nama Anda?' I said.

Silence. Then a haughty voice spoke. 'I have no idea what you are talking about, whatever it is you want.'

'Sorry,' I apologized, 'it seems I have the wrong number.'

I rang the second number. A male voice said, 'Hello.' I could feel the tension coming down the phone line. I knew then it was Delminico. Nonetheless, I also asked him his name using the same Indonesian phrase. He laughed softly and replied, 'Nama saya Anthony. Thought I might be hearing from you.'

'So, what's the story?' I asked. 'Best you spit it out because my employer is going to want answers when I show it this document I received earlier tonight from you know who.'

Delminico said he understood. I heard the shuffling of papers.

'Battersy,' Delminico said, knowing that Cuthberson would have told me about him, 'was a madman. Very right wing politically. Racist. Hated the black Africans. He was always trying to get RAF colleagues to go to events on the pretext they were gatherings of old flyers, when they were actually political meetings in support of that white politician fellow out in Southern Africa who flew for the RAF in the war. I only got sucked in once. Battersy was an officer and I was an NCO; he more or less ordered me to go. Unfortunately, I didn't have the backbone or means to leave immediately I twigged what was going on. Battersy had driven me there for that reason. So I just got pissed on the free beer.'

'That's fine,' I said. 'But it doesn't explain why you set that long streak of misery on me.'

'About a fortnight ago I had a visit from a South African fellow named Kelvin Fullerton. Showed me his passport. Kelvin said he was trying to find a cousin of his, Geoffrey Fullerton, whose mother was about to expire at some great age. Her dying wish was to see her son again. Geoffrey was wild and headstrong and had lost touch with other family members several years ago after moving to England. The only person Kelvin knew of who could assist in tracing Geoffrey was James Battersy. Geoffrey was apparently an associate of Battersy's. But Battersy was dead. Someone had suggested that Battersy's former RAF colleagues might be able to help. I had served under Battersy in number 32 Squadron and Kelvin found me from RAF records.'

'So Kelvin's found you. What then?'

Delminico cleared his throat. 'Kelvin confided that Battersy had politically influenced Geoffrey. The two had been active in a London-based organization supporting white rule in Rhodesia. It was all very embarrassing, but if I was able to point him to any RAF person who had been an associate of Battersy's, particularly anyone who might have also been with the same organization, that could open up fresh leads. I wasn't nimble enough in my brain. I should have said I knew nothing about the group or anyone linked to it. But Kelvin seemed like a nice chap and I did recall silly Garrick once showing me a copy of minutes he'd typed of a political meeting Battersy chaired. I gave Kelvin Garrick's name, wished him good luck and thought that was the end of it.'

Delminico paused to sip something, water presumably. I also heard the turning of a page. I wondered if I was jumping at shadows by thinking he was very well organized – speaking notes seemingly prepared and glasses of water by his side. The water tumbler was set down on a wooden table and Delminico continued. 'But on Monday this week Kelvin reappeared. Said he had an odd request but there was 1,000 quid in it for me. My RAF pension has been considerably eroded by inflation; I was interested, but cautious. I said, "Tell me what you want and I'll decide." '

'And what did Kelvin ask and what did you decide?' I said, trying to hurry Delminico along.

'Kelvin said something about the newspapers going ballistic on Wednesday with a story on Rhodesia. Told me to expect a call from Garrick regarding the minutes of a meeting on Rhodesia Garrick had in his possession. I knew Kelvin meant the minutes that Garrick had typed for Battersy. Kelvin said, "Tell Garrick to give the minutes to the Foreign Office, before he gets into trouble. Your RAF records show you worked in the British Embassy in Jakarta. You will know a suitable Foreign Office person to whom you can direct him." I asked the obvious questions. All Kelvin would say was that he was assisting the police on a confidential matter relating to the minutes.'

'And?'

'I told him to fuck off,' Delminico said. 'The whole thing was far too strange for my liking, more like your line of work. But he just gave me the Foreign Office telephone number as if I had said *yes*. All I had to do was tell Garrick to ring the FO and give him a name. Then I could say I had health issues and I'd be cut out of the loop. When I told him *no go* again, Kelvin was not so friendly anymore; got nasty in fact. Said if I didn't comply I'd be putting my family at risk. I live alone since my wife died. All I have is my kids; they're my life. I'm not as strong as I used to be and couldn't risk putting them or their families in harm's way. Reluctantly, I agreed. You must understand I was scared stiff, for the kids and grandkids, not for myself. I felt I had no option. Thinking back to my time in Jakarta, your name came to mind in the circumstances.'

Delminico seemed to be crying. I wasn't sure. His extra-loud sniffling sounded fake to me. 'So you took the grand and did what he asked.' It was a statement not a question.

'Yeah,' Delminico whispered.

'OK,' I said, 'let's leave it there. Someone from the office will be down to see you in due course. You may need to make a formal statement to the plods. I really don't know at this point.'

'Night, Joe,' he said, and hung up.

◆━◆

The immediate effect of Delminico's version of events was to draw my mind to a droll joke currently doing the rounds. The set-up question was: *What's the difference between the IRA and Dublin Gas?* The punch line answer was: *The IRA gives a three-minute warning.* I was not drawn to the joke's dark humour, far from it. I was drawn to its subtext – that the IRA relied on publicity to achieve its political objectives. In other words, the IRA did not deal in non-attributable outcomes, much less the subtlety of which Mrs O'Hare had spoken. On the contrary, being openly known as a threat to public safety was its stock in trade. But the IRA had not bothered to claim responsibility for the earlier Ladler material. And now, in channelling the minutes through me, it was forsaking the opportunity to build, with or without attribution, on this initial embarrassment of the UK Government. The Service would deal with the minutes privately as it did every other internal problem, irrespective of how much gravitas my handing them over engendered. Yet Delminico had just detailed the hoops the IRA had jumped through – the planning, the expense, the risks. Where was the corresponding benefit? The Service inconvenience angle no longer cut it.

I realized then Delminico's confession had told me two things. It had confirmed once and for all that Mrs O'Hare was not IRA. And it had also revealed there was something else, something obscure and no doubt sinister behind the O'Hare group's determination that I should furnish the Service with the minutes. But as to the group's end objective, I had no idea. There were no fairies at the bottom of the garden. The thought that the exercise was intended for my benefit simply didn't enter my head.

The mystery of it all caused me to reflect on my conversation with Delminico. There is a rule good spies follow when building cover, or legends as the romantics like to call it – deviate from the truth only when absolutely necessary. Delminico appeared to have adopted the same approach. I suspected he was intimidated by this Battersy maniac, as reflected in his warning to Cuthberson, and had attended more WRR meetings than he liked to admit. Whoever the O'Hare group was, it likely found Delminico's name regularly appearing in the WRR records and had come to know he served with me in Jakarta. With that, Delminico self-selected as the lynchpin in the group's quest to have me deliver the minutes to the Service. Delminico had admitted to accepting a bribe, under duress allegedly, to direct the minutes to the Foreign Office. It was not hard to imagine him agreeing for the same consideration to voluntarily direct the minutes to me.

But Delminico's cover story meant he could not plausibly hold a copy of the minutes. He had to find a credible conduit to me. That being so, it was no leap of faith to conclude that Delminico had proposed Cuthberson as the credible conduit, subject to the O'Hare group confirming Garrick still had his copy of the minutes. Delminico had tacitly admitted this; telling me he alerted Kelvin from South Africa, the man who approached him with the bribe, to Cuthberson and how Kelvin on his return visit effectively confirmed Cuthberson's possession of the document. Garrick was the ideal choice. His ingrained RAF training guaranteed he would obediently follow any instruction from Delminico, his former senior NCO; and his explanation for having the minutes was watertight.

Equally, though, I knew that unless I'd badly misjudged Delminico his story would collapse under expert questioning. I was sure *Kelvin* so-called was part of the O'Hare group. But I very much doubted he had peddled a long lost cousin story. That, however, was a secondary concern. More worrying was Delminico's line he had chosen me at random to be the recipient of the minutes. Once that fiction was revealed, the Service would want to know why Delminico had been instructed to direct Cuthberson to come to me. It was no consolation that I might get away with it by playing dumb when the investigators set on me. Being specially chosen to receive the minutes would preclude my promotion and snuff out any hope I had of gaining the Washington station head appointment.

My nerves were jangling when after completing one more urgent task I rang Martin Mumford at his home. 'Martin, something has come up that you need to know about this evening. Unfortunately, it's not possible to go to Reggie.'

Mumford was typically unflustered. 'Should I come to the office?' he asked.

'I can come to you,' I replied. 'Best we do it that way.'

'Sure thing,' he said. 'See you shortly.' I liked the way he was prepared to rely on my judgement.

CHAPTER 28

REGGIE

Martin lived in Wimbledon, close to the All England Tennis Club. It was a lovely area but how he and his family put up with the crowds each year during those two weeks in July was anyone's guess. Tonight, however, that was the last thing on my mind as my taxi wound its way to his home. I gave Martin the WRR minutes, not mentioning the suspicions I had about Delminico. I didn't need to point out Reggie's name; Martin's raised eyebrows told me he had seen it. It was nearly 11 pm by the time he stopped asking questions. 'Right,' Martin said, 'given the risk of more press allegations, we should pay Reggie a visit, right now. Then I may need to brief the DG.' I had anticipated that Martin would likely want to update the Service chief and prepared for it.

Reggie Sullivan's modest home was in Fulham. Cheap houses were the means by which civil servants like Reggie managed to live in such posh suburbs without over capitalizing. On the way, Martin told me he would prefer I wasn't there, me being Reggie's subordinate. But it was getting late and he couldn't interview Reggie without a witness. It took a little time to rouse Reggie. Martin smiled at me when a light went on upstairs. 'I hope he hasn't been sucking too hard on the gin bottle,' he said dryly.

Reggie was in pyjamas with a dressing gown tied loosely around him. His scowl disappeared when he saw Martin Mumford standing before him. He ushered us into the sitting room, glancing enquiringly at me as he did. Mumford spoke the instant we were all seated. He thrust the minutes at Reggie. 'Reggie, what can you tell me about this meeting you apparently attended?'

Reggie looked at the document trying to understand what it was. 'Yes, yes, I do recall this event,' he said, stroking his chin. 'What a bunch of inconsequential no-hopers.' He placed the minutes on the coffee table in front of him and stared at Mumford. 'You'll have seen that a fellow called James Battersy chaired the meeting. Jimmy and I served in the RAF and stayed in touch after I joined the Service. Jimmy was hyperactive; it didn't surprise me when he died of a heart attack a couple of years ago.' Reggie nodded at the minutes. 'He told me we were going to an RAF reunion,' he said. 'But once there, not one of the promised names was to be seen. I was right peeved and sat up the back ignoring everyone. I had no idea they were going to list me as an attendee.'

I could tell Reggie was telling the truth. He pursed his lips to continue but Martin broke in. 'You were a Service officer at this point, Reggie, and this was a meeting of people actively working against government policy, however unimpressive they might have been. You knew the rules. You should have reported the incident.'

Reggie scratched the back of his head. 'So I should have, Martin,' he said ruefully, 'so I should have. But honestly, they were such a bunch of ...' He settled for shaking his head after struggling unsuccessfully to construct a suitably critical description.

'I do accept it might have seemed trivial at the time,' Mumford said. 'But we have to presume the *UK News* and its fellow travellers will know you are Service. You know as well as me that with a little effort and friends in the right places, Service middle managers can usually be identified. Right now there's a risk of these rags leading their Saturday morning editions with salacious headlines similar to what we saw earlier in the week with Freddie Ladler. If that eventuates, your attendance at the WRR meeting will build on Wednesday's effort and give the whole beat-up some credibility.'

Reggie was crestfallen. 'I understand completely, Martin,' he said, wringing his hands in anguish.

Mumford went on. 'Taken in isolation, Reggie, I would usually keep a minor indiscretion like this between you and me. But in the current circumstances, I do have to brief the DG tonight because of possible media fallout tomorrow. Sorry, but that's what has to be done.' Reggie looked at the clock on the mantelpiece. It was now past midnight. He shuddered, bemused that after so long something as fringe as this should rebound on him.

With that, we all sat in momentary contemplation. Then a light switching on behind a pair of frosted-glass sliding doors, followed by the doors beginning to open, broke the still of the night. The design of the doors was such that they were slid apart by means of shallowly recessed handgrips. The effect was that, for an instant, the person opening the doors was obliged to stand with both arms fully extended in open view of any sitting room occupant.

Alerted by the light switching on, we were all looking up when the doors finally opened. Standing there, arms outstretched, was a young woman. With the light shining behind her, the nightgown she wore was rendered transparent. I could clearly make out her firm breasts and the dark nipples appointing them, and below a wild bush of jet-black pubic hair. The stirring in my loins reminded me of how long it had been since I was with a woman. Reggie was mortified. He jumped to his feet. 'For God's sake, Annica,' he said, shepherding the woman back into the hallway. A tense conversation ensued followed by the sound of the woman crying. 'Go back to bed, Annie,' Reggie was heard imploring her. 'I'll be there shortly.'

Reggie re-entered the room. Bad had just become worse. If one subscribed to the trilogy of bad luck theory, a meteorite was about to hit Reggie's house. 'The maid,' he said simply, a hangdog look on his face. 'From Sardinia. Glenda's at her sister's.' Martin and I glanced at each other both understanding that neither of us passed moral judgement on Reggie for shagging the maid while Mother was away. But whereas my tolerance came from knowing the loneliness of an empty marriage, Martin's derived from the distraction of Reggie having sex with a foreign national. Knowing that Reggie would not have declared the liaison to the Service, thus leaving himself open to blackmail, Martin, ever the pro, was fixed on the possibility of the Service being exposed to a security risk.

Reggie stood there. I sat mute. We both waited for Martin to speak. 'It's time for us to go, Reggie,' he said eventually. 'We will talk later. But first I need to use your telephone if I may.'

'Certainly, Martin,' Reggie said, as if an obliging valet in a high-class hotel. Right arm outstretched, he squired Martin to the instrument sitting on a small mahogany table in the hallway.

Martin rang a number and waited patiently for it to be answered. A gruff voice could be heard to say, 'Jameson.'

'Colin,' Martin began, it was strange to hear the DG, Sir Colin Jameson, being called by his Christian name, 'we need to speak before the morning. I'll be with you shortly.' I didn't hear the muffled response. Martin replaced the receiver. 'Let's go,' he said to me. We left without a backward glance at the hapless Reggie.

'Martin,' I said as he drove, 'I thought some media talking points might be needed. In the taxi to your place, I roughed out a few words for the top floor's possible use.' I had in fact written the points in the office after talking to Delminico, before I called Martin, knowing for certain they were not necessary but nonetheless giving great care to their content. I might have been terrified by the events swirling around me, but was also driven to take every opportunity to repair my standing with the Service bigwigs damaged by my indiscipline towards the head administrator Richard Sampson in the aftermath of Agnes's death. The DG was my primary target but if I happened to impress Martin on the way through then well and good. It was all about building personal capital with them; positive memories they would store away for future retrieval as and when my name arose in one decisional context or another.

But if Martin was impressed he didn't show it. 'Let me have a look at them when we get to Kew,' was all he said.

We pulled up outside a beautifully restored cottage on Bushwood Road at the back of which sat Kew Gardens. Mumford was gone only about twenty minutes. He'd clearly had a very direct conversation with the DG. He started the car. 'Where in Brent Cross are you, Joe?' he asked. 'Time to get you home.' I made noises about getting there under my own steam. 'It's past one in the morning,' Martin said. 'If I left you to your own devices we'd never see you again.' He laughed at the suggestion. 'I need to brief you anyway. The DG liked your media points. He thought they were very good for something drafted in the back of a taxi.' I disguised my pleasure at hearing this. I had been sure Martin would tell the DG the points were my own initiative but not so sure about them winning the chief's approval. 'The DG,' Martin continued, 'was about to brief Bill Rimmington as I left. Rimmington will go down to Brighton first thing this morning to quiz this Delminico fellow.'

My warm feeling evaporated. Rimmington was in charge of Service internal affairs. A former copper, his steely doggedness gave him a menacing air. Delminico wouldn't last ten minutes with him; Rimmington would then come looking for me. Martin was speaking again. 'Naturally, I had to tell the boss about Reggie's undeclared attendance at the WRR meeting and the business with the maid.' Martin shook his head. 'Reggie, Reggie, Reggie,' he mused out loud, 'what have you done?'

✦

The telephone on my bedside table jangled, reminding me of that awful night when I received the news that Agnes had been killed. It was 7:30 am. 'Joe,' Martin Mumford's voice said, 'Delminico's dead. Suicide the Brighton police say. Shot himself, apparently.'

'Christ almighty,' I exclaimed, genuinely shocked. 'I did tell him he may be formally interviewed, but he seemed OK with that.'

'Who knows what happened?' Martin replied. 'Come into the office at ten and we'll discuss it then.'

I reflected on the latest turn of events as I drove my little Ford Anglia into Century House, where I could park underneath given it was a Saturday. I didn't believe Delminico had killed himself. The only logical conclusion was the O'Hare group had murdered him so as to cover tracks. But as to what tracks I had no firm ideas. For now, though, I had to push aside such disturbing thoughts and focus on the attention that would be paid to me at the office.

Mumford chaired our meeting. Other than me, Bill Rimmington and an off-sider were also present, as well as three or four Service others. Rimmington opened the batting. 'Special Branch,' he said, 'contacted the Sussex constabulary at 7 am, just on three hours ago. They were instructed to take Delminico to Brighton Crowhurst Police Station where I would later question him. When the police could not rouse Delminico, they forced entry. They found his body in the study. No sign of any break-in. Initial indications are he died of a single gunshot wound administered under the chin, the bullet exiting the top of his skull via the roof of his mouth. A Smith and Wesson pistol has been recovered and is undergoing forensic testing. It's not clear how Delminico was in possession of the gun. He was not the registered owner of it or any other weapon.'

Mumford asked me to go through the events of the day before, Friday 11 May, up until the time I had called him. I did, emphasizing that a woman posing as Delminico's sister had contacted Garrick Cuthberson in the days before the story on Freddie Ladler broke.

This proved, I said, that someone was running a smear campaign against the Service. The point of this blindingly obvious observation was to cause those gathered to think the Freddie Ladler story ran deeper than first assumed. They could hardly have thought differently. Mentioning Cuthberson also had its purpose – the O'Hare group's strategy relied on him confirming my story.

My biggest headache was Rimmington. He was watching me, and his twitching copper's nose was telling him my involvement wasn't as innocent as I'd made out. I reasoned my main point of vulnerability was a neighbour Rimmington may interview who had seen Mrs O'Hare come to my house. I had no alibi for such a visitor. But on thinking it through, I began to relax. Mrs O'Hare was a professional. Not only did she walk to my home from a distance, much like a local returning from church, but on arrival she had dwelt just seconds on my doorstep before pushing into the house and away from the gaze of any casual observer. And her precisely timed departure told me her driver was not static at her pick-up point but rather passed by it at a pre-arranged time.

I also thought of how Delminico would have wilted under Rimmington's pressure and admitted he had been instructed to direct Cuthberson to come to me. It was of no little relief to have escaped Rimmington's tricky questions on the subject – a frankly welcome unintended consequence of Delminico's elimination I assumed.

Unsurprisingly, therefore, at no point then or afterwards did I ever think I might have been the intended beneficiary of Delminico's murder; that as with the delivery of the WRR minutes to the Service, I had to be seen as snow-white. Not until *our source* came over did I learn that Shukhov had judged my protection from the instruction issue as reason enough alone to order the KGB London station to arrange Delminico's murder. I do believe a Lithuanian assassin specializing in this sort of thing was flown in specifically for the job.

But for all of Shukhov's protection, my instinct to be chary of Rimmington proved to be well on point. Although it was not until January 1990, nearly six years on from that Saturday morning meeting of 12 May 1984, that Rimmington almost undid me. And even then, I was unaware of the close call as it played out. Only some time later did I learn of it, and its unanticipated character.

CHAPTER 29

HENESHAW

Monday morning at headquarters was tense. Just after lunchtime, Martin Mumford called Heneshaw and me to his office. 'Effective as of tomorrow morning,' he said without preamble, 'Reggie takes up a placement at Fort Monckton. Pending a promotion round permanently to fill Reggie's vacancy, each of you will act in the job for three months. Right, who wants to go first?'

I looked at Mumford, not thinking about going first or second but how being asked to act as a middle manager was evidence that any top floor image problems I might have had as a result of my hospital bed disobedience towards the head administrator Richard Sampson had now subsided. Delivering the WRR minutes to the Service and writing the media talking points for the DG had clearly erased past sins. I was on a roll. 'I'll go first, Martin, if that's all right with Rupe.' The realization I was over the Sampson incident had made me chirpy; the *Rupe* bit was an intended turn of the knife.

Heneshaw smiled through gritted teeth. 'OK, fine,' he said.

'One last thing,' Mumford added, 'there's a US presidential election this November coinciding with the selection of our next Washington station head. The CIA would prefer we don't appoint Freddie Ladler owing to the recent white supremacist stuff in the newspapers. Both keep that in mind when you're acting.' I hid my delight; I'd not even dared to hope that the Rhodesia beat-up would cause the CIA to embargo Ladler from the Washington posting. It was also the first I had heard of Heneshaw's interest in the position.

Martin rarely spoke so openly. But it was actually a sign of things to come. Martin, you see, was the senior Service officer who debriefed *our source*. His news on Freddie Ladler was in fact the first instalment in the comprehensive briefing he would later provide me on the saga that my story became. This briefing took place in December 1991, more than seven years after the Reggie Sullivan incident, following Martin's debrief of *our source* and completion of other enquiries. Henceforth, I shall call it Martin's *Final Briefing*.

———◆◆———

In July, around the halfway point of my three-month acting stint, we received a *Secret* cable from our Bern station recommending a recruitment attempt. The proposed target was a Soviet, not Russian but an ethnic Kazakh. His name was Yerik Massimov, a junior scientific attaché at the Soviet Embassy in Bern. The station reported that Massimov often made work trips alone within Switzerland. In the station's estimation, this made him important enough to go after, his lowly embassy ranking notwithstanding.

I was keen to pursue the opportunity. Mumford's implicit warning that my acting performance would be crucial to my promotion prospects meant a moderately decent scalp like Massimov snared on my watch would not go astray. But I didn't want to display my eagerness to Heneshaw, who had oversight for Bern station. Finally, after a week of contrived indecision, towards the end of which – surprisingly, given the benefit to me – Heneshaw became keen to progress the recruitment, I proposed to Mumford that we offer Massimov 2,500 US dollars per month to work for us.

Bern station's reporting indicated that Massimov was most susceptible to recruitment when visiting the Institute of Plant Sciences in Zurich. When there, he seemed to throw all caution to the wind, concentrating more on the city's clubs and brothels than on how to grow cabbages, splashing money about hand over fist in the process. On receipt of Mumford's go ahead, I instructed the station to pitch at Massimov when next he was off the leash in Zurich.

Come the day, Wednesday 1 August 1984, I looked forward to Bern station's cable advising Massimov was in the bag. It never came. Instead, the station chief, Justin Cox, called on the secure line. Heneshaw and I were on speaker at our end. 'I approached Massimov in the lobby of the Howard Hotel,' Justin said. 'He was immediately angry. "I told you no more contact until the university job is confirmed," he said. He then clammed up, realizing he'd mistaken me for someone else, and bolted from the hotel.'

I looked at Heneshaw, who shrugged his shoulders. 'Neither Rupert nor I have a clue as to what's got into him,' I told Justin. 'Make some discreet enquiries and see what you can find out. And keep me informed.' Heneshaw and I both knew that Justin's investigation would include speaking to the CIA station in Bern.

—◆—◆—

Justin never got the chance to sound out the CIA station – the Americans beat us to the punch. Unbeknown to *most* of us, the CIA had a concentrated interest in Massimov and was close to recruiting him. But following Bern station's approach, a rattled Massimov had told them that all bets were now off. After obtaining video footage from the Howard Hotel, the CIA went apoplectic.

It started the next morning when Tommy DeLuca, the CIA station head in London, came in *to rip the Service a new asshole*, to use Tommy's quaint expression. Martin had asked me to be present. I was nervous knowing I largely carried the can for the fiasco. Tommy could be very intimidating. But it was a privilege to watch Martin in action. 'Please don't carry on like a complete prat, Tommy,' Martin said, after first allowing DeLuca to blow off steam. 'We don't have

ESP. How could we have known you were chasing after the same body?' DeLuca glowered but didn't answer. Martin continued, but this time with deliberate hostility. 'If you, and I mean the royal you, the CIA, had the common decency to ask us to steer clear of him, we would have considered the request. Now get the fuck out of here before I have the wardens throw you in the street.'

Deluca stormed out. With that, Mumford ordered me to close the door. I did, dreading what was to come. 'This is not great, Joe,' Martin said, 'and unfortunately you'll have to take the lion's share of responsibility. It was your op after all. Our political masters will curdle under US pressure. We'll need to make a *mea culpa*.'

'But Martin,' I protested, 'that's tantamount to agreeing to seek American approval for every single thing we do.'

'No, it isn't,' he said forcefully. 'It comes down to judgement about when to consult and when not. I know you're anxious to be promoted. But the bald fact is the ability to make the right call eight out of ten times sorts out who advances and who doesn't.'

Mumford could sense my rising testiness. 'Sometimes it can be counterproductive to try too hard, Joe,' he said, electing to end our conversation and save me from saying something I'd later regret. On returning to my office, still stewing over Martin's rebuke, Heneshaw and I passed each other in the corridor. I glanced at him. What caught my eye was how pleased Heneshaw looked, which in the circumstances I found difficult to fathom.

❖

My acting stint was six weeks past when the October promotion round took place. I had made it to the final interview and foolishly allowed my hopes to rise. But when the telephone on my desk rang on Friday 16 November 1984, it was back to earth with a thud. Brian McGowan, the administrator with whom Freddie Ladler and I had done the root and branch review, was now head of Placements. 'Joe,' he said, 'the middle manager promotions will be announced on Monday. You've missed out.' I started to speak but Brian talked over me. 'The Massimov matter back in August told against you. But I can also tell you the DG is pleased with the way you picked up yourself. I can further advise that for candidates like you who made it to the final interview but were unsuccessful, an additional vacancy will be up for grabs in April next year. There are no guarantees you will be selected to fill this extra spot but you will be considered.'

Brian's advice of an extra position was cold comfort. Even were I promoted in April, the new Washington station head would have already been in place for two months. My gloom deepened as I thought of Agnes. If it weren't for the horrible events of October 1983, she would now be finished with HOPE in India and safely back in the UK. Wearily, I headed home for the weekend.

Come Monday afternoon the promotions circular issued. It took some willpower to look at it. A woman called Alison Meagher had been bumped up to fill Reggie's vacancy. I'd heard only good things about her. Taking a deep breath, I flicked to the next page. 'Fucking hell,' I said, the words involuntarily escaping my lips: Rupert Heneshaw to head of station Washington; and Frederick Ladler to lead a new outfit called the Falklands Intelligence Unit.

***

The reason for Rupert Heneshaw's smugness in the corridor I had noticed when returning to my office after receiving Martin Mumford's dressing down was not revealed to me for many years. When it was, Martin was again my source. Only this time, his information came not as part of his *Final Briefing* but in 1996, nearly five years after the day in December 1991 when Martin and I sat closeted for eight hours in the study of his Wimbledon home.

***

At the time of the Massimov operation, a former marine called Maurie Sanity was attached to the CIA London station. Sanity retired from the CIA in 1992. Loud and brash, those he worked with used to joke that Sanity was a walking misnomer. In 1996, twelve years after Bern station's pitch at Massimov, Sanity was diagnosed with inoperable brain cancer; he knew he wouldn't see out the year. Since Massimov Sanity had carried a guilty conscience. With the end in sight he wanted to unburden himself. He contacted the CIA.

The gist of Sanity's deathbed confession was that in July 1984, when drunk, he told the MI6 officer Rupert Heneshaw about Massimov and how the Americans had come to know the Kazakh was a prime mover in the Soviet biological weapons program. He did so prompted by Heneshaw mentioning the Service's interest in apparently the same person. Sanity said he warned Heneshaw the Brits should back off, telling him that Massimov pretended to be a drunken womanizer while all the while the Americans were secretly negotiating a deal with him. 'It's taken nearly two years,' Sanity said he told Heneshaw. 'But we're now close to terms.'

The CIA contacted the Service to seek an explanation. Up on the top floor it was recalled that I had carriage for the pitch at Massimov. Mention of my name still caused the odd political palpitation. The Service overlords were wary of giving the Lambert matter new life in Whitehall. A safe pair of hands was required. Names were mooted. Finally, the senior executive decided that one of its own, Martin Mumford, should question Heneshaw.

Mumford wrote to me after interviewing Heneshaw. He explained the political sensitivities involved and how my comment on his record of discussions was crucial to properly rounding out his report. I returned to England especially for the occasion.

'Freddie Ladler hosted a dinner party in the middle of the same week that Bern station had proposed a pitch at Massimov,' Heneshaw told Mumford. 'Several from the CIA's London station were there, Maurie Sanity included. We proceeded to get drunk. But after a couple of drinks, one of the Americans left. I said something to Sanity to the effect that Barney must be slowing down in his old age.

' "He's flying tomorrow," Sanity whispered to me. "Our Bern boys have a scientific wallah in play, a Sov, and want some help."

'I remarked that our people over there had just this week cast the rule over a scientific fellow from the Soviet Embassy. Sanity asked if he was a Kazakh. I played dumb and said I wasn't sure. Sanity then became anxious and warned me the Brits should back off.'

'And what followed?' Martin asked.

'Nothing initially,' Heneshaw said. 'Sanity knew he had blabbed and soon went home feeling remorseful. The next morning, I began to consider what to do with the gold he had dropped in my lap. Usually I would not have hesitated to arrest Bern station's collision course with the Americans. But I also knew that significant blame would fall to Lambert if the station interfered with the CIA's efforts to recruit Massimov. This caused me to think.

'The one big advantage I identified was that Sanity would swallow glass before admitting to spilling the beans. I contemplated the possibility of not alerting the Service. Sure, the Americans would moan if the station interfered with their plans, but that would wash over once they had Massimov on board. So I decided to give Lambert a kick in the nuts while I could. You'll appreciate I was very tired and not a little hungover when making this decision.'

'Yet that's where you left it,' Mumford said. 'Even after you'd caught up on your sleep and were thinking more clearly.'

'Lambert had been unduly cautious in proposing the Massimov operation to you,' Heneshaw had explained. 'If that was any guide, another opportunity to damage him may not have arisen. Lambert and I had a dust up in the men's toilets back in 1980. He had just been promoted ahead of me and I could tell he was revelling in my disappointment. Ever since I had wanted to get even. I wasn't about to risk that bumpkin again being promoted at my expense. That was the clincher. That's why I stuck to my chosen course of action.'

⸻ ◆◆ ⸻

And the implications for Heneshaw in admitting he did not alert the Service to the American interest in Massimov, preferring instead to visit harm on me? None really. Heneshaw had shrewdly summed up it was now a different time. Once she knew the facts, Alison Meagher who succeeded Sir Colin Jameson as the DG in 1993 – nine years after her elevation to Reggie Sullivan's middle manager position – opted for the political safety of doing nothing. A slap on the wrist for Rupert and a telephoned apology to her American counterpart, there was no time to dwell on the past.

CHAPTER 30

OBLAST

I'm told the snow fell voluminously in Western Russia in January 1985. I'm also told that General Shukhov took advantage of this to enjoy a week's cross-country skiing before returning to work in mid-January. He started the year by reviewing Operation Oblast and decided that, after its initial spurt, it now needed fresh impetus. He said all of this to Colonel Dmitri Aleshkovsky, head of the elite Active Measures Department and the man who in 1990 became *our source*. But first he had to wait a week because Aleshkovsky was still on leave. Two years on, Aleshkovsky's deputy, Major Zamir Umarov, would tell a third party – which then told the Service – how Shukhov had been mightily displeased when so informed. He had rudely declined Umarov's offer to see him in Aleshkovsky's stead.

When he did get to open up to the third party, Umarov explained he had never won Shukhov's confidence. He was an Uzbek Muslim and Shukhov was not prepared to indulge anyone who wasn't from good Russian stock. Umarov had specifically recalled Shukhov's rudeness in January 1985. 'I was insulted,' he said. 'Only a year earlier I had completed an arduous assignment as station head in Jeddah. I had done an exceptional job under intense scrutiny from the Saudi security services. Yet on return to Moscow that arsehole of a general, Shukhov, had blocked my promotion.'

——◆—◆——

Martin Mumford's *Final Briefing* fully detailed Aleshkovsky's meeting with Shukhov first thing the following Monday. 'This was a watershed moment for two reasons,' Mumford was to tell me. 'It was Aleshkovsky's first hint that Shukhov's bond to Operation Oblast extended beyond a close professional interest. It also led to the events directly following, the significance of which Aleshkovsky said he could never have guessed at in his wildest dreams.'

<hr>

'The press coverage on Ladler was ideal,' Aleshkovsky began brightly, once he and Shukhov had dispensed with the preliminaries. 'And with London station's smooth elimination of the Brighton go-between, Delminico, Lambert was unhindered in passing the WRR minutes to his Service. The success of this phase of Operation Oblast is reflected in the Sullivan fellow's shift to Fort Monckton.'

Aleshkovsky, however, had adopted an apologetic tone before continuing. 'But Lambert's promotion status,' he said, 'remains unclear.' As Shukhov's displeasure visibly mounted, Aleshkovsky had hastened to explain. 'We usually track senior MI6 officers through UK academics and journalists who periodically deal with the British intelligence establishment. But our contacts are telling us that since last May's bad press on Rhodesia no new senior MI6 staff have been sighted. I think this is MI6 applying the lesson of the WRR minutes, of how this Reggie Sullivan's status being comparatively well known exposed MI6 to the risk of more bad press coverage.' Aleshkovsky was right. Eight months earlier the now risk adverse DG had ordered that newly promoted middle managers should avoid all but essential public contact.

A raised hand caused Aleshkovsky to pause. 'Even if you are correct, colonel, this is not a progress report,' Shukhov had said, his eyes now flint hard. 'It is no more than back-fill and excuses.'

Shukhov had then taken a deep breath, seemingly restraining himself. 'I can see your knowledge of Operation Oblast needs to be expanded,' he said. 'You should be aware just how fortuitous it is that Lambert's objective in visiting Phoenix Investments related to his wish to be posted to Washington as head of station. Strictly for your own information, Operation Oblast never intended anything but Lambert's promotion and his posting to Washington as MI6 station chief. I know back in March 1983, when first announcing Oblast, I told the steering committee that head of station Bonn and Brussels were other possibilities. But that was a security measure, a precaution in case we had a talker in our midst.'

Shukhov lit a cigarette and motioned Aleshkovsky to continue. Aleshkovsky noticed that Shukhov was now smoking *Camels* instead of the odious Latvian things. But given the general's edginess, Aleshkovsky's focus was on delivering a forward-looking briefing. 'Sir,' he said, 'the incumbent MI6 head in Washington has not yet been replaced. If Lambert takes up the posting, we will know his promotion has been achieved and that the objective of recruiting him while alongside the Americans remains in reach.'

Shukhov did not respond, his unspeaking stare telling Aleshkovsky he wanted more. By his own admission, Aleshkovsky filled the vacuum unwisely. 'Our strategy has by no means failed if Lambert does not become Washington station head,' he said. 'If promoted, he will still be senior in MI6 and his recruitment will offer many other meaningful intelligence opportunities. It is a matter of degree. It just means our strategy has succeeded to a lesser extent.'

Aleshkovsky then told of the uneasy silence that ensued. Shukhov broke it by heaving violently from his chair, its screeching on the office floor as it slid backwards startling Aleshkovsky. 'Listen to me you fucking *krestyanskiy*,' Shukhov growled, his heated use of the Old Russian word for *peasant* rich in menacing ferocity. 'All I want to hear is how you intend to achieve Operation Oblast's objectives. Don't give me this bullshit about degrees. Unless you want to see yourself posted to forward operations in Afghanistan, you will ensure Lambert's promotion and his posting to Washington. Get that through your thick head. And once he is in Washington your Department will fast track his ingratiation with the Americans. The objective is for Lambert to spy for us from within the American inner sanctum. When it suits us best, we will shop him to his own side. As a result of his betrayal while in the Americans' confidence, the US–UK special relationship on intelligence cooperation, the engine room of the Western intelligence effort against the Soviet Union, will be crippled for decades. Oblast has no room for degrees. Now get me results, and soon.' Aleshkovsky saluted and pirouetted. He left the office, he later told Martin Mumford, with more spring in his step than he actually felt.

'How was it, Dmitri Aleksandrovich?' Aleshkovsky's deputy Zamir Umarov asked him on return to the Active Measures Department.

The two men were friendly despite their different backgrounds. Aleshkovsky trusted Umarov. He was occasionally indiscreet with Zamir when needing an outlet for his frustration. 'It's all close hold, Zam,' Aleshkovsky said. 'But between us I can tell you we're leaving a trail of bodies like Hansel and Gretel trying to pull in some Brit. We even topped his girlfriend in a fake car crash for God's sake. The *gruppenführer* is like a mad dog with a bone.'

The Nazi ridicule caused both men to snigger and the tension to ease. Aleshkovsky returned to his office. He needed to think. It was when reflecting on Shukhov's white-hot anger that Aleshkovsky first began to wonder if the general actually had skin in the game.

The extraction of Aleshkovsky and his family to the West – his wife and four young children – took place in March 1990. The Russians at the time were largely focused on vehicular traffic crossing from Russia into Finland and Norway. A decision was taken to have Aleshkovsky commandeer a military plane to fly he and his family to Vladivostok in Russia's Far East. Invoking the feared authority of the Active Measures Department he headed, Aleshkovsky somehow pulled it off. The family's exit thereafter entailed a bribe to a ship's master and some delicate negotiations with the Japanese as regards the vessel making an unscheduled stop at Akita on the island of Honshu, ostensibly for boiler repairs.

Later, once safely in London, Aleshkovsky told Martin Mumford his relationship with Shukhov had deteriorated in February 1985 when he advised the general that Rupert Heneshaw had taken up as Washington head of station. 'Shukhov was grimly dismayed,' Aleshkovsky said. 'He angrily ordered me to determine Lambert's promotion status without further delay.' Unable to rely on his usual sources to identify senior MI6 officers, Aleshkovsky chose innovation. He tasked all KGB station heads, known as *Residents*, to report the name and rank of any MI6 officer within their jurisdiction. 'I had calculated,' Aleshkovsky informed Mumford, 'that this blanket approach would soon reveal Lambert's promotion status.'

Aleshkovsky began to receive responses. One was a report in March 1985 from the KGB Resident in Paris. 'He informed me,' Aleshkovsky said, 'that Frederick Ladler, an MI6 middle manager, had recently visited France in his capacity as head of the MI6 Falklands Intelligence Unit.' Most UK casualties incurred during the 1982 UK–Argentina Falklands War had resulted from Exocet missile attacks on British warships. Ladler's main task was to stymie any Argentine effort to rejuvenate its warfare capacity such that it could potentially resume hostilities, in particular to obtain more Exocets from the French manufacturer. Aleshkovsky told Mumford his Resident never did learn the substance of Ladler's discussions in Paris. But he did discover that Ladler told the French he would be in his current job at least until UK–Argentina diplomatic relations were restored. 'We in Moscow, of course, knew that would be some years off,' Aleshkovsky said.

But as Aleshkovsky admitted to Mumford, the Ladler material was virtually the only item of interest his grand plan elicited. 'By late April 1985,' he said, 'I was deeply frustrated by the lack of progress on something as basic as Lambert's promotion status. So, inspired by Shukhov's example of simply asking Lambert why he called on Phoenix Investments, I decided to do the same thing.'

------◆---◆------

That's how it was, one cold and rainy Saturday morning in early May 1985, that a dapper man of about forty sporting a beautiful cashmere overcoat approached me in the car park of Sainsbury's Brent Park supermarket as I loaded groceries into my car. 'Mr Lambert,' he said in pucker English, 'Valerie O'Hare sends her best wishes. She would like to know if you managed to get promoted as a result of the little help we were able to provide last year?'

The man's mention of promotion prompted recall of Brian McGowan's advice the previous March that I was to be promoted. Brian, though, had been apologetic. 'It's a complicated story involving Legal and others,' he told me. 'All you need to know is that we're announcing your promotion during this current round only it's to take effect as of 1 October and not in April as planned.'

'Well?' the man said, jolting me back to the present.

I tried to think of a suitably cutting response but my distracting thoughts prevented me. 'I'm being promoted on the first of October, actually,' I said huffily. It was the best I could manage in the moment. But then my anger took over. 'Who the fuck are you O'Hare people?' I yelled, grabbing the man's overcoat lapels and shaking him hard. Other shoppers paused to watch.

The man ignored my question and with strong arms removed my hands. 'Thank you for confirming your promotion as of 1 October,' he said evenly. Then he looked down at his expensive overcoat, the lapels of which I had twisted out of shape. 'You should not be so ungrateful,' he spat in a flash of anger. 'Your promotion was our intention all along.' The man immediately calmed himself. 'Please don't make a scene,' he said, straightening his coat. 'The last thing either of us needs is a policeman asking questions.' With that, he turned and walked away.

I was too bewildered to run after him. The words *Your promotion was our intention all along* rang in my ears. My astonishment came not from the man reinforcing the conclusion I had reached the night I spoke to Anthony Delminico, that the O'Hare group's strategy was something more complex than a plan to inconvenience the Service. No, it was that seemingly goaded by my shaking of him, the man had just solved the piece of the puzzle I could not fathom. He had just told me that the O'Hare exercise – Freddie Ladler; Reggie Sullivan; Cuthberson and Delminico – was all aimed at helping me. And with that understanding came instant, clawing apprehensiveness: if there is one surely immutable rule of the universe it has to be there is no such thing as a free lunch.

<hr>

'The combination of Shukhov's apparent personal interest in Operation Oblast and Lambert's failure to win the Washington posting,' Aleshkovsky told Martin Mumford, 'had made me cautious. I wasn't overly perturbed by Shukhov's threat to send me to Afghanistan. But I'd seen it happen and had my family to consider. I wasn't about to push my luck. Once I knew the date of Lambert's promotion, I rushed to Shukhov's office.'

'Sir,' Aleshkovsky briefed Shukhov, 'you will recall that in February a man called Rupert Heneshaw took up as head of MI6 station in Washington. I can now advise Lambert takes up a promotion to the Washington station head level as of 1 October, while his rival, Ladler, although eligible for the Washington appointment, will be tied up on other matters for several years.'

Aleshkovsky told of Shukhov having a coughing fit when starting to respond. 'He was literally barking,' Aleshkovsky said. 'It was a good minute before he settled down.'

When Shukhov was able to speak he noted that the delay in my promotion taking effect was actually advantageous. 'We need to convince this Heneshaw to go home,' Shukhov told Aleshkovsky. 'In line with the gentlemen's agreement we have with the West, no physical harm must befall him, his wife or children. But if, for example, the brats are unable to adjust to life in Washington, Heneshaw may be compelled to put family before career. Get me a plan so I can explore this angle. If Heneshaw goes home maybe Lambert can still yet take up the Washington position.'

Aleshkovsky said after leaving Shukhov his mind was racing. 'I was preoccupied with coming up with a plan for convincing Heneshaw to go home. Yet at the same time I was thinking about the general's coughing. It sounded consumptive and explained why he had switched to smoking *Camels*. But I knew, and suspect Shukhov did too, that by now the damage would be done. It was the first sign I'd seen that his health was seriously on the wane.'

CHAPTER 31

WASHINGTON

Of all those Aleshkovsky gave up, Martin Mumford was to tell me, it was William and Barbara Whetstone where he evinced the most regret. The Whetstones were Russians and so-called illegals – having entered the United States from Mexico over a decade earlier posing as US citizens returning from vacation in Cancun. The surname they took belonged to a two-year-old boy who in 1955 drowned in a pond on the family potato farm outside Sonna, Idaho. Aleshkovsky had met the Whetstones, then using their real names, at the time of their entry into the KGB's illegals training program, where later they were paired. Like Aleshkovsky, both Whetstones were former Red Army cadets; this drove his empathy.

Rupert Heneshaw and his family lived in Falls Church, Virginia, across the Potomac River from the British Embassy in the District of Columbia. Barbara Whetstone was a teacher's aide at the Omar N. Bradley High School in Falls Church, a position specially chosen for the access it gave her to many of the foreign diplomats and US government officials residing in the area. Heneshaw's son, fourteen-year-old Timothy, was enrolled at the school.

To this day, I don't know how Barbara Whetstone was able to plant marijuana on Timothy. All Mumford could tell me at the time of his *Final Briefing* was that Aleshkovsky had devised the plan and Shukhov had approved Barbara being tasked to implement it. In any event, when the police were called to the school on Friday 23 August 1985, 200 grams of the drug were found in Timothy's gym shoes.

———— ◆ ◆ ————

Fast forward to the first week of October 1985 and I'd been in my new middle management position for a whole three days. But I was far from content. Even though I'd been promoted, the companion objective of the Washington posting now seemed unattainable. After Heneshaw, Ladler would likely be posted there given by then the Rhodesia beat-up would have been and gone. In the new era where station chiefs regularly did four-year stints or more, the wait could be as long as a decade. Even if I did succeed Ladler, it would probably be all too late. Hence only listlessly did I reach for the handset when the telephone rang.

Martin Mumford's voice caused me to sit up in my chair. 'Washington station chief's fallen vacant,' he said. 'You expressed an interest in the position early last year in your letter congratulating me on my promotion to the top floor. Still keen?'

'Yes, yes, Martin, definitely,' I managed to croak out, my mind now a disbelieving whirl. 'But how come it's suddenly available?'

Martin didn't answer the question. 'Let me speak to head of Placements,' he said. 'Either McGowan or I will revert to you.'

Two months later, in early December, the deputy ambassador from the embassy in Washington, a senior Foreign Office diplomat on home leave, called into the Service to introduce himself, knowing I was soon to take over as Washington station head. Our conversation turned to Heneshaw. 'The State Department informed Rupert in early September,' the deputy said, 'that the marijuana found on his son was a trafficable quantity. It directed that Timothy should leave the United States by the end of November.' The State Department was the American federal agency responsible for managing foreign diplomats in the United States. 'Rupert of course continued to plead his son's innocence,' the deputy said ruefully. 'But State had made up its mind.' The deputy noted that Rupert had not personally been asked to leave and could have remained in Washington. 'I understand,' he said, 'that Rupert did consider sending the family home and staying on. But eventually he decided he would miss too much of Timmy's development.'

It was not until much later that I learned of the Russian plan to curtail Rupert Heneshaw's Washington posting. Despite the passage of time, I felt nonetheless a tinge of regret for Heneshaw's son who then was just a boy. But later still, on hearing of Heneshaw's electing to discredit me rather than alerting the Service to the CIA's work-in-progress recruitment of the Kazakh scientist Massimov, I became more sanguine. Years and years had passed. *What goes around comes around*, was all I thought.

I arrived in Washington on 19 December 1985 to take up the position of MI6 station chief. My assignment was notionally for four years. It was twelve years to the day since my inauspicious debut for the Service in East Berlin. The first three months took place in the usual blur of arrival preoccupations. The introductory side was unrelenting, particularly over the Christmas and New Year period. At this time, I christened myself the *plumber with leaky taps* in that while I was adept at the social interaction my job demanded, I was happiest when alone with my memories. For the unversed, the equivalence is of a plumber out fixing up everyone else's leaky taps but putting up with leaky taps at home. I took an apartment in McLean, Virginia and braved the daily commute to the District.

It was clear from the attitude of the CIA people I first encountered that Heneshaw's legacy lived on. They were polite to a fault and did what had to be done, but no more. In my own interests I even tried to argue Heneshaw's case, making the obvious point that he had done nothing wrong; it was his son who had gone off the rails. The Agency guys, though, felt they had been burned. It was a barrier I didn't need and one that had to be overcome if I was to fulfil my secret quest to identify Agnes's killer.

Washington station was the Service's largest, some twenty-one people in all. My number two looked after day-to-day affairs. This freed me to concentrate on the bigger picture, with no issue more prominent than my liaison with the CIA. The station staff trawled Washington's big global community, with Eastern Bloc diplomats, journalists and academics always a high priority. Mindful of the nothingness of many of the agents Jakarta station had on its books when I arrived there, I was discerning when approving recruitment proposals to London. *No empty vessels* became my mantra.

The Americans were relaxed about us conducting operations on their turf provided we avoided American citizens, as we were relaxed about them doing the same in the UK, reciprocal citizenry terms pertaining. This ostensibly happy state of affairs was underpinned by an agreement that any resulting product was always to be shared, even if sources were not usually revealed. The Service suspected the Americans often withheld information they collected and, equally, were not averse to targeting British citizens when it suited them. But as a sign of Britain's international decline and its strategic reliance on the United States, we honoured the agreement to the letter for fear of incurring big brother's wrath.

1986 rolled by. I worked ferociously hard at ensuring the station ran at maximum efficiency and in cultivating CIA contacts. The Agency was a broad church. Many of its people were robust and rough-hewn. I was always hail-fellow-well-met in their presence and grateful that my working class origins equipped me to pull off this act. The bookish ones were usually the more senior and hardest to get close to. They scared me. Incredibly intelligent individuals, I worried each time we talked about this defector or that they would see through me and perceive my real intent.

Aleshkovsky told Martin Mumford it was a Friday evening in late September 1986. 'I recall winter was fast approaching,' he said. 'I had requested a meeting with Shukhov and got in to see him towards the end of the day. Shukhov suggested I sit on his office sofa.'

'Can I offer you a glass of vodka, Dmitri Aleksandrovich?'

'Despite our often-testy relationship,' Aleshkovsky said, 'I had warmed to Shukhov as it became clear his health was failing. He poured our drinks, the exertion of it causing him to gasp for breath.'

'Emphysema,' Shukhov said, once his lungs had absorbed enough oxygen for him to speak. 'It will cause me to cease working at some point and eventually kill me. To your good health.'

'We downed our vodkas in a single gulp,' Aleshkovsky said, 'and then a second glass. I was surprised by Shukhov's apparent interest in my family and my children's progress at school. It was not until we were on to our third glass that he turned to business.'

'Tell me about Operation Oblast,' Shukhov had said. 'Are the Americans warming to Lambert?'

Aleshkovsky said he could feel the effects of the vodka and had referred to his pocket book notes. 'I reported,' he said, 'that nine months into his Washington assignment, Lambert appears to be well settled. I explained that the length of his meetings at the CIA headquarters in Langley, Virginia suggested a growing level of trust, albeit so far there was no sign of him attending social events at the homes of senior CIA people.

'Even so, I told Shukhov we did have an indication of an incremental improvement in Lambert's personal relations with the CIA leadership. This took the form of a recent sighting of him lunching in Georgetown with Charles Kudermann, the CIA deputy director. I finished with my assessment that while Lambert appeared to be on his way to winning the Americans' confidence, it would be slow going unless we instituted measures to foster closer ties.'

Aleshkovsky said Shukhov had considered this at length. 'Let me take you into my confidence, Dmitri,' he said finally, the glint in his eye gone and his tone now serious. 'Something I rarely do with anyone in this madhouse. You should know I am personally invested in Oblast. Katya Vasilievna Lyubimova, remember her?'

Aleshkovsky told Mumford that Shukhov's admission of a personal investment in Operation Oblast came as no surprise – he had suspected it for over a year now. 'But his mention of Katya, the Soviet agent Joe Lambert had recruited in London in the summer of 1979, as the subject of his personal investment,' Aleshkovsky said, 'was a new development. I was certain the vodka had not loosened Shukhov's lips. He was choosing his words very carefully. "I do, general," I had replied with deliberate blandness. "I recall she was uncovered as a British agent in May 1980." '

All of a sudden, Aleshkovsky said, there was tension in the air, as if Shukhov was about to reveal something very secret about Katya. But an instinct seemed to have stopped him at the last moment. 'The general owed his career, and in all likelihood his life, to trusting no one and always holding his cards close to his chest,' Aleshkovsky said. 'I have no doubt he intended a moment of substantial openness but ingrained caution prevented it.'

'I was close to Katya's father,' Shukhov eventually said. 'It killed him when we executed her. When we discovered Lambert was behind her role in compromising the entrapment of the British scientist in Vienna and her recruitment as an ongoing agent, I devised Operation Oblast and the plan to use Lambert as a pawn to destroy the US–UK intelligence relationship. It's an ambitious outcome I'm seeking. That's why I've been so demanding of you.'

'Speaking intensely had caused Shukhov to labour for breath,' Aleshkovsky said. 'I waited for him to recover.'

'With the assistance of an oxygen mask,' Shukhov said once composed, 'I hope to work until such time as Oblast reaches its conclusion. After that, I'll go to the dacha to die. The tumblers are falling into place, Dmitri, and I have no time to waste. Right now, this very instant, I want you to feed Lambert some red meat. Make the Americans love and revere him. I have in mind one of our US Navy sources – *Contraband*.'

'*Contraband's* real name,' Aleshkovsky told Mumford, 'was Ritchie Ross. He was a social misfit, a former submariner who had spied for us since 1983 in retaliation for the US Navy a year earlier declaring him unsuitable for at sea service because of his drinking habits.' Aleshkovsky recounted how the Soviets could not believe their luck when after the ban Ross was posted to a shore job at the King's Bay submarine base near St Mary's, Georgia. 'It amazed us,' Aleshkovsky said, 'that the Navy redeployed him to a position with access to sensitive documents. For over three years he had been passing us highly secret material on nuclear-powered submarine propulsion systems. But by September 1986 the creeping introduction of computing, and the electronic footprint this created, meant his use-by date was fast approaching. I agreed with Shukhov that Ross was an ideal choice to be given up.'

'Good,' Shukhov said. 'We will give the CIA plenty of time to fully weigh and appreciate Lambert's value and then around March next year introduce a woman I have handpicked. I propose to call her Sunlight. I will tell you about her shortly into the New Year.'

'Shukhov was now physically exhausted,' Aleshkovsky said. 'He did offer me a fourth vodka but only to be polite. I left feeling light-headed and clear at the same time. I now realized that Shukhov was engaged in a personal crusade linked to Katya – even if at the last minute he had decided to withhold the actual how and why.

'Nonetheless, what he did say explained why he was throwing a fortune at Operation Oblast and moving with such precision. It also explained why he was prepared to kill Lambert's girlfriend and her co-workers, however uneasy I still felt about that. And I could now better understand why he had ordered the tidy-up killings of the Indian lorry driver and attesting witnesses involved in the woman's death, and separately that of Anthony Delminico, the ex-RAF fellow in Brighton we used to channel the WRR minutes to Lambert.'

CHAPTER 32

EPIPHANY

My apartment in McLean, Virginia came with two side-by-side car parks. As I had only the one car, it was not uncommon in my early days to arrive home late from the office to find that someone, usually another tenant's visitor, had parked in one of my two spots. I objected to this because when returning home late and tired it suited me to swing into the bays leaving my car straddling both slots. I had complained to building security and the infringement of my parking space had ceased.

I reacted angrily, therefore, on the night of Friday 17 October 1986, when arriving home exhausted at 11 pm I spied on entering the underground garage a sky blue Chevy Camaro parked in one of my bays. As I drew closer, I could see the car carried diplomatic corps plates. The licence number, however, was not one I recognized. I resolved, once I found out to which embassy the vehicle belonged, to make my displeasure abundantly clear.

I pulled in to the vacant slot and to my amazement saw the shapes of two persons sitting in the Camaro's front seats. A tall blond man I had never seen before emerged from the driver's side and opened my passenger-side door. 'You'll have to forgive the diplomatic plates on my car,' he said amiably. 'When you check you'll find they belong to Sao Tome and Principe. They're not genuine. It's just that diplomatic plates were necessary to get past the front security office.'

My reaction was to fire off a rapid volley of questions mixed with aggressive bluster. 'Don't get feisty,' the man said. 'We need to speak and of course my colleague,' indicating with his head to the second man still seated in the Camaro, 'is not here for his good looks.'

The blond man was now seated in my front passenger seat.

'And?' I asked icily.

'My people have certain information that the American Government would be pleased to receive and we have decided you should give it to them,' he answered calmly. I tried to speak but my incredulity prevented me from finding the right words. 'It concerns a US serviceman, a *matelot* called Ritchie Ross,' the man went on, 'who has been passing high-grade information to the Soviet Union for three years. He is currently based at King's Bay in Georgia.'

'And who might I say told me this?' I asked abrasively, my voice rasping with tension.

'Whom I represent need not concern you,' the man replied. 'That is because next Friday night you will attend the Austrian Embassy's national day reception.' He threw back his head in what appeared to be genuine amusement. 'Those lazy schnitzels refuse to work on Sunday, when Austria's independence day actually falls this year. But I digress.'

The man was matter-of-fact again. 'At the function a person by the name of Sukhan Kuliyeva will approach you. He is attached to the KGB station here in Washington working under consular cover. He is from Turkmenistan and because of that doesn't get any of the sexy work. Perhaps that is why the FBI has not identified him as an intelligence officer. But Kuliyeva has done good work among the Turkmen community in New York City. As a reward, his KGB masters have tasked him to take what he believes is the first step towards recruiting you into a deception operation.

'Please proceed carefully,' the man continued. 'You should not let on you are expecting Kuliyeva's approach. Kuliyeva will demand money. The plan, so far as he is concerned, is for the first batch of documents he sells you to be high-grade intelligence provided by the source, genuine US Navy documents. Kuliyeva has been told this is to snare you and set you up to be sold bogus information. And the first tranche of documents will be genuine. But unbeknown to Kuliyeva, the documents will also allow the Americans unambiguously to identify Ritchie Ross as a traitor.

'You will report the Kuliyeva contact to London and recommend the obvious – that the Americans be made aware the documents on offer will identify a US traitor. Naturally, you will refrain from mentioning that Kuliyeva does not know the documents will reveal Ritchie Ross's name and, if necessary, deny his later claims to this effect. In due course Ross will be arrested. You will also recommend that the Americans be informed of Kuliyeva's identity. London is certain to agree. The Americans are always deeply resentful of undetected KGB officers. Mr Kuliyeva will be expelled, returning to Moscow to an uncertain fate, unfortunately.'

The sheer ruthlessness of the apparent Soviet intention to throw Kuliyeva to the sharks reminded me of my own vulnerabilities. 'Look,' I said, 'you need to understand I've already had people drop things in my lap and lightning rarely strikes twice.'

'I take it that is a reference to Mr Garrick Cuthberson,' the man said. 'My people have seen no indication the Americans know about him, his WRR minutes and the second Rhodesian matter concerning Mr Reggie Sullivan. If we are correct, your coming across Kuliyeva will not arouse American suspicions.' He looked at me questioningly. I stared back, expressionless. Yet, somehow, he seemed to have detected the truth. 'Perfidious Albion,' he said in mock reproach, smiling broadly. Soberly, he continued. 'Nor should you worry about London's reaction. Your contact with Kuliyeva will occur during normal diplomatic business and not be seen as out of the ordinary. Added to which, Kuliyeva's approach will not be inconsistent with the disaffection often displayed by non-Russian Soviets who feel poorly treated by the Russians. Your head office is always anxious to please the Americans. It will be salivating at the prospect of alerting them to a traitor and providing the name of a previously unidentified Soviet intelligence officer.'

I reached across the man and locked the front passenger door. It was a waste of energy. All he had to do was lift the locking button. But it symbolized how I felt. 'I'm assuming you're from this O'Hare group that wants to pretend it's my fairy godmother,' I said as menacingly as I could. 'I know you've got nothing to do with the IRA. You are not getting out of this car without telling me exactly who you are and why your people want to help me.'

The man showed no alarm. 'My instructions,' he said, 'are to say nothing about our organization. But I do understand your inquisitiveness. Yes, I do act on behalf of the O'Hare group as you choose to call it. We are an international coalition that wants to address global inequality. Our belief is that you, a product of the British working class, being in a position of power in the British Secret Service is a step towards our objective of a fairer world unconstrained by the shackles of rightist ideology.'

'OK,' I said, far from convinced. 'But how do you know what the KGB's Washington station intends to do this time next week and more to the point why is it doing what you say it plans to do?'

'Mr Lambert,' the man said patiently, 'we have men and women from all walks of life working for us. Information regularly comes our way. As to why the KGB station proposes to proceed as outlined, I would simply encourage you to accept it has its reasons.'

'Sounds like a load of cobblers to me,' I retorted. The man shrugged and didn't answer. 'Where is your organization based, then?' I asked belligerently.

The man looked at his watch. 'I can spare you no more time, I'm afraid. Just do as I ask and I assure you your photograph will soon take pride of place on the mantelpiece at Langley.'

I watched the man and his companion drive away, knowing for certain he'd been selling me a line about the O'Hare group. Slumped at my kitchen table and deeply fatigued, I tried to think it through. Slowly my thoughts crystallized, and when they did the moment of epiphany dawned. The man's knowledge of the internal workings of the KGB's Washington station was surely the key. Whereas previously the Rhodesian incidents involving Freddie Ladler and Reggie Sullivan offered no inkling of a link to the Soviets, a Soviet connection now existed.

The more I thought about it, the more obvious it became that this O'Hare business was actually a front for a complex Soviet orchestration. Who else had the resources and organizational skills, not to mention the utter ruthlessness? Anthony Delminico's death; Ladler's besmirching; Cuthberson, Reggie and the WRR minutes were all somehow connected. With startling clarity it dawned on me that Agnes's death was not a case of tit for tat revenge. 'It's a part of this Soviet play,' I exclaimed loudly. But in that instant, as my words reverberated around my dark and silent apartment, I also knew this changed nothing. The Soviets had butchered Agnes, whatever their reasons. My resolve to identify Agnes's killer and take retribution surged anew.

But what was the Soviet play? Why had they previously gone to such lengths to assist me, and why now were they willing to give up a source and an operative for nothing obvious in return? The answer immediately hit me: the Soviets had a very big fish to fry and for some reason inflating my credentials was central to it. The guaranteed effect of my alerting the Americans to Ritchie Ross and the Soviet spy Kuliyeva told me that much.

As to the Soviets' end point I had no idea, other than they were prepared to play a long, long game in getting there. But if the Sovs wanted so badly to cosy up to me I would see where it took me, only from here on with my *eyes wide open*. In the interim, if what they were giving me caused the Americans to take me to their hearts I would happily use it. After all, it would probably come down to a race between the Sovs and me to see who got to the finish line first.

——◆—◆——

The man who drove out of my apartment garage was Finnish by birth Aleshkovsky later informed us. He had worked for the Russians for a number of years, many of those while living in the United States. Aleshkovsky said that when asked by the KGB Resident how things had gone, the Finn had replied, 'Reasonable but no more. Lambert has seen through the IRA cover and because of that I was forced into giving him the international coalition spiel.'

'The Resident, who knew a little but not the lot, rang on the secure line to warn me of this,' Aleshkovsky told Martin Mumford. 'I alerted Shukhov, telling him that now the Kuliyeva phase had been introduced, it was only a matter of time before Lambert would work out we were pulling the strings.'

When Mumford asked about Shukhov's response, Aleshkovsky said, 'He was worried, certainly, as was I. But all he said was something to the effect that provided we can get over this step, he was confident Sunlight could do her part.'

CHAPTER 33

KULIYEVA

Friday 24 October 1986. After the usual problems of finding a car park, I entered the front door of the grey sandstone Austrian Embassy. A Germanic-looking Ambassador with brilliantly shined shoes headed the reception line. He shook my hand before quickly losing interest in me. I mingled and chatted. Somewhat nervous about what was supposed to unfold, I allowed myself a second glass of the *Grüner* Veltliner dry white wine the Austrians so prefer.

The reception was scheduled for two hours. After an hour nothing of note had happened. The mid-point speeches took place.

Thereafter, a Viennese orchestra was pressed into service and guests invited to dance. I fell into a meaningless conversation with an intense German woman. She asked me if I had ever been to Vienna and did not smile when confirming, in response to my tongue in cheek question, that she meant the Austrian capital and not the town in Northern Virginia across the river from Washington DC. I affirmed I had but spared her the fact I hadn't gone there as me. The woman asked where I usually stayed. 'The Erdberger Wien,' I lied.

'Ah, well then,' she replied, 'you must go there for your work.'

I took this as a reference to me being an impecunious civil servant unable to lodge at the Erdberger without the assistance of the long-suffering British taxpayer. Inspired by the truth of her insult and the growing conviction that Kuliyeva was a no-show, I was about

215

to go home. Then I felt a tap on my right elbow. A short, bespectacled man swarthy in complexion smiled at me. I gratefully excused myself from my German tormentor. 'Mr Lambert,' the man said, 'please accept my business card.' *Sukhan Kuliyeva, Consular Section, Embassy of the Soviet Union* it read.

Hiding there in plain sight, amid the hubbub going on around us, Kuliyeva cast his net. 'I am Turkmen,' he said in stilted English. 'The Russians treat people like me with contempt. I have a proposal. An American serviceman, known to me only as *Contraband*, is selling secrets to the KGB. For 10,000 US dollars, I will provide you with certain documents. They will facilitate measures to help the US authorities counteract the damage the traitor has done. Provided you do not reveal me to the Americans, for a suitable fee I can offer you other valuable information on an ongoing basis.'

'Whoa, hang on cowboy, not so fast,' I said. 'I would need proof there is an American traitor as you claim. I might add that ten grand is a very steep asking price, especially as you don't know the traitor's real name. Money doesn't grow on trees. How about five if you can prove to me you're genuine?'

Spy to spy, I admired the way Kuliyeva held his nerve. I had fully expected him to meet me halfway on the money. But he knew the key to enticing me into his disinformation sting was not to devalue his product. 'No, 10,000 it is,' he said, 'take it or leave it.' I pretended to think this over while Kuliyeva coolly feigned impatience. 'Meet me at 4 pm next Thursday at the Air and Space Museum,' he said, 'in front of the lunar landing capsule. I will bring the proof you require, you bring the money.' With that, he faded into the crowd. The last I saw of him he was capably dancing the Viennese waltz with a blonde piece a foot-and-a-half taller than him.

I returned immediately to the embassy and cabled a modified report of my encounter to London, one indicating that Kuliyeva was selling documents purporting to identify a US traitor. I noted the

Thursday deadline and made the usually persuasive observation that I assessed the offer to be genuine. I finished with the assertion that, provided the documents revealed the traitor's identity as promised, the hefty price tag would be justified. But I wrote my dispatch already knowing Kuliyeva's material would clearly finger Ritchie Ross. I left out the bit about Kuliyeva, unaware he was poised to expose a live KGB asset, preparing to sign his own death warrant.

The question of whether to reveal Kuliyeva's identity to the Americans required more nuance. Aided by Martin Mumford's wise advice in the aftermath of Rupert Heneshaw's sabotage of the pitch I led at the Kazakh scientist Massimov, I knew not to be too eager in pursuing my desired outcome. Accordingly, I provided two options. One was not to reveal Kuliyeva's identity. Instead, we would share his intelligence with the CIA in accordance with the standing agreement. The second was to inform the Americans of the likely presence of an undetected KGB officer in their midst, the word *likely* included for the benefit of my readership. The risk, I noted, was Kuliyeva's expulsion and the loss of his product. I recommended the second option, risk notwithstanding. Alerting the Americans to Kuliyeva would allow them to decide whether to kick him out or string him along. It was their country after all. I knew Mumford would understand my preference for consultation. He would also be influential in London's decision. For three days I sweated on a response, hoping for the go-ahead on the second option and the deep ingratiation with the Americans it offered.

'Joe, Joe, please have another piece of pecan pie,' CIA deputy director Charles Kudermann's wife implored me. 'It's so nice to have you to Sunday lunch. We want you to feel right at home.'

'For God's sake Betsy leave the man be,' Kudermann said. 'He's a big boy. If he's hungry he'll have more pie when he wants it.'

Kudermann smiled warmly at me. 'Let's go into the study,' he said. 'We can have a glass of bourbon while we're waiting for Bill to drop by.' We sat in floral-patterned lounge chairs. 'It's not every day, you know, Joe,' Kudermann said, 'that the CIA Director makes a social call. It's really a gesture to say how grateful we are for your efforts with Kuliyeva. Turns out this Ritchie Ross character was really mixed up. A loner: no friends, no family and an alcoholic with a chip on his shoulder; just ripe for turning.'

Jesus Christ, I thought, *he could be speaking about me.*

Hearing Kudermann list Ritchie's vulnerabilities prompted me to think of the Service's attitude to loners. Nought had been right about its eventual evolution, to the point today where natural reclusiveness was no longer automatically considered symptomatic of a security risk. I was no doubt a beneficiary of this maturity. Even so, my foundational years were in a less enlightened organization. From that perspective my ill-starred marriage to Kathleen had not been a mistake. And after all, I reasoned, it had served a purpose for both parties.

The recall of my marriage of convenience made me yearn, not for the first time, for Agnes to have been Kathleen. The futility somehow reminded me that since Agnes's death I had reverted to total obsession, not as the dedicated careerist of yore but as her uncompromising avenger. From out of nowhere it struck me how this relentless pursuit had left me unable to differentiate between right and wrong: the lack of remorse I felt over things like Delminico's murder, the crucifying of Reggie Sullivan and Kuliyeva's recent fate signified the outlier I'd become. A jarring unpleasantness overtook me. Nought's prophecy of moral incompetence, I realized, had come true. *So here I am*, I thought, *hiding in The Far Grass, condemned forever to pad alone across spying's frozen landscape.* Waiting there in the CIA's inner sanctum for its Director to come and shake my hand, I suddenly felt chill. It was the thought that many twists and turns were still to come before the dangerous double game of death and deception set in train by my visit to Phoenix Investments fully unfolded. How prescient I was.

———◆◆———

There is simply no greater indicator of status than a car park, especially a reserved place under the CIA main building. And that's what I was given: *UK Liaison* the brass plate on the wall proclaimed. CIA officers who had previously avoided eye contact were now going out of their way to greet me in the Langley corridors. As promised by my tall, blond visitor that night in October last year, my photograph was in pride of place on the CIA's mantelpiece.

Robert Sandilands was a scholarly man of about fifty who went by the vague title of *Director, Reception Analysis*, which translated into him having responsibility within the CIA for processing Soviet defectors. 'Robert,' I said, seated in his office, 'now that it's February and everyone's back at work, my first project for 1987 is to build up my station's knowledge of current KGB structures. We've been tardy on this and I'm keen to address the information gap. We're particularly weak on Soviet clandestine ops against foreign personnel. Wet affairs used to be the province of the Spetsnaz Directorate and psyops, honey traps and naughty pictures, that sort of thing, used to be run out of Directorate *K*. I've seen nothing suggesting this has changed, but as to whom heads the various sub-directorates and who is coordinating we currently have little clarity. I was wondering if you had someone who has stepped over in the last little while who might have that sort of knowledge?'

My request for information on KGB structures was calculated. I had chosen the topic because the Americans could not assist me with it. They preferred to worry about what they were doing rather than trying to keep track of how the opposition was lined up on any given day. The structures enquiry was also designed to gain access to a defector with knowledge of recent happenings in Lubyanka head office and avoid me being saddled with a nonentity who had just jumped the fence at some out of the way Soviet embassy.

Robert stared unblinkingly at people while thinking. It reminded me of Edis Aksu, the Service officer whose objectivity spared me from summary dismissal after the Konrad debacle in East Berlin, and had the same unnerving effect. 'We're always happy to take requests for additional defector information from the MI6 head in Washington,' Robert said. 'Especially from you, Joe,' he added with an unnatural smile. 'Let me see if there's anything we can offer you. If so, we'd be pleased to receive a list of questions.'

'Actually, Robert,' I said, in a cold, business-like voice, 'at a luncheon hosted by the deputy late last year, which I was pleased to attend, Director Casey spoke of a new era in US–UK intelligence cooperation. In that spirit, as head of MI6 station Washington, I will no longer accept the UK being treated as an unequal party when making *ad hoc* requests for defector information. With the commencement of this new era, to use the Director's own words, we will no longer submit questions and accept answers to them filtered through the lens of US perceptions. If you have someone who can help, I expect to be able to speak directly to that person. Check with Kudermann if you feel the need. I am here seeking the level of cooperation to which the Director referred, not asking to be babysat.'

Sandilands stared at me; his warmth had gone. But the mention of the Director had made him cautious. 'I will speak to the deputy as you suggest. If he agrees, we will look at what may be appropriate. Good afternoon,' he said, curtly dismissing me.

I fretted I had overplayed my hand. Kudermann had seen the Director metaphorically slapping my back and, reflecting on it, I wondered if he might have been my best bet. That said, it would have looked odd if I had gone direct to Kudermann without first raising the matter with Sandilands, the officer in charge of the line area. It was a whole week before my assistant advised that Kudermann's office had called seeking an appointment with me.

❖

Kudermann and Sandilands were waiting when I was ushered into the former's office. No handshaking routine this time. 'It's an irregular request you've made, Joe,' Kudermann said bluntly. 'And Robert and I are not particularly at ease with it. Defectors are a very sensitive business. The long-standing practice has been to accept defector information requests from head of MI6 Washington, but this has always been conditional on the incumbent submitting a list of questions. I see no reason to depart from this arrangement.'

'Charles,' I said, using the familiarity of Kudermann's Christian name to remind him of the praise lavished on me at his home, 'you were there when the Director told me that my work on Kuliyeva was the harbinger of a new era of UK–US intelligence cooperation. You will also recall the Director lauded my advice to my Service not to run Kuliyeva until he ran out of goodies but rather to give the US the option to kick him out – which duly occurred. Now you seem to be saying the Director did not mean what he said.'

Kudermann wasn't enjoying the conversation. We both knew the Director had been laying it on hoping to encourage similar instances of cooperation. But Kudermann also knew that admitting this was out of the question. He needed to put the conundrum to bed, once and for all. 'You have misinterpreted the Director by some distance,' Kudermann said. 'But in light of our Services' special relationship, I am prepared to offer you an exception to the rule. I do so on the clear understanding that in accepting this offer, or indeed your declining it, the favour you did us will henceforth be fully repaid.' He glanced briefly at Sandilands. 'The offer is for you to speak to someone who came in just over a week ago. The interview will be for a maximum of thirty minutes. No notes will be permitted. We will, of course, be listening. And one last thing: with immediate effect we are rescinding your parking rights. You will now have at your disposal the public parking lot, which I understand offers visitors to the CIA the facility of metered parking.'

I made noises about being hugely disappointed with this tepid interpretation of *a new era in cooperation* and feigned indecision before accepting the offer on the table. I believe I also uttered the word *petulant* when talking about my ill-fated parking space. But Kudermann had shut down; he wasn't listening. *No more lunches at chez Kudermann for Joey boy*, I thought grimly as I was escorted from the building, in the truest sense of the word.

For all that, Kudermann kept to his promise. On Monday 23 February 1987 in a heavily guarded safe house in Bethesda, Maryland I sat across the table from a tired and nervous yet still alert Major Zamir Umarov, formerly deputy director of the KGB's elite Active Measures Department presently headed by Colonel Dmitri Aleshkovsky. The CIA, of course, was the third party to whom Umarov had vented his spleen over his disrespectful treatment at the hands of General Shukhov back in January 1985.

CHAPTER 34

UMAROV

At the time of his *Final Briefing* Martin Mumford noted how Aleshkovsky had reconciled to Umarov's deception of him. 'It was clear when debriefing Aleshkovsky,' Martin told me, 'that by then he regarded himself and Umarov as peas in the same pod. He spoke about Zamir's defection without so much as a hint of emotion.'

Aleshkovsky informed Mumford that Umarov had taken three weeks leave commencing in late January 1987. The family – Zamir, his wife and two children – was planning to ski at a resort in the Ural Mountains. Zamir had provided a hotel telephone number in case of emergency. 'But he also knew,' Aleshkovsky said, 'that I rarely bothered my staff while they were on leave and refreshing.

'Two days after Zamir should have returned to the office,' Aleshkovsky continued, 'there was still no sign of him. I put out a trace only to find the Umarov family had been allowed to drive into Finland because their passports contained valid exit visas. Further investigations revealed that a letter using the forged signature of General Shukhov had authorized the visa issue. I tasked the KGB station in Helsinki to follow up urgently. It reported that Zamir's car had been found abandoned at Helsinki-Vantaa airport but the Finns could find no record of the Umarovs leaving the country. I knew then Zamir had flown the coop. I had sent him to a conference in Lyon the preceding November. I remember thinking, once it was clear he had gone, I bet that is where whoever it was got to him.'

Then, Aleshkovsky said, a mere forty-eight hours later on an appropriately bleak Friday morning, crisis had turned to catastrophe. 'This took the form,' Aleshkovsky said, 'of a report from the Washington Resident suggesting that the CIA's grasp of Lambert to its bosom, triggered by his giving it Ritchie Ross's name and the unearthing of Sukhan Kuliyeva, had been released without obvious explanation. From socializing with the Director at the deputy's home late last year, Lambert had recently been seen in a convenience store seeking parking meter change before proceeding to Langley for what turned out to be a very short meeting. The report cautioned nothing was definite. But I didn't need to read further. As with Umarov, I knew instinctively this was also bad news.'

Aleshkovsky's immediate reaction was to think about how he would break the news of the dual setbacks to Shukhov. 'The general was due back at work the next Monday,' he said. 'He had just spent two weeks supposedly on leave but in fact at a sanatorium in Sochi where the doctors were trying to remove some of the shit that was clogging up his lungs and slowly suffocating him.'

◆——◆——◆

'This is Mr John Partridge. He is from the British Government. He will ask you a series of questions. Understood?' Umarov nodded.

'Thank you, sergeant,' I said to the marine who had admitted me to the poorly lit, windowless room. I didn't have much time to get to ask the questions I wanted to ask. But I also knew the listening Americans would be expecting me to concentrate on KGB structures where my professed interest lay. For twenty minutes I probed Umarov on this subject. He seemed bored, and who could blame him? In all probability he mentioned Shukhov but without a record of discussions it was impossible to recall every name he had thrown up. Now with ten minutes to go I decided to chance my arm.

'Tell me,' I said, 'are you aware of any operations past or present against British civilians; private citizens who are not British government employees?'

Umarov rubbed the back of his neck. He was not about to tell me much. He needed to amass as many bargaining chips as he could. 'As I told you,' he said, 'I worked only in one of a number of areas covered by the Active Measures Department. I have no insights, for example, into political or economic operations designed to influence government policy, usually involving the recruitment of prominent trade union officials or academics.'

I realized then Umarov had misunderstood my intention. He thought it was exactly in these areas where I was focused. That's why he was so openly withholding, signalling he wanted something in return. My pulse quickened a little. Umarov's evasion substantially narrowed the subjects he could talk about. 'Those fields you list, Major Umarov, in which you claim no knowledge, are of prime importance to my government. Unfortunately, there is today insufficient time for game playing. I would simply caution that these matters will be revisited and when they are I would encourage you to be more forthcoming if you know what is best for you and your family. For now, however, can you tell me please about any other operations against non-government British citizens of which you have or had visibility, full or partial?'

Umarov's face remained expressionless. But it soon became apparent my question would have pleased him because he proceeded to throw me a bone that involved no burning of capital. 'There was one operation, a recruitment running against a British male for which I was not indoctrinated. My superior, Colonel Aleshkovsky, had tactical responsibility for it. The head of the First Main Directorate of whom I spoke earlier, General Sergei Shukhov, directed strategy.

He treated the operation as a matter of extreme importance. I have no idea about the target person, what he did or why the matter was so important to Shukhov. What I do know is that one day when expressing his frustration at Shukhov's demands, Colonel Aleshkovsky let on there had been several operational killings ordered by the general, including the man's girlfriend in a fake car accident. I do not know her nationality or where she was killed, but if the man was British I suppose it is possible the girlfriend might also have been British. The operation was still running when I left. I have no idea as to its current status.'

It was my turn to be impassive. Umarov had just iced the cake that Agnes's driver, Gulam, had baked in his letter to me over three years ago. I stood and without another word rapped on the door. The marine who opened it wore a watch with a large digital display. The stopwatch function had been selected. It showed I had interviewed Umarov for twenty-nine minutes and forty-two seconds.

⎯⎯◆◆⎯⎯

Aleshkovsky was to tell Martin Mumford of his tenseness as he approached Shukhov's office. 'Shukhov and I had become quite close over the preceding few months,' Aleshkovsky said. 'I hoped this would stand me in good stead. But my worst fears appeared to be realized once I had briefed him. He had been cold and formal, describing the Umarov and Lambert developments as *calamitous*. I wondered if this meant our relationship had now relapsed, or worse.'

But then, according to Aleshkovsky, Shukhov had softened. 'Dmitri,' he said, 'the doctors in Sochi gave me a new type of medicine, a steroid I inhale. Used together with my oxygen mask it helps with my breathing and will hopefully extend the time I have before I get too feeble. I have been cautioned the reprieve will be temporary and my decline could happen without warning. But the relief I'm currently experiencing is timely. It convinces me that with this apparent downturn in Lambert's fortunes, we can afford to be patient in progressing Oblast. We should not be panicked into revising the operation. The objective for now remains to recruit Lambert while he is in the American inner fold.'

Aleshkovsky told Mumford he was sufficiently encouraged by Shukhov's conciliatory tone to put to him it was impossible to predict when, if ever, I would be restored to the CIA's inner circle. Shukhov had apparently pondered this for some time before replying. 'As you note, Dmitri, whatever has gone on in Washington has not resulted in Lambert being sent packing, either by the Americans or his own side. My instincts are telling me his position will improve. The unknown is to what extent. I accept we cannot mount another operation to assist him win favour. That would be far too obvious. But I reiterate we can afford to wait, particularly as that traitorous Uzbek bastard Umarov cannot compromise Oblast. A small mercy, but one for which we can be grateful. He will bring down the house on a raft of other operations when finally he spills his guts but he has no knowledge of Oblast.'

Dear general, Aleshkovsky had thought, *but for you and others like you Zamir would still be here.* 'But I kept that heresy to myself,' he told Mumford with a wry smile. 'The general then proceeded to shuffle his papers,' Aleshkovsky said, 'giving himself time to regain his breath.'

'Let's see if Lambert can recover his status,' Shukhov said once stable. 'I am prepared to wait up to a year if we have to, unless beforehand this illness of mine completely strips the stripes from the tiger in me. If we become certain the Americans will not rehabilitate Lambert we may be forced to review our recruitment plans. But let's see. In the meantime, let me tell you about Sunlight. When the time comes we need her to be ready for immediate deployment to Washington. Who knows when Lambert's fortunes might revive?'

I had no option but to report to London on my interview with Umarov. This was unavoidably a confession, of how I wasted the priceless collateral we had earned with the Americans without so much as a word of consultation with head office. I knew that the admission of unilateralism alone would be sufficient for the top floor to put a large black mark next to my name. But sooner or later the Service would have become aware of my conduct, and to have not reported would have caused me even bigger problems.

The Americans put me in the freezer for three months. They brought me out in time to allow me to make preparations for the DG's annual visit to Washington in June 1987. There was no formal declaration of the thaw. Rather, they relied on car park diplomacy in that one day in May, out of the blue, an unspeaking official gave me a pass allowing me to park in the area reserved for approved diplomats. It was highly symbolic: parking underneath the CIA was a sure sign of being in the inner circle; parking in the public area, with the accursed parking meters, was an equally sure sign of being on the outer; while parking in the outdoor space reserved for approved diplomats, physically situated as it was between the main CIA building and the public car park, indicated a status somewhere in between. The *status quo ante* had been restored; in that as when I arrived I was no longer regarded as on the nose but still someone to be treated cautiously and kept at arm's length.

The DG's visit went well although he was noticeably cool towards me. It was a living certainty the Americans would have chewed his ear over my behaviour, leading me to wonder if I might be recalled. That did not eventuate, principally I expect because the DG did not want to attract the political attention invited by successive Washington heads of station failing to complete their assignments. Instead, the sop he extended to the CIA was a reshuffle of the top floor executive a month after his return to London.

The smiling, affable, stab-you-in-the-guts-when-you-were-not-looking Digby Carhiddy became my boss in place of Martin Mumford. Carhiddy was originally from the automotive industry, he of the David Niven moustache and silver cigarette case. He had entered the Service at a time when the idea of Service operatives in the business world had undergone a growth spurt. From there Digby had skillfully ducked, weaved and manipulated his way up the Service's pecking order, ascending to the top floor in 1982. Mumford's becoming the scapegoat for my apparent rashness deeply upset me. He had always supported me. I hoped one day to explain to him that his judgement wasn't astray.

⎯⎯⎯◆◆⎯⎯⎯

The footnote to discovering Shukhov was responsible for Agnes's death was that my tenuous relations with the Americans and my own Service gave me little leeway to take advantage of the breakthrough. Had I flagged an interest in Shukhov's movements with either, the first thing I would have been asked to explain was why I was seeking this information.

I floated Shukhov's name with my Danish counterpart, a woman with whom I had a good if benign relationship. She wanted to know each and every detail. Rattled, I pleaded secrecy. I knew then I would have to wait until something happened of its own accord, until an opportunity arose. At least my patience had been rewarded in identifying who gave the order to assassinate Agnes. I could only hope for a repeat outcome where coming face to face with Shukhov was concerned.

CHAPTER 35

SUNLIGHT

'Just over a year had passed since the Americans disowned Lambert,' Aleshkovsky told Mumford. 'Things other than Operation Oblast had occupied my attention. Then in March 1988, as the winter thaw was beginning, Shukhov called me to a meeting. For one reason or another I hadn't seen him since January. I was shocked at the deterioration in his health. I saluted. When he looked up his eyes were pained and watery. He looked depressed.'

'Yes – Oblast,' Shukhov said, subdued and speaking slowly. 'A year on since Lambert's setback and still there is no sign of him having access to the CIA any better than that of a third-ranked ally. I know you think I should have acted sooner. But I badly wanted Lambert recruited while ensconced with the Americans so that we might destroy the US–UK intelligence relationship in one fell swoop. I've waited as long as I possibly can and now have to accept the unhappy fact that we must focus on recruiting him in a more limited capacity. Could you activate Sunlight for me, please? Do it under the alternative option we discussed in January, but let her move at her own pace. She needs to be confident when the time comes that her legend is sound.'

'I hurried back to my office,' Aleshkovsky said 'and immediately called in my operations coordinator. I briefed him on the alternative option. It was premised on Lambert having no access to inner

American secrets and him being of most value to us as a senior MI6 head office source. Sunlight was to form a relationship with Lambert while in Washington and allow it to mature for the remainder of his posting, with a view to them becoming an established couple and Sunlight his emotional bedrock. The plan envisaged Sunlight returning to London with Lambert on those terms. Once he was back in head office, she would begin the task of extracting intelligence from him.'

One by-product of my insularity was I had become a small target outside of the diplomatic and intelligence milieu I inhabited. It was not intentional, more a matter of lifestyle. My erratic hours and a 24-hour supermarket close to my home meant I did not shop for food at regular times; nor did I frequent bars at nights or on weekends; and I had no leisure pursuits, let alone any requiring a routine. My only predictable behaviour was the commute from Virginia to the District, always crossing over the Potomac River via Chain Bridge. In order to avoid the traffic crush, you could set your watch on me traversing the bridge at 7:50 am each workday. The security gurus were forever telling me to vary my routine. But I saw no need. It was widely known I was the MI6 station chief, and my staff attended to our clandestine business, things like clearing dead letter boxes. Indeed, I paid no attention at all to possible scrutiny as I moved about. The fact that I talked to the CIA and other US intelligence agencies was hardly a state secret. The Soviet watchers were easily able to monitor my movements.

I was at a standstill on Chain Bridge at 7:52 am on Friday 23 September 1988 waiting for the arrow to turn green facilitating my right turn into the District of Columbia and eventual passage onto Arizona Avenue. Suddenly there was a thump as my car lurched forward having been rear-ended. Fortunately, the impact was not severe and I safely avoided cannoning into the car in front. 'Fuck it,' I cursed, as I looked in the rearview mirror to see a woman with a look of anguish on her face.

I alighted from my car and the woman from hers. Her car had Florida plates. We examined the damage to my car's bumper, which was slight. 'I'm so sorry,' she said in accented English. 'I mistook the accelerator for the brake.' I looked directly at her for the first time. She was an attractive young woman of about thirty, quite tall.

The lights had turned green and there was mayhem, with horns blaring and blocked drivers shouting in frustration. I retreated from my navel-gazing. 'Can you give me your name and number and I'll contact you?' I said in standard motor vehicle accident response. 'We're holding up the traffic and neither of us is injured.' I fished out a notebook from my suit jacket and offered it and a pen to her.

Liliana Leanca she wrote next to her telephone number. 'Can you please do the same for me?' she asked. 'I feel so silly and embarrassed and want to properly apologize to you.'

By now it had dawned on me that obtaining quotes to have the woman pay for the repairs would involve a significant commitment of time. Time I didn't have. Yet the cost of repair would be low. Enforcing my legal rights surely amounted to a case of false economy? I resolved there and then to have my Service-owned vehicle repaired at official expense.

Why then did I still comply with the woman's request? It was, I later decided, because on looking closely at her I had begun to detect her similarity to Agnes. She was by no means a dead ringer. But Liliana's hair, although darker than Agnes's, was similarly flowing. And despite not having Agnes's high cheekbones, her smile, like Agnes, came from her eyes – black in Liliana's case – and was just as warm. Even her stance and manner of speech conveyed a strength of personality reminiscent of Agnes. Not as direct, certainly, but with the same engaging effect all the same.

Returning home the following Saturday afternoon after spending most of the day in the office, I found a message from Liliana on my answering machine. I rang back with the honourable intention of telling her I would attend to the repairs. I anticipated no further contact. But the sweet lilt of Liliana's accented English and her ready laugh captivated me. Liliana said her family had immigrated to the US from Moldova a decade ago and lived in Miami. Sick of living at home, she had moved to Washington two months ago and leased a bed-sit apartment in Arlington, just on the Virginia side of the Potomac. She had recently taken a position at a steakhouse on Arizona Avenue in the District. The thought occurred to me that I probably passed the restaurant when driving to the office. Liliana's job was to greet customers and seat them at their tables. So far she liked the job, even if being a *meeter and greeter* meant she did not usually receive tips. I found myself absorbed by this banality and disappointed when Liliana had to go for fear of being late for work. We agreed to speak again during the next week.

It is a rank understatement to say the spark Liliana ignited surprised me. With Agnes's death and the subsequent passage of time, I'd grown to find emotional comfort in my isolation, albeit until my recent awakening while in the CIA's inner sanctum, when in Charles Kudermann's study, I'd never thought of it as hiding in *The Far Grass*. The spark also conflicted me. I had been resolutely faithful to Agnes in the nearly five years since the Russians had murdered her, not so much as looking at another woman. On top of that, there were the bridges I had burned in seeking to avenge Agnes, something I couldn't walk away from even if I wanted to, not least because I was now embroiled in a major and as yet unclear Soviet play. The other sobering reality was that even were I interested, Liliana was unlikely to have any romantic notions. I was no longer a handsome young man, if ever I had been. Liliana was ten years my junior. Who was I kidding? I should forget about her.

Driving to work the following Monday, however, I found myself looking for Liliana's place of work on Arizona Avenue. It was located two blocks before my right turn onto Massachusetts Avenue taking me to the British Embassy. The effect of passing the restaurant was to instil in me a curious sense of pleasurable lightness. Returning home that night, and the following night, I found myself rushing to the answering machine hoping for a message. When Liliana did ring on the Wednesday night, I guardedly asked if she would like to have dinner. The safety net compromise reached beforehand, born of Agnes's memory and worry about looking foolish, was to tell myself the invitation would be an act of friendship. Even so, I can't deny feeling a rush of adrenalin when she said, 'I would love to.' Liliana did not work Wednesdays and Sundays. We agreed to dine one week later at a restaurant close to her apartment.

I did subsequently declare my relationship with Liliana to the Service. But I was economical with the truth in that, when describing her consistent with her passport as a US citizen, I omitted the complicating fact of her Soviet republic birthplace. The Service security-meisters would argue, correctly, that my intention to form only a friendship with Liliana was no defence to this evasiveness.

❖❖

It is pertinent at this point to address a rather obvious question. Why didn't Liliana's interest in me raise a red flag? After all, I was an experienced intelligence officer who on discovering the O'Hare group was a Soviet plot had earnestly committed to proceeding with *eyes wide open*. Yet here was a desirable young woman, resembling of Agnes and raised in Soviet Moldova of all places, who by some miracle had dropped into my life out of the clear blue sky. There were marginal factors for my denial: I was an isolated and ageing male reacting naturally to Liliana's attractiveness; and Liliana, directed by Shukhov to activate me only once I was back in London head office, showed no interest whatsoever in my work.

But the real reason I blocked out suspicions about Liliana can be traced back to that Sunday afternoon in Charles Kudermann's study, when on becoming aware of my moral incompetence I realized it threatened to condemn me to life eternal in *The Far Grass*. Even so, the revelation had not tempered my long-professed indifference to living or dying so long as I was able to avenge Agnes. Liliana, however, changed all this. Without me knowing it, she had revitalized my will to live. All of a sudden I was scared witless by Nought's warning about spending my life hiding in *The Far Grass* and forever padding alone across spying's frozen steppe.

Over the next six months the envisaged plutonic relationship ensued, during which I told Liliana of Agnes and my continuing love for her long after her death in a motor accident. For her part, Liliana explained that she grew up in Chisinau, Moldova's capital. After her mother died unexpectedly, when Liliana was just fifteen, her schoolteacher father had decided on a fresh start for he and his two daughters. Many rejections later, the authorities had relented and the family migrated to the US. Liliana by now was a young adult. She had studied literature at Moldova State University, but once in the US her initially insufficient command of English prevented her working as a journalist as she had hoped. She had drifted into hospitality work, waitressing and the like, and stayed there.

Towards the end of that first six months, however, I also found myself beginning to think how Agnes would want me to move on with life. Little by little my affection for Liliana began to run. Any voice of recrimination, I would later recognize, was suppressed by her enlivening my fear of living alone in *The Far Grass*. Deep into month seven, Liliana and I kissed passionately for the first time. By the end of the month we were petting regularly.

One Sunday afternoon in early June 1989, just over eight months after Liliana and I first had dinner, we returned to her apartment both buoyed by a glorious day and our walk among the District's fully blooming cherry blossoms. Liliana let our petting explore new frontiers. Soon we were lying on her bed, both naked. To my horror I just couldn't function. Resurgent guilt I expect. Whatever, I was afflicted with some variety of widower's droop. 'Joe,' Liliana whispered, 'I want you to be my big stallion. I want us to make music together.' I took this as encouragement, which did nothing for my performance anxiety.

In fact, Liliana was forewarning me she was going to take control. This she did, not with an exotic sexual technique, but by taking me in her arms and stroking my back, neck and the top of my head with gentle tenderness. Liliana's touch stimulated my dulled senses. I came to experience a burst of affection emitting from me, literally, the fact of it physically passing to Liliana evident from her sharp, instantly corresponding inhalation. Intimacy overrode misgiving. Liliana kissed me deeply, whereupon her sitting astride me I climaxed away over five years of celibacy.

Whether I actually became Liliana's big, music-making stallion is a matter for conjecture. But from then on we were lovers. It was a slower burn than with Agnes; nonetheless the steady increase in emotional outlay did in time come to exceed my upper threshold. And when the telltale effusion of calm and emotional security announced the dowsing of my loner instincts, I recognized that Liliana had become my second *real deal*.

Along the way, as Liliana and I had increasingly immersed, I detected my determination to avenge Agnes start to wane. I made no grand self-declaration formally abandoning Agnes when finally all resolve was gone. Rather, I simply permitted myself to accept that whereas atoning for Agnes's death was once my reason for being, now it was Liliana. Life is for the living I suppose I was thinking.

All I kept from Liliana was my profession, this and the matter of my entanglement with the Russians, their murder of Agnes and my past exploits directed at avenging her. I accepted that one day I would be held to account on any number of these fronts, but committed to deal with them as and when individual reckonings arose, in whatever form they materialized.

CHAPTER 36

KNOWING

Liliana was very pessimistic about Moldova's future. 'The Soviet Union,' she said, 'is in steep decline. This is emboldening many Moldovans to call for democratic elections to evict the Soviets. But our political class is fragmented, weak and lacking the knowhow to govern. There will be chaos when the Soviets lose control.'

'Most countries transitioning to democracy,' I replied, trying to appease her, 'usually experience teething problems.'

But Liliana was not having it. 'In the absence of Soviet authority,' she said forlornly, 'Moldova's divisions will unleash and eventually spiral into a civil war.' According to Liliana, Moldova's main fault line centred on Transnistria, the Russian-speaking territory in Moldova's east. Transnistrians, she said, feared the loss of their way of life at the hands of Moldova's larger ethnic Romanian population, which favoured integration with Romania.

'Soviet weakness, specifically Russian weakness,' Liliana said, 'is already giving impetus to secessionist movements in Transnistria's capital, Tiraspol. As Russia further deteriorates, the sentiment will quickly spread to other centres.' Liliana held grave concerns for the stockpile of Soviet weaponry in Moldova, one of the largest in Europe. 'It is widely accepted in Moldova,' she said, 'that both sides of the Transnistria argument will go to any lengths to obtain these armaments once the Soviet Union forfeits control, especially things like surface-to-air missiles capable of being fired by a single person with a shoulder-mounted rocket launcher.'

Liliana declared Western apathy to this to be confounding, singling out the UK for particular criticism. 'You English diplomats,' she admonished me, 'need to understand that your country risks the presence of disorderly, heavily armed elements in its European backyard should Moldova implode when the clamour for democracy inevitably forces out the Soviets.'

When later the Berlin Wall came crashing down in November 1989, foreshadowing the imminent collapse of the Soviet Union, I knew then that Moldova would soon wriggle out from under the Soviet yoke. All of a sudden Liliana's warning of rogue Moldovans roaming through Europe armed with surface-to-air missiles able to be fired at will didn't seem quite so extravagant.

In parallel with my blossoming romance with Liliana, my work demands continued unabated. The more entwined I became with her, the more equipped I felt to deal with the rigours of office. In August 1989, we landed a mid-level diplomat attached to the Chinese mission to the United Nations in New York. It was quite a coup. But although this won me some kudos, I would have had to recruit the Chinese President to fully repair my relations with headquarters. That much was rammed home when shortly after I received advice that Freddie Ladler was to replace me the instant my four-year term expired the coming December. The message's subtext was plain to see: *Don't be fooled into thinking the Chinese recruitment means you are forgiven.*

By now my affection for Liliana ran so deep that I had come unques-tioningly to accept her feelings for me were the same. One evening in early December, however, two weeks from my scheduled departure, the warning bell jangled with sufficient volume for reality finally to intrude.

Liliana and I were discussing future plans. The Service's literally telegraphed attitude towards me had been playing on my mind. It would be a bleak existence working in headquarters. A clean break seemed attractive. On the spur of the moment, I told Liliana I could do well to resign. 'We could travel the world,' I said. 'The sale of my London house would finance us. You could turn your hand to journalism; perhaps write a book on our exploits. We'd be fine.' Liliana was wide-eyed. She tried to match my enthusiasm but was visibly lukewarm. I took her reservation to be surprise, born of the fact she was unaware of the Service's dictate I should depart Washington the minute my time was up.

But what did provoke my concern was that shortly after, Liliana became highly agitated. From voicing muted support for my resignation, she switched in an instant to uncharacteristic vehemence, her emotions appearing to boil over. 'Under no circumstances should you resign,' she told me heatedly, before screaming at me, *'You must not resign.'* This alarmed me. Anyone could see that behind her out of character outburst there was more than worry I might be making a rushed decision. Her momentary loss of poise gave the impression my proposition had panicked her. This raised more questions than there were answers. I decided for now to agree not to resign. With unmistakable relief, Liliana perked up. 'Yes,' she said, 'I will join you in London in the New Year after I have visited my father to explain why I intend moving to the UK.' I hoped our disagreement was a misunderstanding and tried to blot out the gnawing sensation it might not be.

London, Friday 22 December 1989. On leaving Washington on 19 December as instructed, the exact fourth anniversary of my arrival, I had returned direct to London and my home in Brent Cross. On the flight back I decided I had to clarify things with Liliana, once and for all. She had told me she would be working double shifts in the days following my departure, in the busy lead-up to Christmas, after which she would go to Miami to spend time with her father. Liliana insisted I should not ring her until 2 January, when she would be back in Washington; it was too difficult otherwise.

My deliberations, however, had taken me to the point where I was no longer prepared to wait. I decided to ring her right then, at the restaurant where the staff would be preparing for the lunchtime crowd. I knew Liliana would not appreciate the call, having earlier told me never to ring her at work because the boss did not allow staff private calls. But enough was enough. I was determined that Liliana should tell me what was going on.

The phone connected in the distinctive burr of the American ring. A harassed-sounding male answered. I apologized for the call but said I needed urgently to speak to Liliana Leanca. 'Man,' he said, 'so would I. She left work early on Wednesday night and yesterday morning her husband rang in sick for her, saying she would be off for a couple of days. Said she had laryngitis and couldn't speak. I guess people get sick but she has really let me down. If you're speaking to her, tell her to get her ass in here.'

The husband mention made the hairs on the back of my neck stand up; not because I actually thought Liliana had a husband but because someone had called posing as such. I rang Liliana's apartment – no answer. I sat quietly, thinking. Then on a hunch, I rang a contact in the American customs and immigration service in Washington. It was just after 7 pm in London. The five-hour time difference made it early afternoon in the District of Columbia. 'Danforth Rickkerts,' I said lightly, 'how are you big guy?'

'Hey, Joey Lambert, what's up?' the giant black man replied.

'I'm back in Blighty you bloody reprobate but have a loose end I need to tidy up tonight. If I gave you a passport number could you do a check on any known movements in recent days?'

'For you my man anything is possible,' Danforth said, chuckling. I had with me a copy of the foreign persons contact report on Liliana I had lodged with the Service. I read out her passport number. Click, click, click on the lumbering computer at the other end. 'Yep,' Danforth said, 'departed state side at Dulles 2300 local Wednesday 20 December. Turkish Airlines direct flight to Istanbul, ETA 1615 plus one local.'

I wasn't massively surprised. Since the night that Liliana had imploded at the thought of me resigning, supposedly from the Foreign Office, I had known something was up – my *eyes wide open* antenna had finally switched on. That Liliana was a KGB plant tasked with recruiting me was high among the possibilities I had considered. Her undisclosed travel coupled with the husband revelation had just confirmed it, of this I was certain, beyond all reasonable doubt as the lawyers like to say.

***

Liliana, it transpires, had alerted General Shukhov that her lapse might have raised my suspicions of her. Shukhov in response ordered her to attend a crash meeting with him on 22 December in Sofia, Bulgaria. Had the general been in better health they would have met closer to the US. Liliana's KGB controller also directed her to ensure there was no contact between us from the time I departed Washington on 19 December until 2 January. His calculation was that, although Liliana would be absent from the US only for forty-eight hours, it was prudent she be free to undertake more travel abroad if Shukhov required it.

I learned later that on the night of 20 December, Liliana flew to Istanbul on her KGB-obtained American passport and thence to Sofia on false papers provided by the Soviet consulate in Istanbul. After five hours dead to the world in a Sofia hotel on the night of 21 December, she was roused for her meeting with Shukhov commencing at 6 am sharp on 22 December. The meeting spanned three intense hours, during which she received her updated instructions. Liliana was exhausted but there was no time for sleep. Retracing her steps to Istanbul, she boarded a mid-afternoon Turkish Airlines flight arriving back in Washington on the night of 22 December, some six hours after I called her apartment.

———◆◆———

Armed with all the facts, it didn't take long to understand the Soviet intentions. Agnes had been killed so as to tear an emotional gap in my life and Liliana had been chosen to fill it. It was no fluke that she shared many of Agnes's traits: the tenderness and intelligence; the engaging smile; the mannerisms; the hair. You could bet Liliana had been selected as my recruiter for this very reason. Being Moldovan was no barrier. People from Eastern Europe regularly immigrated to the US. In any event, she couldn't easily disguise her accent and had to be comfortable answering questions about her background, however innocently put.

Word of my breakdown over Agnes's death had circulated widely in New Delhi. I was sure the KGB's plan predicated on this, presuming that once emotionally hooked the fear of another life-shattering event would open me up to recruitment. Liliana hadn't pitched before I left Washington. It followed, therefore, that the KGB planned for her to move on me once she was in the UK.

As to the large time gap between Agnes's death and Liliana's approach, some five years, I was less certain. The Soviets had clearly sought to aid my career advancement, indicating an intention to assist me climb the Service's higher rungs before recruiting me. This obviously took time and partially explained the lag. But how could they have been sure I would not have found someone else in the period before Liliana's introduction?

I decided the answer lay in the fact that I was built differently to the average Joe Bloggs. I thought of it in terms of thresholds of emotional outlay. With Agnes and later Liliana I had identified that above an upper threshold my natural inclination to hide in *The Far Grass* was suppressed because I was emotionally secure; whereas with Kathleen, to whom I'd once been married, my experience was of an emotional outlay falling below a lower threshold, with my resulting indifference to the threat of rejection offering a form of emotional security. I was positive most men had similar thresholds. But my relationship history had shown the gap between the high and low ends, when my loner instincts were prone to trigger, to be abnormally large. My guess was the Soviets had detected this particularization; they were big on psychoanalysis and other profiling. They had relied on this confident another woman capable of filling the void was unlikely to come into my life.

This analysis assuredly had more than a grain of truth to it. But I didn't know at the time that, driven by his own secret agenda, General Shukhov had delayed Operation Oblast well past the deadline for activation recommended by the KGB psychologists.

CHAPTER 37

COUNTERING

I mused deeply over the ensuing days. My only rush to anger –real, deep and raw – was when recalling that Liliana's faked affection had duped me into abandoning Agnes, luring me from the emotional safety of *The Far Grass* to where I had instinctively retreated in the years following Agnes's death. By the night of 27 December I was clear on what I had to do.

Martin Mumford was cool upon opening his front door mid-morning Thursday 28 December. His carrying the can for my indiscretion with the Americans nearly three years earlier clearly still rankled. He did not invite me in; instead, we talked for over two hours in his back garden, after which Martin drove us to the cottage near Kew Gardens that was home to the DG. There we were quickly ushered inside. Digby Carhiddy, my current boss, arrived shortly after. For three hours the four of us sat closeted in the DG's timber-panelled anteroom at the front of the house.

Late on 31 December Martin rang. 'The DG's just returned from Washington,' he said. 'It's clear to go. As soon as you're finished on 2 January I'll come and get you and we'll go to Kew.' He hung up, not responding when I wished him Happy New Year.

I didn't need to act light and airy when I rang Liliana as scheduled on 2 January. She knew I'd called her workplace when she was in Sofia. 'Thanks to your lot,' I said sourly, 'I'm in a colossal bind with my employer.' I knew that Liliana would grasp my veiled reference to the criminal offence of withholding information on Anthony Delminico's murder and my many other acts of serious misconduct. 'I have no choice but to listen to your proposal.'

'We can get an outline to you tomorrow,' Liliana said.

'No,' I spat back angrily. 'It has to come from you. I'm not starting all over with a London functionary I've never met before. I'll pick you up at the airport. You should stay here as planned.'

A pause, possibly to consult someone who was listening. 'Give me a week to make arrangements,' she said when back on the line. 'I'll take a morning flight from Dulles on 10 January.'

'Never lose sight of the fact that the Soviets must believe the Service knows nothing of Liliana's visit,' Martin Mumford said on leaving the DG's home later on 2 January, several hours after my conversation with Liliana. 'It's a key aspect of this exercise.'

'I'm conscious of that, Martin,' I replied. 'If we can pull this off, I hope it will compensate for the trouble I've caused.'

'You've cocked up massively, Joe,' Martin snapped in a rare loss of control. 'But for the DG you'd be in a prison cell.' Martin steadied. 'We're keeping the indoctrination list very tight. It will not be expanded beyond we four – the DG, you and me, and Digby. Service others helping out will be told only what they need to know.' We drove to my home in silence. 'OK,' Martin said on arrival, 'see you at the Matilda West Gallery in Kew Gardens, 10 am sharp this Saturday, 6 January – the curator's office at the back.' Martin stared at me. 'We're at *the off*, Joe. You're now supposedly on leave until 30 January. No overt contact with the Service unless it's readily explainable. We'll communicate as planned.'

The technical people were at my home first thing the next morning, 3 January, posing as removalists delivering furniture. My second bedroom was the focus of their attention. Here they built a room within a room just big enough for two people. Its entry was via a heavy door that shut much like watertight doors I'd seen on ships.

'This room is now the only place in the house where you can speak openly,' the team leader warned me. 'Your house has an exposed left flank which the Soviets will access to attach an encoded radio microphone under the roof eave ahead of their agent's arrival.' The team leader briefly looked puzzled. 'The top floor,' he said, 'has directed us not to sweep the house's exterior.' I knew why but said nothing. 'The Sovs,' the leader said, resuming his briefing, 'will hear everything in the house bar in the safe room. But we will have audio both in the safe room and in the house. To avoid the Soviets becoming aware of our listeners, when outside the safe room you must act as if there is no Service monitoring.'

⚫⚫

I met Liliana at Heathrow when she arrived in the late afternoon of 10 January. She was nervous. So was I. Once at my home, I took her to the second bedroom. Her eyes widened but she said nothing. We entered the safe room; closing the heavy door electronically shielded us from the external world. 'Outside of these four walls,' I said, 'you are not to mention this room.'

'Of course,' Liliana replied calmly, smiling at me. Her pleasant conformity was surprising. It was as if a switch had been thrown transforming her earlier tenseness into relaxed warmth.

'We will talk in here tomorrow,' I said. 'If we need to speak securely when outside the room we will use notes.'

I then took Liliana for a Chinese meal. She wasn't thrilled but this was the arrangement. Mid-meal I went to the lavatory, where I greeted Harry Brandt. Harry would be a staunch ally. He had never forgotten my acceptance of him into the Service at a time when many were resisting it. 'Tell the DG, Martin and Digby she passed the first test,' I said softly. 'I'll conduct the second test in the morning. If she passes it I'll raise the sitting room blind after ten thirty. In the event, I'll make the eyes and ears pitch soon after and, if successful, that night prepare Operation Fife for activation.' Harry knew all about the eyes and ears pitch, but beyond its name nothing of the DG's creation dubbed Operation Fife.

Liliana spent her first night on the couch. After breakfast the next morning I led her into the safe room. 'OK,' I said, 'you'll know by now that I've told my Service all about us. I'm cooperating with it to try and make amends. That being so, we are about to go out to the sitting room where, for the benefit of your listening friends, you will make the offer you've been sent to make, which I will pretend to consider. Let's go.' But before opening the safe room door, I handed Liliana a note. She read it quickly before looking searchingly at me, her eyes sparkling as she did.

Liliana sat in one of my sitting room armchairs, her legs curled beneath her. 'Joe, I know you are angry with me,' she began. 'But I do want to be with you. Before then, though, much work needs to be done. All Soviet republics are currently experiencing upheaval fuelled by Western disinformation and temporary economic decline. For the sake of the Soviet Union this revolution nonsense must stop. Until such time as Soviet patriots can seize control in Russia, you must help us counteract the West's support for the liberal reformists.' Liliana uncurled from her chair to kiss me. Her tenderness told me it wasn't all in the line of duty.

'Well that's all very noble, Liliana,' I said. 'But what about me?' My scorn might have been scripted for Soviet ears but it came easily. Bitterness still lingered over Liliana playing me. Her affection reminded me I'd abandoned Agnes because I had been selfish and weak. I returned to script as the rush of heat subsided. 'If tumbled,' I continued, 'my spying along with all my other misdeeds would see me locked up and the key thrown away.'

Liliana appeared to consider this. 'We would protect you,' she said. 'Why don't you come to Moldova and see for yourself, to Chisinau and get a feel for a proud Soviet republic?'

'And how would I do that?' I asked with a pained voice. 'Service officers just can't decide to visit the Soviet Union.'

'Simple,' she said. 'Your Service does not know I am here and you return to work on 30 January. Tell it you plan to holiday in Portugal for a week, leaving, say, on 19 January. That will give me time to make arrangements for our onward travel to Moldova.'

'I suppose a trip to Portugal would not look unusual at this time of year,' I said cautiously. 'Let me sleep on it. I'll make a final decision on the recruitment tomorrow.' With that, I stood and raised the sitting room window blind. The time was half past ten.

The note I'd earlier handed to Liliana in the safe room had read: *When you pitch at me suggest we travel to Chisinau leaving on 19 January, on the pretext of me taking a week's holiday in Portugal.* I'd used a note even though we were in the safe room; I didn't want the Service listeners to know I'd set Liliana a test.

Liliana had passed her first test the night before by keeping quiet about the safe room. The safe room note was a second test to gauge her reaction to me possibly making a secretive visit to Chisinau. I wasn't exactly sure why Liliana had cooperated in both instances, but whatever had caused her warmth towards me since arriving at my home was clearly a factor. Even so, there was still a long way to go, that fact best known to Operation Fife's indoctrinated four – the DG, Martin, Digby and me.

⁕ ⁕

Back in the safe room, I asked Liliana why she was working for the Russians. 'My father became political after mother died,' she said. 'The Soviets threw him into prison where his health began to fail.' Liliana took a deep breath. 'Then Colonel Shukhov headed the KGB in Moldova. I went to his office. Shukhov said if I worked for him, he would release my father. If not, he would be left to rot. So, I agreed.' She smiled sadly. 'My father is not in Miami, Joe; he lives in a village north of Chisinau. He is the KGB's insurance.'

'And you?' I said. 'Where do you usually live?'

'I have a small apartment in Chisinau,' Liliana said. 'Shukhov has allowed me to stay there to be close to my father.'

'Give me the apartment's address.'

Liliana did not stop to think. 'Strada Alexei Sciusev 69.' This confirmation was important; at least to we Operation Fife indoctrinated four. 'But why do you ask?' she added warily.

'We want you to be our eyes and ears in Moldova once elections are held and the Soviets lose control,' I said, 'to warn us of threats to British commercial aircraft from rogue Moldovans armed with surface-to-air missiles. You'll report to a cut-out we'll arrange.' I paused for effect. 'You will also know better than me that Moldova risks a civil war if militants are left to run free.'

Liliana shuddered at the civil war reference, her reaction consistent with the conclusion I had reached in Washington, the one on which I was now betting the farm. It was time to press my case. 'There'll be a bloodbath in Moldova if you don't work for us,' I said pointedly, 'one you would likely have prevented.'

'I often dream of Moldova burning,' Liliana reflected sadly, biting her lip in such distress as to stir my protective instincts. 'I agree with you. It is my national duty to help avoid a civil war.'

———◆◆———

That night, I handed Liliana a second note. It was the Operation Fife olive branch I'd been directed to extend: *Why don't you sleep in my bed?* Liliana's eyes fiercely interrogated mine before she nodded slowly. The night was frigid. I had an electric blanket somewhere but didn't look for it, which in hindsight told me something. Liliana and I snuggled for warmth, our touch reviving powerful memories. Yet I was also careful to ensure we nestled quietly. I was worried about my own listeners, not the Soviets'.

'We're out of milk,' I yelled on leaving the house the next morning. In the supermarket dairy section, I whispered to Harry Brandt's back. 'Tell the DG and the others the olive branch seems to have been accepted. I will activate Operation Fife later today.'

That afternoon, seated in my sitting room, I gloomily told Liliana how I had been trying to convince myself I could do prison time but now realized I could not. 'On pain of being betrayed to the Service,' I said fearfully, 'I have no alternative but to spy for the KGB.' I sighed audibly. 'But first I have to see Chisinau as you suggest. I need to know it's a place to where I could defect.'

'I understand,' Liliana said evenly. 'Let me speak to my people about our Chisinau travel. It's best not to ring from here.' I handed her a third note at the door. *Tell them Shukhov must come to Chisinau to give me his personal assurance I will be extracted at the first hint of detection. Say I'm so scared you think I could still pull out.* Liliana gulped, but she left without saying a word.

I pondered the Service's strategy while Liliana was out. As a double agent, I was supposed to feed in chaff designed to hasten the Soviet Union's demise and the KGB's with it. For her part, Liliana's eyes and ears role would begin in March after Moldovans, in elections to be held then, had ousted the Soviets. But there were more balls in the air than our strategists knew. Not only was there Operation Fife – its details known only to the DG, Martin, Digby and me – but unknown to any other – the DG, Martin and Digby included – there was also my private endgame attaching to it.

On Saturday 13 January, the day after my contrived decision to become a Soviet spy, Martin Mumford briefed Service others that Liliana would travel to Moldova on 19 January to await activation, while later the same day, my work done, I would fly to Portugal for a well earned holiday. My boss Digby Carhiddy was also active on 13 January. He was off to Canada, to Toronto, for an overnight visit. Digby would later admit to using the trip as his chance to rescue the Service from the DG's dreadful folly, and to hopes of praise for his grit at the highest UK political levels.

CHAPTER 38
RIMMINGTON

For long after the Saturday morning meeting in the Service on 12 May 1984 called by Martin Mumford to discuss Anthony Delminico's death and the Rhodesian smear campaign running against the Service, I had remained wary of Bill Rimmington, the long-time head of Service internal affairs, and his evident suspicion of me. But by January 1990, after close to six years had elapsed, hearing nothing to suggest that Rimmington had made progress on the Rhodesian matter had combined with my many other distractions to lull me into a false sense of security.

As it transpires, Rimmington had decided to retire at the end of April 1990. Renowned for hating loose ends, he returned from holidays in mid-January determined to devote his last three months in service to clearing up the Rhodesian mystery. Martin Mumford was later to tell me this and also detail Rimmington's endeavours. Martin did so in December 1991 as part of his *Final Briefing,* after he had debriefed *our source* Aleshkovsky and completed his ancillary interviews, including the one he did with Rimmington.

Rimmington's usual practice was to review unresolved investigations in conjunction with the police Special Branch. By the time he began his last spurt on the Rhodesian issue a policewoman called Margaret Otten had been three months in the Special Branch Chief Superintendent's chair. It seems Otten was happy to oblige on 15 January when Rimmington suggested that, apropos of the Rhodesian matter, she issue an information request on the Met and regional networks asking for information to hand which might have an intelligence implication, however minor.

No sooner had Margaret Otten's telex been sent than on 16 January Durham police contacted Special to advise that a recently arrested man claimed to have information about spies he would share in return for leniency. His name was Leslie Stratton. Rimmington doubted that Stratton would have much to offer but nonetheless took the night train to Durham. First thing on the morning of 17 January he interviewed Stratton in the holding cells at Aykley Heads police headquarters. Leslie had resorted to armed robbery to pay the bills. He told Rimmington life was so much better when he drove for that crazy Irish outfit.

Stratton said he had dropped an Irish woman called Mrs O'Hare in Brent Cross one Sunday afternoon in early May 1984. Along the way, she had made a vague reference to *spooks*, and Leslie knew that *spooks* were spies. 'I was astonished to find that the drop was barely a quarter-mile from Joe Lambert's house,' Rimmington told Mumford. 'I'd always known he was hiding something. Fifty years of policing had been telling me so.'

Stratton had also recounted how his pick up instructions were to pass by certain locations at ten minutes to the hour for as long as necessary. 'After a couple of no-shows,' Rimmington said, 'this Mrs O'Hare was waiting at the 3:50 pm location, which was also a comfortable walking distance from Lambert's home. After that, Stratton dropped her at a phone box near Cricklewood station where she proceeded to make a call.'

———◆◆———

It was Brian McGowan who informed Mumford on Rimmington's next step. 'I was in the office late on 17 January,' McGowan said.

'I had been the Service's head administrator for over a year by then. Rimmington rang. He was just back from Durham and seeking approval for an internal audit first thing the next morning.

'When Rimmington came up,' Brian said, 'I was surprised to see he wanted to put the cleaners through Joe Lambert. When I told him my staff movements advice indicated Lambert would be holidaying in Portugal for a week from 19 January, he argued Lambert should not leave the country. But Rimmington didn't know Lambert's entry in my movements advice contained the *Star*. I told him that, despite the proximity of Mrs O'Hare's drop-off to Lambert's house, I would not ban Lambert's travel without more to go on. I authorized his audit on those terms.

'Rimmington was too disciplined to dispute my decision,' Brian said. 'He settled for asking for Lambert's departure details. I told him it was on British Airways at 11:55 am on 19 January.'

<hr>

The *Star* was an asterisk, really. It only ever appeared on the highly classified movement advices issued to the top floor executive. It was designed to warn them when private staff travel might have operational implications. The unannotated movement advices distributed to Service others – the likes of Rimmington – sat at the other end of the classification spectrum.

<hr>

Rimmington told Mumford he did not sleep well on the night of 17 January. 'I knew I was on the threshold of something major and needed to unearth it before noon on 19 January. I was out on the corridors on 18 January as people began arriving at work.'

Rimmington said that after drawing some blanks, the now computerized records in the domestic documents registry linked

Lambert's name to a bogus driver's licence in the name of Brian Spinks. 'The licence had been issued on 9 January 1984 to a Grantly Worthington who returned it on 13 January,' Rimmington said. 'I asked for the old issue card and found a notation showing that Joe Lambert had possession of the licence from 9–10 January.

'I spoke to Worthington twenty minutes later,' Rimmington said. 'All he knew was Lambert needed the licence for a close hold, *Need to Know* purpose. After getting back the licence, Worthington had asked a registry clerk called Thelma Morton to record Lambert's temporary possession of it.'

Rimmington was then informed that Thelma Morton had left the Service in 1988. He requested her personnel file but had to wait until it arrived from the archive. 'When I did get to see it, it was 3:30 pm,' he told Mumford. 'The file showed a forwarding address in Huddersfield.' When Rimmington could find no Thelma Morton in the telephone directory, he had enlisted the help of the West Yorkshire police. Thelma went by her married name of Cooper and it had taken them over two hours to find the number.

Rimmington was a details man. He was able to provide Mumford with a precise summary of his conversation with Thelma Cooper née Morton drawing on the copious notes he took. 'Thelma was initially unconcerned when I rang at half past six on the night of 18 January,' Rimmington said. 'I asked her about the entry on the issue card reflecting that Lambert had taken temporary possession of the licence drawn by Worthington in January 1984.

'At first Thelma could recall nothing of note. She said she was not permitted to ask about the licence's use; her job was only to make sure the records were up to date and accurate.

'But suddenly Thelma began to cry. I had seen a lot as a copper and whatnot and was usually unflappable; regrettably, I lost my temper momentarily. "Stop snivelling, woman," I demanded, "stop it this instant. Tell me why you are crying."

'She said one word. "Bruce."'

'I was totally perplexed. I yelled, "Bruce what?"'

'Then she told me. "I told Bruce Branton that Joe Lambert had possession of the licence on 10 January." '

Rimmington told Mumford it had taken some time to clarify who Branton was and what he wanted, and more time to find out he was no longer with the metropolitan police service. 'But by 10 pm,' Rimmington said, 'I had a phone number in Edinburgh. Branton was not pleased to be dragged from his warm bed. When I asked him the obvious he assumed the worst and refused to speak to me without his lawyer present. By now it was nearly 11 pm. I told Branton I would be on his doorstep in six hours and then rang Margaret Otten. She had previously offered me the use of the Special Branch helicopter. I told her I now had an urgent need for it and suggested she come with me in case we needed to wield a policing power against Branton. At 5:40 am on 19 January we rang Branton's front door bell.'

—◆—◆—

Brian McGowan again, when interviewed by Mumford. 'My home phone rang just before 7 am on 19 January. It was Rimmington. He had been up all night and was ringing from Edinburgh. He told me he now had incontrovertible evidence that a Soviet operative had sought information on a bogus Service driver's licence at a time when Joe Lambert had it in his possession.

'I learned later,' Brian said, 'that Rimmington had given Branton a written guarantee of immunity to get him to talk. And now informed, Rimmington was in full flow. He forcefully put to me that Lambert should be detained and urgent investigations conducted into why he had the licence and why hostile foreign intelligence elements became involved.'

Brian told Mumford he could tell from the confident tone of Rimmington's voice that he had the evidence of which he spoke.

Brian judged this sufficient to overcome the protection of the *Star*. 'Thank you, Bill, I understand,' he had said. 'I will have a team go to Lambert's home immediately and bring him to the office.'

———◆—◆———

On 15 January, four days before Rimmington's Edinburgh visit, while in my sitting room, I told Liliana I had to lodge my travel details with the Service for it to release my personal passport. This was true. It was a standard requirement for officers privately travelling abroad. Going into Century House that day, therefore, would not alarm the listening Soviets. Upon joining the DG, Martin and Digby, the DG began immediately. 'Digby was in Canada at the weekend,' he said. 'There's a headache with the Operation Fife sepop. The separation operation, that is.'

Digby cleared his throat. 'The Toronto people organizing the sepop,' he said, 'need to employ sub-contractors on the ground and pay them in US dollars. But they won't pay them from our election grants for fear of revealing the channel they use to send that money to Moldova. We'll have to pay for the sepop in cash, which means you'll have to carry the funds. Here's what we propose....'

As I was leaving, the DG told me he had decided to *Star* my travel plans in the movement advices circulated to the top floor executive. 'The security risk is low,' he said. 'And you never know, it might smooth your way in some form or another.'

On return home, I told Liliana the visit to the Service had unnerved me. To her and the listening Soviets, I said I wanted to pull out of the Moldova visit and abandon my recruitment. 'Don't make any rash decisions,' Liliana cautioned. 'It's only natural that going into headquarters would unsettle you.'

I vacillated for a time. 'I'll go ahead as planned,' I said finally, trying to pretend that greed had overcome my fear, 'but only if I receive five grand US in cash on arrival in Lisbon.'

'Let me speak to my people,' Liliana said wearily.

I was now on heightened operational alert. The world of espionage was such that even at the best of times a Soviet defector could walk through the door of the largely unindoctrinated Service and give up my plans to visit Moldova. True, I didn't have Rimmington in mind, and I'm sure nor did the DG when, at our meeting in Century House on 15 January, he told me I should exercise all care in taking the final step in Operation Fife's preliminary planning. That's why on 16 January, I found myself in Berkshire, in Reading, paying cash for flights to Lisbon for Liliana and me on a Portuguese budget carrier departing at 6:30 am on 19 January. My British Airways flight at 11:55 am on 19 January remained in place, just in case of any random check by a Service unindoctrinated.

I met Harry Brandt in the supermarket on the evening of 18 January. 'All's set,' I said. 'Tell Martin and Digby that Santa's on his way.' As usual in recent times, Harry had no idea what I was talking about. But his loyalty guaranteed he would ask no questions.

Service listeners, of course, had heard Liliana's seemingly unprompted suggestion that she and I go to Moldova and later my supposed demand to visit there. These were conversations that, unavoidably, had to be had for the benefit of the listening Soviets. But the wider Service never got to know of them. The top floor indoctrinateds – the DG, Martin and Digby – had first call on the transcripts prepared, which they had Mavis, the DG's ancient gatekeeper, amend. The listener transcripts distributed to Service others, to the unknowing unindoctrinated who thought I was engaged only in Liliana's recruitment, thus contained words like *inaudible* and *muffled* where mention of travel to Moldova once existed.

But in the case of Liliana and my secret early departure on 19 January, it was not dialogue destined for transcription that the listeners would encounter but unscripted actions. The DG was worried that a diligent listener monitoring my house could interpret the unexpected change of plan as something untoward and alert a Service unindoctrinated. The coded message I passed to Harry, therefore, was a signal to Martin and Digby to brief the specially selected Service listeners who would be on duty from midnight to noon on 19 January. They would be admitted to a higher category of clearance, one imposing severe penalties in the breach.

CHAPTER 39

DIGBY

By the time the Service security detail scrambled by Brian McGowan reached my house on the morning of 19 January, Liliana and I had just landed in Lisbon. I didn't need to act nervous; I was petrified. My hand shook as I put on a show of greedily counting the 5,000 dollars the Soviets gave me on arrival before stashing it in my backpack. And by the time the security detail discovered our early morning departure from Heathrow, we were in a Soviet safe house, had surrendered our passports and been issued with false papers for the Air Moldova flight to Chisinau the following day.

Digby rang the DG around lunchtime on Saturday 20 January 1990, the day after Liliana and I travelled to Portugal. 'Flash in from second base advising that Drake drove to location Zebra this morning,' Digby said. 'Seems he has Albatross with him as Gordon predicted.' Digby was conveying a message from the MI6 station in Moscow advising that Aleshkovsky had just driven to Kubinika, the military airbase outside Moscow. His passenger was Shukhov, as the Uzbek defector Zamir Umarov had said he would be.

'Thank you,' the DG said. 'Could you let Martin know?'

'Certainly,' Digby replied.

Digby was later obliged to explain to the Service why he had not contacted Mumford. 'The DG had just made a rash and damaging decision,' was his response when questioned. 'And I was the only one on the top floor with balls big enough to protect the Service from it. It was demeaning to be treated as a messenger boy.'

Exactly a week before telephoning the DG, Digby had called on a Moldovan priest in Canada, in Toronto. After handing over 20,000 US dollars for the quite distinct matter of electioneering, Digby had turned to other things. 'The *add-on*,' Digby later told the Service, 'was my means for rectifying the DG's reckless decision to give carriage for a vital UK security interest to Lambert's untested Moldovan agent over sources I had personally selected.' The security issue troubling Digby was the Service's need for early warning of threats to British commercial aircraft from rogue Moldovans equipped with surface-to-air missiles.

Digby said the priest knew that instructions had to be followed to the letter. Failure to do so would result in withdrawal of the election funding. 'Therefore,' Digby argued, 'making clear the sub-contractors were not to implement the *add-on* until they had completed the Operation Fife sepop ensured the *add-on* would not impede Fife. I told the priest that, on those terms, the sub-contractors would be paid 5,000 US by our person on the ground.'

When probed, Digby had taken the high road. 'I had to do what I had to do,' he claimed. 'Otherwise, the Americans would have regarded the Service as a laughing stock.' The investigators were not entirely silly. They pressed Digby who ultimately proved to be all hat and no cattle. When the cave in came, Digby's irresistible craving for power was revealed. The *add-on,* he admitted tearfully, was directed at contrasting the DG's flawed judgement with his own verve and analytical acumen and bringing this to Whitehall's attention. It was also intended to earn the Service he aspired to lead invaluable American gratitude.

Our departure from Lisbon was uneventful. It was an era when airline passengers – and their cabin baggage – were only cursorily scrutinized. The Portuguese customs officer at the departure gate certainly asked me no questions. Nonetheless I kept my backpack close at all times. After all, it contained five grand US in cash. Oh, and as well, buried under the money safe in its exquisitely embossed leather container was the nine-inch, antique silver rapier bequeathed to me by Nought as a dying father would his son. With one thrust of this razor-sharp implement into the soft skin beneath Shukhov's chin, I would kill him. The unarmed combat techniques taught to me on joining the Service would finally have a role in my life.

Liliana and I arrived in Chisinau in the early afternoon of 20 January and made our way to Liliana's apartment. The meeting with Shukhov was to take place in the apartment early the following afternoon. We then walked to the Central Park of Culture and Leisure and stood in the frozen tundra next to a small fountain, looking out at an ice-filled lake. 'This is the first chance we've had to speak freely since you came to the UK,' I said, smiling at Liliana.

But she was in no mood for small talk. 'You're up to something,' she said, her eyes ablaze. 'I know the US dollar payment you demanded means nothing to you. I just hope you know what you're doing.' I could have easily said *Amen* but remained silent. 'Tell me, Joe,' Liliana asked, now softer, 'what convinced you I could be recruited by an appeal to my conscience?'

'You're a patriot,' I said simply. 'It is plain to see from your anxiety over a possible civil war between Moldova's ethnic Romanians and Transnistrian separatists that you are wedded to Moldova and not a discredited Soviet ideology. I've known that since Washington.' A chill wind blew off the icy lake but Liliana appeared not to feel it. 'Mind you,' I added, 'when I told the Service about you in late December, it was not convinced. Several pro-Romanian contacts have recently been cultivated. Some senior people believed that sufficient reliance could be placed on these.'

'And what caused your senior people to change their minds?'

My thoughts turned to Digby Carhiddy. Digby had led the charge on farming pro-Romanian contacts. It was his idea to use expatriate religious groups in Canada to funnel money to pro-Romanians in Moldova to assist them contest elections in the coming March that civil unrest had forced the communists to schedule. But I made no mention of Digby. 'I argued the obvious,' I said instead. 'The pro-Romanians and the Transnistrians are at loggerheads. Neither of them would hesitate to paint the other in a bad light. If we were to obtain early warning of Moldovan irregulars obtaining abandoned Soviet weaponry, how could we be sure we were getting a reliable read-out from either side?'

Liliana suddenly changed subjects. 'If your Service leaders are so enamoured with the pro-Romanians, why is my cut-out to pose as an employee of a private UK aid organization?'

I wondered if she was testing for signs of fabrication. 'Your cut-out's cover organization is called HOPE,' I replied. 'It is well known to me. And, yes, that's precisely the point. To influence elections is one thing but agent running is another. After some time, one top floor executive and then the DG came to agree that both the eyes and ears asset and the cut-out should be impartial.'

My explanation took me back to that long day of 28 December, when first Martin Mumford in his back garden and later the DG in his cottage's anteroom had come to align with my way of thinking. Only Digby, who had invested so much personally in his pro-Romanian networks, had objected. His seething resentment at being overruled by the DG was still on display two weeks later.

'But even if my impartiality explains my recruitment,' Liliana interjected, 'it still doesn't explain why you want Shukhov in Chisinau without your own Service knowing.'

'I swear I will tell you everything when this is all over,' I said.

Liliana laughed softly at my ducking of her question. 'You know, Joe,' she said soberly, 'we in Moldova let our hearts rule. The moment I entered your house, I knew instantly I wanted to be with you. And when you suggested I sleep in your bed that second night your eyes told me you felt the same way, even though you were still trying to be angry with me and no doubt had your reasons for making the offer. Whatever you do, do so knowing that although my love for you is why I didn't alert my people to your safe room and other plans, it is your love for me that led me without knowing why to convince Shukhov to come to Chisinau.'

———◆—◆———

In bed that night, I thought of how for years I had schemed to kill Shukhov, even before I knew him by name. I never thought the day would come. Too tense to sleep, I replayed over and over that Saturday morning of 6 January at the Matilda West Gallery in Kew Gardens, four days before Liliana's arrival in the UK, when the DG had detailed Operation Fife, while Martin, Digby and I sat there listening intently. How the American debrief of the defector Umarov had revealed that Shukhov was dying. How Umarov had nominated Aleshkovsky, the KGB star and head of the elite Active Measures Department, as Shukhov's heir apparent and the man who would build Russia's stand-alone spy agency from the ashes of the KGB when the Soviet Union collapsed. But how Aleshkovsky and his family would then be eliminated, simply because they were part of the old Soviet regime. Yet Umarov, knowing Aleshkovsky, could guarantee that if forced to choose, the colonel would always put his family first. If Shukhov could be lured out of Moscow, Umarov told the Americans, Aleshkovsky was certain to follow. And once free of the Kremlin's galvanizing influence, Umarov was sure, Aleshkovsky would come to recognize the stark reality he faced.

The DG had harked back to the day of 28 December in his cottage's anteroom, when I first proposed to demand that Liliana come to London when I rang her on 2 January. 'Once you suggested it, Joe,' he said, 'I immediately identified the possibility of a bolt on to the base operation whereby Liliana would orchestrate Shukhov's use as a decoy to entice Aleshkovsky out of Moscow. The CIA is confident that Aleshkovsky's defection will cripple Russia's efforts to stand-up a successor to the KGB. It green-lighted Operation Fife when I was in Washington just before the New Year.' The DG directed I should proceed as planned and, once Liliana was in London, persuade her to arrange for me to meet Shukhov as part of my supposed recruitment. Chisinau was the most plausible location. If Liliana had an apartment there that would be ideal. 'Digby,' the DG explained, 'will organize a side operation, a sepop, to separate Aleshkovsky and Shukhov for about thirty minutes.' Digby had confirmed this was so. Then all that remained, the DG had said with chilling simplicity, was for me to execute Operation Fife as my hugely secret planned pitch to Aleshkovsky was officially known.

The DG had emphasized that operational security was paramount. 'Liliana must not know of our interest in Aleshkovsky,' he said. 'To ensure he is kept out of it, we'll make her think that luring Shukhov to Chisinau is Joe's own unauthorized initiative.' The DG's face by now was grey with strain. 'It is also critical,' he said, 'to keep Operation Fife from the wider Service. Others will be briefed on the base op to recruit Liliana as an eyes and ears asset in Moldova, including the involvement of this HOPE outfit. But Joe's travel to Chisinau must be closely guarded. Otherwise, conjecture about an additional objective vis-à-vis Liliana risks exposure of Operation Fife and its design on Aleshkovsky, and with that Russian quarantine of him.' In the event, the DG had warned with ominous understatement, the Americans would be substantially unimpressed.

And lastly, the DG had sought views on whether Liliana would agree both to her eyes and ears recruitment and, believing it to be for me, arranging Shukhov's travel to Chisinau. Fifty-fifty Digby had estimated. I waited for Martin. 'Joe,' he said finally, 'has rebuked Liliana for her deception. But she will fully cooperate only if wholly devoted to him.' We had all stared at Martin. 'Once Liliana is in his home,' he said, 'Joe must extend her an olive branch, shall we say.'

The DG's brow had furrowed. 'I'm more than a little concerned,' he said, 'with the optics of Joe romancing Liliana while supposedly running an eyes and ears recruitment designed to exploit her unease over a possible civil war in Moldova. It could create precisely the type of Service speculation I want to avoid.'

Martin had smiled grimly at the DG. 'Even if Liliana agrees to the eyes and ears role, Colin, she will baulk at Shukhov unless Joe first offers her an olive branch. He must, without our side knowing.' Martin wasn't just hoping. Rather, he somehow sensed that Liliana and I really did love each other. It was this he wanted to ignite. He said so. 'It has to be love,' he had whispered in our ungrasping ears.

✦

Lying there as Liliana slept in my arms, I again returned to that day of 28 December, this time to when I had confessed the whole ghastly lot to Mumford in his garden and later to the DG and Digby in the DG's anteroom – starting with the Russians killing Agnes. But there was one key variable: rather than admit to a plan to kill Shukhov, I depicted my antics as a quest for closure – a need to understand why Agnes died. They were not impressed, as I knew they would not be.

The prepared salve I offered that December day was Liliana's recruitment as an eyes and ears asset in Moldova reporting to a cut-out working under HOPE cover. I proposed to the DG, Martin and Digby that when I rang Liliana on 2 January, I hint at becoming a Soviet spy but insist she stick to the KGB plan to recruit me in

London. And once Liliana was in the UK, I added, I should leverage her evident concern over Moldova's future so as to convince her she could prevent its slide into civil war if she worked for us. There was much discussion, but ultimately only Digby demurred.

At the time, though, it was not Liliana's recruitment at the forefront of my mind but rather my private endgame. Then, as on 6 January at the Matilda West Gallery, when the DG had asked the same question, I was unsure if Liliana would comply – in the case of my private endgame for her to arrange at my behest a meeting with Shukhov, at which I would kill him. That was my driving ambition.

My restored resolve to kill Shukhov derived of course from my fury that I had been hoodwinked into abandoning Agnes and lured from the sanctuary of *The Far Grass*. This emotional charge was still coursing powerfully within me that Saturday morning at the Matilda West Gallery. When Operation Fife was unveiled as the near duplicate of my private endgame, my intention to kill Shukhov remained the one secret I did not share with the others.

CHAPTER 40

SHAKESPEARE

At 2 pm sharp on Sunday 21 January 1990, there was a short rap on the door of Liliana's apartment. The time had come. For some reason my mind was filled with thoughts of Bootle, particularly the Bootle docks. Try as I might, I could not be rid of them. Liliana moved to answer the door. I touched her arm to stop her. She watched, puzzled, as I hung a small towel over the Juliet balcony looking onto Strada Alexei Sciusev. Then I nodded to her.

Greetings were made in Russian, followed by the sound of shuffling footsteps along the short hallway. The door to the living room opened. I held my breath, unsure what to expect. In stepped an older man white-haired and shrunken, the loose-fit of his casual attire indicating he had once been much larger. A younger man, ramrod straight and of unmistakable military bearing, also in civilian clothes, supported him. The younger man pronounced himself as Aleshkovsky. He held an oxygen cylinder. The plastic lead extending from it curled around the older man's ears so that the lead's two prongs inserted in his nostrils would stay in place. I sat on a small couch. Liliana would translate if Russian were spoken. Nought's rapier, free from its container, nestled in the inside pocket of my jacket.

'Mr Lambert,' the older man said in English, each word uttered only with considerable effort, 'I have been waiting to meet you for a long, long time.' He gripped Aleshkovsky's arm, releasing it only once he was lowered into a straight back chair he had nominated with his eyes. 'I am close to the end,' he said. 'If I am any judge, the travel here to Chisinau has just about done for me.'

Looking at Shukhov in person for the first time, my unshakable resolve to kill him – my restored ironclad commitment – instantly evaporated. Dismayed by this and its suddenness, flailing and seeking protection from my own condemnation, I willed myself to picture Agnes deferring to Shukhov's state of decay: *Anger's such a counter-productive emotion*, she would say. But thoughts of Bootle, those that were niggling me and would not let go, overrode the obfuscation. I was again a young boy on the Bootle docks learning to talk the talk because I was too scared to fight the fight. My plan to kill General Shukhov would never be fulfilled, in his sickness or his health. When the chips were down I didn't have the stomach.

Oblivious to my inner turmoil, Shukhov had paused to gather what breath he could. Now he spoke, snapping me from my wallowing. 'Two things quickly, while I can,' he said, his bushy eyebrows rising as he leant forward in my direction. 'You want to recruit Dmitri I take it?' Aleshkovsky recoiled at this, vigorously shaking his head. I'm sure I looked stunned too. Shukhov smiled. 'Do you think I am such an old fool as to fall for this nonsense about you wanting personal assurances before we can recruit you? I can smell traps like that from five miles away.' He turned to look at Aleshkovsky, the craning of his neck causing him obvious discomfort. 'You must accept their offer, Dmitri. The socialist dream is over. It's every man for the lifeboats. There will be purges and God knows what before the dust settles. That's the Russian way; it will never change. You're part of the old regime. Your card is marked along with that of your wife and children.'

Turning back to me he ordered me like the man accustomed to command that he was. 'Give Dmitri the papers you want him to sign. Give them to him right now so he can sign them while I'm alive to see it.' Returning his gaze to Aleshkovsky he said, 'You'll understand, Dmitri, that putting your signature on these forms is not something you can later repudiate. The Presidium will suspect you for signing them, whatever the circumstances, and only execute you and your family quicker than it would have anyway. Sign them now my boy. Sign them so I can die knowing that I've given you and those who sustain you a chance at life.'

A moment of hesitation, followed by the flourish of a pen. And with that Colonel Dmitri Aleksandrovich Aleshkovsky embarked on his defection to Her Majesty's Secret Service. 'Go to the Moscow Circus in the Lenin Hills next Friday night,' I told him. 'Someone will contact you there to begin making extraction arrangements.'

'And the second thing, General Shukhov?' I asked, looking up as I returned the signed forms to the hidden pouch inside the lining of my rucksack, my instincts urging me to keep things moving.

Shukhov was exhausted and ghostly pale. I had to lean forward to hear what he was saying. 'Katya Vasilievna Lyubimova, you will know her. She is imprinted on your soul.'

Thinking it was a question, I nodded before I realized it wasn't. 'What about her?' I asked, my mouth suddenly dry.

'She was my daughter,' Shukhov said, lifting his watery eyes to mine.

We all looked at him, dumfounded. 'General ...' Aleshkovsky gasped, his mouth agape, unable to find other words to say.

Shukhov appeared not to notice the reaction. 'Not by my lawful wife,' he said, looking at me. 'An indiscretion, actually, one I tended to keep quiet. But I loved Katya more than you could imagine. My world changed when I signed her execution papers. I was no longer objective. I wanted to destroy you on finding out it was you who recruited her.' Shukhov was not inventing. He was slipping away and had time for nothing but the truth. I wanted to ask about Katya's mother and understand who had raised her, who it was that Katya so badly wanted to protect when we recruited her. But the questions would not form in my mind. It was all too late. The innocents had already been punished.

No longer with the strength to turn to Aleshkovsky, Shukhov spoke to the floor. 'That's the real reason, Dmitri, why I waited far too long before activating Operation Oblast. My judgement was flawed. I didn't care a fig for the damage we might cause the US–UK intelligence relationship. But I needed the resources of the Soviet state for what I wanted to do and a plausible reason for using them, one I had to pretend was a huge secret. I did want Lambert here to betray the CIA from within its privileged inner sanctum but only so I could extract the full measure of revenge. I wasn't satisfied by the thought of him going to prison, even for a long time; I wanted his betrayal to be on a scale where the Americans would run a wet affair against him.'

Shukhov stopped to take several shallow gasps of air before continuing. 'I did toy briefly with executing him ourselves. But issuing orders infringing the gentlemen's agreement was guaranteed to attract political attention and invite discussion. There had to be a better way. I devised a plan for the Americans to do the job for us. That's why I kept waiting and waiting, in the hope of achieving the ultimate revenge. But then Lambert became unloved by the Americans and in February 1988, after a year of waiting to see if his situation improved, my illness sharply worsened, without warning as the doctors had said it might. I quickly became chronically ill and too feeble to continue the fight. I was spent. I had no option but to settle for the alternative of Lambert's recruitment in London.'

After all this time, I thought, *all this bloody stress and worry, I now finally know it was Shukhov's own agenda driving events.*

I wanted to reflect more, to think about everything that had happened to me. But I couldn't wait. Shukhov was fading. And more than anything I wanted him to tell me the one thing I already knew. 'Agnes?' I asked softly.

It was now Shukhov's turn to strain to hear. 'She was to you what Katya was to me,' he replied eventually. 'Her death was not a an eye for an eye if that is any consolation; like Katya she was just another operational requirement in this unholy life you and I have chosen.' Shukhov stared at me. We both knew the unpleasant truth. Shukhov's gaze turned to Liliana. 'She was to replace your Agnes,' he said, smiling at Liliana with sad fondness. 'But I was too clever by half; she was too much like Agnes. No doubt Liliana has told you about her visit to Sofia in December?'

'Some, but not the precise detail,' I replied cautiously.

Shukhov continued, wheezing and labouring as he did. 'I guessed what likely had happened when Liliana reported she might have alerted you to her being a Soviet agent. That's why I was unconcerned that calling her to Sofia risked you confirming your suspicions during the forty-eight hours she was gone. And when you did, it didn't matter. You already knew the truth in your heart.'

Shukhov began to cough violently, the rattling sound resembling the tearing of plasterboard. With much effort he steadied himself. 'I know Liliana very well,' he rasped. 'She and Katya were so alike. She was like a second daughter to me, particularly after ... that ... with Katya.' Shukhov's voice trailed off, only to rally. 'The Sofia meeting substantiated everything I suspected. Liliana is too good to have made so fundamental a mistake. The funny thing is that *she* didn't grasp the reason for it. I guessed you would demand she come to the UK. I told my people to allow that. I wanted her to understand she warned you because she had fallen in love with you. My dying gift to my second daughter, my only living daughter.'

We stared at each other, both reflecting on how alike and intersecting our respective journeys of vengeance had been. 'How were you going to get back at me, Joe?' Shukhov asked after a time. 'What was to be the personal touch you intended in culmination of this clever plan to entice me to Chisinau?' I was taken aback by his forthright familiarity. But he was now stripped bare and no longer knew formality. I took the rapier from my jacket and showed it to him. Liliana gave a start and Aleshkovsky sat forward in his chair. Shukhov smiled. 'Today certainly, but even a year ago I doubt you would have got me with that.' To my surprise and consternation in equal measure, I found myself laughing with, not at him.

The ensuing quiet was suddenly shattered by the sound of splintering timber. *The fucking sepop*, I thought. I'd been happy to trigger it by placing the towel over the apartment balcony as called for in Operation Fife. But only because I had calculated that killing Shukhov would be easier without Aleshkovsky present and in all certainty coming to the general's defence. Now, however, it was an unwelcome interruption. Two men ran into the room. They were young, strong and rough-looking. The others sat transfixed. I alone knew the intruders were the sub-contractors arranged by Digby Carhiddy, but I knew nothing of Digby's *add-on*. I was to find out about it just minutes later. 'The master key did not work,' one man blurted in Russian as Liliana translated.

'Are you Shukhov?' the other man asked Aleshkovsky.

'No,' yelled Aleshkovsky, rising from his seat in the same instant to confront the intruders. But both men had handguns. Aleshkovsky stopped. Unarmed, there was little he could do.

'What do you want?' Liliana demanded with fierce indignation.

Ignoring Liliana, one of the men began an obviously prepared recital. 'We are Transnistrian patriots,' he said falteringly, struggling to remember his lines. 'We need to speak privately to General Shukhov. Without more Russian support for Transnistrian independence,

Moldova will soon become part of Romania. We need to consult the general on this now, right now, before those wretched Moldovans wanting to suckle from the Romanian teat have their way and there is a Romanian flag flying over Tiraspol.'

Shukhov appeared to be sleeping, his head inclined to one side as though he was straining to hear a bird sing. Yellowy-tinged fluid seeped from his mouth, trickling down his neck and onto his shirt collar. We waited for Shukhov to respond, we and the intruders alike. But the general did not. Indeed, he could not. For the Great Russian Bear was dead.

There was a moment of confusion. Aleshkovsky was first to recover. He took Shukhov gently in his arms while mouthing something in Russian, a religious liturgy I assumed, and laid his body on the hearthrug before lightly kissing Shukhov's snow-white forehead. The sub-contractors looked at one another. I heard one say *add-on* in English. With that, the other turned to Liliana. He spoke in Romanian and I didn't understand him. But I did detect the question, 'Liliana Leanca?' Liliana nodded in confirmation. The man then raised the arm in which he held his pistol.

I immediately sensed what he was about to do. The rapier still in my hand, I lunged forward as he fired two rapid shots into Liliana's upper torso. The recoil of the discharging gun pushed him slightly backwards, resulting in my rapier contacting only his arm. My forward momentum caused me to fall to the floor. The shooter yelled in pain and his companion in alarm. The injured man's gun fell to the timber floor of the apartment and slid over its smooth surface in the direction of Shukhov's body over which Aleshkovsky crouched. The sub-contractors stood still exchanging bewildered looks. One looked down at me and said in English, 'Money?' That was the last word he ever spoke. Aleshkovsky, having picked up the fallen firearm, shot him and his companion dead, both with perfect headshots delivered from a kneeling position.

As if in slow motion, I crawled to Liliana and took her in my arms. The flow of blood from her chest told me the worst. It was the scene of a Shakespearean tragedy. The two slain men off to one side, Aleshkovsky sitting in vigil over the dead body of Shukhov, and me cradling the lifeless second love of my life, unable to think of anything other than my preordained destiny to forever hide in *The Far Grass*.

CHAPTER 41

STILLED

I later told my people in London how Aleshkovsky took control. He had called the local KGB office before instructing me to change into clean clothes. Initially I couldn't react and stood there rooted to the spot. He had slapped me hard across the face to get me moving. The bodies of Shukhov and Liliana had been removed by a Russian military ambulance by the time I left for the airport in an unmarked car and my onwards journey on the night flight to Rome. A windowless van arrived just as I was leaving, its job to dispose of the sub-contractors' bodies. I was barely functioning. But once in Rome I was able to draw on the 5,000 dollars in my rucksack to buy a hotel room. Only when in the room did I discover I had managed to return Nought's rapier to its embossed presentation box and bury it in my carry bag. I had no recollection of doing so. It took a whole day before I was able to make any impression on the British Embassy. Eventually, however, travelling under a temporary travel document issued in my real name I returned to London into the waiting, if decidedly untender, arms of the Service.

The DG deigned not to see me. 'You're too much of a political hot potato,' Brian McGowan said genially as he spread a raft of papers before me. As the Service's head of administration, he was to manage my exit. 'Under the Act, Joe, we could have thrown the book at you on any number of fronts; criminal charges aplenty. But the Minister judged you had made an important contribution to the recent recruitment of a high-ranking Soviet source and that, overall, it was best to avoid the hoo-ha of a trial and be rid of you quietly.' I nodded. 'But you haven't got off scot-free,' Brian cautioned. 'There's a financial penalty involved in the form of us withholding your pension, as the Act entitles us to do in cases of gross indiscipline.' I didn't respond; my spirit was too sapped for further bureaucratic battle. 'Sign here, here and here,' Brian said perfunctorily. 'And date it as of today, 7 February 1990.'

I did. 'That's it?' I asked.

'That's it,' he confirmed. Brian stood to leave. 'One last thing, Joe,' he said softly, 'even though technically it's now none of your business, Digby's also resigned. Not on the DG's Christmas card list at the moment, not by a long shot. A Service investigative team is shortly to interview him. He will likely face charges for arranging Liliana's death.' I raised my eyebrows but said nothing. 'Rupert Heneshaw is set to be elevated to the top floor to replace Digby. Rupert's done a lot of good work over recent years. His promotion will be announced next week.'

'I see,' I said. 'I'm sure Freddie Ladler will be upset to miss the promotion, even though he and Heneshaw are bosom buddies.'

Brian laughed, recalling the enmity between Ladler and me he had first witnessed long ago. 'The Minister has now approved the upgrade of Washington head of station to a senior executive position,' he said. 'The relationship just continues to grow and grow and the station's responsibilities with it. We'll need to hold a promotion round, but Ladler's a dead certainty to get it.' Brian snapped his briefcase closed. 'If you say a word about anything I've just told you about Digby, Heneshaw or Ladler, I'll garrotte you.' He smiled, knowing I wouldn't. 'Just treat it as my parting gift.' Brian closed the door behind him as he left.

Martin Mumford saw me out. We walked in silence initially. 'On hearing your story,' he said as we approached the wardens' counter at the front entrance, 'I admit I wasn't very happy with you. But I now accept any advantage you took of me was incidental to your plan to kill Shukhov. Anyway, life's too short for grudges.'

Martin reflected for a moment. 'Our friend you just signed up will in due course give us the full story of your saga from the other side's perspective. Come back to London, say towards the end of 1991. You know where I live. I should be done with debriefing Aleshkovsky by then and have completed the other interviews I need to do. I'll let you read what I might and where I can't give you papers, I'll tell you what I can.' That promise, of course, became in its honouring Martin's *Final Briefing*.

Outside on the street, Martin shook my hand. 'Joe,' he said, 'you had all the makings of a first-rate officer. Pity you squandered the chance.' I watched him turn and re-enter the Service.

———————

I returned to Brent Cross, not directly to my home but to the local real estate office to put my house on the market. The next day I travelled to Hungerford, to the memorial wall in Saint Saviour's Cemetery. In conversation with Agnes, I explained about Liliana and how fate had led me to love two women. I told Agnes I now needed to return to Moldova to find Liliana's body, contact her father and arrange for her proper burial. I asked for understanding, telling Agnes that she and I would be closer together as a result of the means I'd chosen for fulfilling my obligations to Liliana.

Finally, I told Agnes of my shame on discovering I had no stomach for my perceived duty to avenge her. I said I always knew she would have regarded my plan to kill Shukhov as a retrograde step at odds with her forward-looking philosophy of forgiveness. But full of guilt and negative energy I had ignored this. When I found to my surprise I liked Shukhov, my shame in not killing him was replaced by relief. I told Agnes how this came to tell me the revenge I sought was only for myself. I realized then that all she would ever want of me would be to ensure we were always together. I could guarantee that. No matter where I went or what I did the vial of her ashes sent to me by her mother would be by my side.

Returning to London late at night, I was up early the next morning for my trip to the HOPE office in Ruislip. Rebecca Normington the CEO greeted me on arrival. 'We're pleased to have you on board, Joe,' she said. 'To be honest, I was relieved when told by the Foreign Office it was now unable to fund the proposed HOPE office in Chisinau.' She smiled. 'We pride ourselves on our low pay and poor conditions. When I told the Foreign Office man we were still keen on opening a Chisinau office, he mentioned your name and that you had recently resigned from the diplomatic service. We were thrilled to receive your letter of interest. After decades of Soviet domination, Moldova will be finding its feet in the wake of the elections to be held early next month. Your diplomatic experience will be invaluable on the ground.'

I arrived in Moldova on 14 March 1990 coincident with my forty-second birthday. This was by design. I wanted my birthday to mark a new beginning. Alone – certainly. But not hiding in *The Far Grass* of which Nought had warned. In one way or another, I was now with both my loves. I had joined the Service when I was nearly twenty-four. It was as if I were a bobbing cork in the ocean that had taken over eighteen years to still.

www.ingramcontent.com/pod-product-compliance
Lightning Source LLC
Chambersburg PA
CBHW051650180726
48284CB00006B/1944